★

Alone in the Apocalypse

America Destroyed: After the Solar Flare

A J Newman

Books by A J Newman

America destroyed:After the Solar Flare

Alone in the Apocalypse   Adventures in the Apocalypse*
*To be published late spring 2017

After the EMP series:

The Day America Died New Beginnings
The Day America Died Old Enemies
The Day America Died Frozen Apocalypse

"The Adventures of John Harris" - a Post-Apocalyptic America series:

Surviving   Hell in the Homeland   Tyranny in the Homeland
Revenge in the Homeland....Apocalypse in the Homeland   John Returns

"A Samantha Jones Murder Mystery Thriller series:

Where the Girls Are Buried   Who Killed the Girls?

Books by A J Newman and Cliff Deane

Terror in the USA:

Virus: – Strain of Islam

These books are available at Amazon:

http://www.amazon.com/-/e/B00HT84V6U

✪

As usual, this book is dedicated to my many friends who think that I am bat shit crazy for believing that the Apocalypse is due any day now.

The Apocalypse is coming. Will it be the result of a solar flare, EMP blast, or a failed economy?

Those *are* the questions. It *is* on the way.

This series portrays my vision of regular Americans, how they prepared for and dealt with the issue of survival in a world gone mad.

I am a prepper and will be prepared, will you?

Thanks to my wife, Patsy, who keeps after me to write more books so that I can pay for my prepping, guns, golf, and whiskey.

Thanks to: Patsy Newman for beta reading and proofing.

Thanks to: LTC Clifford T. Deane, US Army, Cavalry, (ret) for proofing, editing, and his contributions to the accuracy of the military, jargon, tactics and color commentary.

✪

This book is a work of fiction. All events, names characters, and places are the product of the author's imagination or are used as a fictitious event. That means that this is all one big yarn that was written purely from my imagination and not a bit of it is true. It might come true in the future.

✪

Prologue

"A Coronal Mass Ejection (CME) is a large cloud of plasma containing an electromagnetic field that is ejected from the Sun. The event releases super-heated particles traveling at immense speeds, and when those particles hit the Earth, they cause a geomagnetic storm, which is capable of wreaking havoc on electrical components.

This novel proposes that a solar body striking the sun would result in a far more massive CME and could lead to an ELE (Extinction Level Event). Since the charged particles would take several days to travel from the sun to the Earth, mankind would have days to think about The End Of The World As We Know IT.

"A CME from the recent major solar flare would take several days to reach Earth." – quote from INQUISTR

A massive CME hitting Earth would set civilization back 150 years. Kerosene lamps, wood cook stoves, and doctors without x-rays, modern medical devices or miracle medicines would become the norm.

People with pacemakers would drop like flies following a CME strike. Diabetics, heart patients, and people living day to day with the help of some miracle drug will die during the first year.

Many of the people on drugs for psychiatric reasons will become violent or suicidal when they run out of the drugs. Death, chaos, and lawlessness would prevail.

My series "After the Solar Flare" attempts to tell a story about how everyday normal people, in a world turned upside down, fight to survive.

I hope you have as much fun reading this series as I did writing them. Thanks to my readers for allowing me to share my imagination with you and remember to recommend this series to your friends.

If you like this novel, please post a review on Amazon.

"Even during an Apocalypse, you should be nice to people except for those trying to kill you. Kill Zombies and the bad guys, but be nice to people."

A J Newman

Main Character List

-

-

Matt Jones – Divorced, high school chemistry teacher, became a prepper a few years back when he became disillusioned with the government, politics and the world in general.

Patty Gale – She and her husband own the General store in Pinedale. She becomes friends with Matt and begins prepping. She becomes his love interest.

Mary Williamson – Matt buys his new home from Mary. She and her husband were preppers. She becomes a good friend and confidant.

Frank Williamson – Former NASA scientist who was part of a team that discovered a disaster was in the making. He was an extreme prepper. Dies before the story starts.

George Gale – Patty's husband is an alcoholic, abusive to Patty and a miserable person.

Sam Nolin – Matt's fellow teacher, mentor, and prepper.

Sheriff Bob Alton - Sheriff of Sublette County.

★

After the Solar Flare

Alone in the Apocalypse

★

Passing a planetary system in the Pegasus Arm of our Milky Way Galaxy, a cold, rogue star hurtling toward the Black Hole in the galactic center ripped the three outer planets out of their orbits. Their star Alpha Omega was destroyed a million years ago. The planets were thus destined to travel billions of miles to their eventual fate.

Chapter 1

Matt Jones

South America

I'm Matt Jones, and this is my story about how I survived the Solar Event known as "The Flare" and the end of the world, as we knew it.

I decided to write my story because it was mid-winter in northern South America and damned cold outside. The snow was knee high to a giraffe, and I was bored. I was also out of whiskey, and my next batch of home brewed beer was two weeks from being ready to drink. Yeah, yeah, I know, the four Ps. Piss Poor Prior Planning on my part. I'm really not an alcoholic, but there isn't much else to do on a snowy South American winter's day. Well nothing, I should put in print anyway.

I started writing about two years after The Flare and continued writing most every day since.

Yes, a huge solar flare hit our world, and within the first year, 80% of the human population was gone from the face of the earth, leaving only bleached skeletal remains to witness their passing.

I started calling the event "The Flare." Some of us were ready for an apocalypse, others rose to the occasion, some preyed on others to survive, but mostly people starved to death or killed each other.

Riots, warfare, looting, gangs, rape, and murder, all happened exactly as predicted. Pay attention; a teaching point comes now: Never underestimate what people will do to feed their loved ones or themselves.

People taking antidepressants, drug addicts, alcoholics and smokers went half-crazy several weeks into the event. Withdrawal from drugs and cigarettes is bad enough without a bunch of wackos running amok in your town because they can no longer get their chill pills.

Disease from rotting bodies, poor hygiene, lack of sanitation, bad water, rats, and so much more reasons took the biggest toll of all. The truth is when people are dying by the billions, the ability to dispose of the bodies quickly becomes an impossibility, which, of course just exacerbates the disease problems.

Oh, the horror didn't stop there. Plagues of rats, spiders, ants, birds and every manner of critters were terrifying............damn, I hate spiders.

10

About 90 percent of the civilized world was not prepared for TSHTF; however, many people in Africa, the Amazon, and the Outback in Australia hardly noticed the disaster until civilization moved next door and it got very ugly. I'll get into that later.

I know it's a damned ugly picture that I'm painting for you. I am thrilled that you have also survived the passing of humanity's pitiful attempt at civilization if for no other reason than you may read, and hopefully, pass on my 'History of the Solar Event.'

I chopped off my writing last month, and the first part is titled, "Alone in the Apocalypse." I just hope I can find a way to publish the darn thing since Amazon Kindle died along with the internet. Perhaps I can get a copier working and publish it myself. Then, again, maybe you're reading my original manuscript, and then you can pass it around. I hope you save it for future scholars.

Okay, back to you. Again, if you are reading this, you survived. That is a major accomplishment. Pat yourself on the back.

It's probably a good thing you didn't come looking for me when I was writing this because I tend to shoot about half of the people that I meet.

Okay, hold on, in my defense, they were all bad, well, most of them. They were thugs, government officials, and thieves, and yeah, I do feel bad that a few were good people trying to do the best they could.

Here comes a "yeah but," I was just protecting what was mine. So, there you have it, that's my story, and I'm stickin' to it.

Yes, I know my writing is sloppy even though I wrote in my best cursive for the first seven chapters before I found an old typewriter. My typing is much better, but old typewriters don't have spell check.

It came as no big surprise to me that the office supply section of Lopez's General Store didn't have much stolen from it. I have plenty of paper, enough typewriter ribbons and boxes of those little thingies that let you put white stuff over the errors. I also have a real dictionary and thesaurus, but you know the biggest problem with those is that most of the time you don't know, that you don't know how to spell a word.

My writing should improve greatly after chapter nine since I found several books on writing and literature at the local high school after I found refuge in a warmer climate. If you are a Grammar Nazi, go read War and Peace and pass this manuscript on to someone who appreciates a good story. My story.

I chose the title "Alone in the Apocalypse" because I moved to Wyoming from Smyrna, Tennessee, alone, to get away from politics, work, political correctness, and people.

I will tell you a little about myself since I am the hero of my story. Also, how I ended up in Wyoming before the shit hit the fan. That's TSHTF abbreviated. I use it quite a bit.

***

-

I was a high school Chemistry teacher at North High School in Nashville. The school was somewhat run down, but I liked teaching back then.

I was married to Jane, and we had two Springer Spaniels, Gus, and Tina. We had a beautiful house in Rutherford County that I inherited from my parents who died in a plane crash. My parents left me the house, and a half interest in their auto repair shop. My brother, Buddy, got half the business and some cash. I

12

also inherited Dad's 1949 FI pickup, and Buddy got mom's 1967 Mustang.

I hope I'm not moving too fast, but we have to get the character development stuff out of the way.

I guess what I'm getting to is Jane and I had it made. The house was paid for. She was a realtor, and I made a fair salary teaching at the high school. Of course, there was also the income from the auto repair business.

It was amazing how quickly I started to hate teaching and how I began to detest that 30-mile drive to work on Highway 24 every day. Now, don't get me wrong, my students were great, but the school was filled with wannabe gangstas, spoiled brats, and a lazy asshole administrative staff.

Jane loved her job and apparently loved a fellow co-worker more than me. This realization had come with the divorce papers about a year before the lights went out.

She told me that we had grown apart, and didn't want anything from me except the divorce. I received custody of Gus and Tina, the Springer Spaniels.

She married her lover and moved to Brazil because of his new job as a construction manager north of Rio.

I thought I was a good husband to my wife Jane but found myself single and lost. I had been with Jane since college, and now I was 36 years old and the target of half the divorced women with three kids in Tennessee. Yep, I was in play. The problem was that I did not *want* to be in play.

Near Nashville, TN

The few friends that I had were always trying to set me up with their sister, friend, or neighbor. Yeah, I went on a few dates and found myself running like hell to get away from women with marriage on their mind after each first date. I stopped dating, worked out at the fitness club, and became a Prepper.

I became a Prepper because of Sam Nolin, a Physics teacher at the high school, bent my ear at lunch one day about the high probability of a major solar event happening in our lifetime.

He told me about how a major solar flare would destroy the nation's electric grid, ruin our electronic devices, and even kill cars and planes. Sam also told me that North Korea could also cause the same damage with a couple of airburst nukes. I was sold.

Sam laughed one day and said, "Matt, your old truck will be running when all of the new vehicles are dead on the side of the road. I bought a '74 Chevy Suburban last week to be my Bugout vehicle."

I replied, "What's a Bugout vehicle?"

"It's a vehicle that will run after an EMP blast or solar flare destroys the electronics in the modern vehicles. You need it to get to your Bugout location and for transportation after the lights go out."

"Do you have a Bugout location?"

"Yes."

"Where is it?"

"The first rule of a Bugout location is that its location is a secret. You don't want every Tom, Dick, and Harry showing up to take your food."

I replied, "Oh."

I thought, *oh shit. This could be serious.*"

Sam told me to go to the internet and look up "Carrington Event." Numerous articles explained the danger and the effects of a coronal mass ejection or solar flare. Below are my favorites.

"Carrington-class CME Narrowly Misses Earth

May 2, 2014: Last month (April 8-11), scientists, government officials, emergency planners and others converged on Boulder, Colorado, for NOAA's Space Weather Workshop—an annual gathering to discuss the perils and probabilities of solar storms.

The current solar cycle is weaker than usual so you might expect a correspondingly low-key meeting. On the contrary, the halls and meeting rooms were abuzz with excitement about an intense solar storm that narrowly missed Earth.

"If it had hit, we would still be picking up the pieces," says Daniel Baker of the University of Colorado, who presented a talk entitled The Major Solar Eruptive Event in July 2012: Defining Extreme Space Weather Scenarios. "– NASA SCIENCE/SCIENCE NEWS

"Experts Warn the Next Carrington Event Will Plunge Us Back Into the Dark Ages" –Infowars 2014

"Earth misses possible total destruction from Solar Flare." Newalk Publications – January 20, 2019.

Therefore, I started prepping. I watched the prepping show reruns on the History and A&E channels, bought a bunch of freeze-dried food, put a Bugout Bag together, and made sure my old Ford was in top mechanical condition. Keeping the Ford in great shape was easy since I owned half of an auto repair shop. I became a little paranoid. Hell, my friends and fellow teachers thought I was more than a little nuts. Prepping was all I talked about and spent most of my time doing each day.

Then one day there was an event at school that enabled me to spend all of my time prepping. I had been out to lunch braving the cold rainy day and returned to school with one of my fellow teachers. I was walking to the admin's office just after lunch when I heard yelling coming from a classroom up ahead on the right.

"Bitch, you can't give me an F. The coach will cut me from the team."

"Tom, calm down. Put that knife away."

There was a scream, I ran to the room and looked in to see what was happening. A large boy had a knife to Mrs. Wall's throat, backed up towards the door, and stopped in front of me. The students panicked and screamed at the boy holding the knife.

I looked for something to use as a weapon and saw a fire extinguisher. I quickly removed it from the enclosure raised it in the air and struck the knife-wielding assailant on the back of the head. He fell to the floor, and the knife rattled across the floor.

Mrs. Walls had a shallow cut on her throat but was otherwise okay. She collapsed onto her chair as one student called 911. Several students came up to me and thanked me for saving their teacher's life.

The EMT's arrived, pronounced the attacker dead, treated Mrs. Walls, and then took her to the hospital to be examined. The principle separated me from the thankful students and took me to her office.

"Matt, did you have to kill him? Why didn't you wait for the police to handle the attack? His parents are going to sue the school. What do you have to say for yourself?"

16

I was enraged by her ridiculous comment and replied, "I saved Mrs. Walls' life, and I'm not sorry that the scumbag student was killed in the process. Had you and the school board done your jobs that boy would have been behind bars years ago. The little bastard killed a cat and hung it from our flagpole. He broke a boy's leg because he wanted his seat on the bus. He kicked Mrs. Bean because she made him go to the principle for disrupting class. He was a turd, and you should have dealt with him years ago."

"Go home. You are suspended."

"Screw you. I quit."

***

When I left her office, two Police Officers "invited" me downtown to assist in the investigation.

I spent four hours that night telling my story, filling out forms, undergoing seemingly unending interrogations, and finally, in frustration, I lawyered up. I called the law office that handled my parent's estate, and they referred me to a criminal attorney. Smart move, I was out of there 20 minutes after he arrived.

In the community, I was either a hero or child murderer depending on which channel you watched on TV.

I stayed in my house for a week to avoid the reporters and cameras while I rethought the direction of my life. After a week of navel-gazing, I called Sam and sought his advice.

"Hey Sam, how's the wife and kids?"

"We're all okay. How are you? I think it's horrible how the media is treating you."

"Sam, this is one of the best things that ever happened to me."

"Really and how did you arrive at that conclusion?"

"I was sick and tired of the daily grind at school. That school and most schools in the country are falling apart due to the government spending money on everything, except what was needed.

I couldn't stand the administration letting those bastard kids get away with being hooligans.

I felt sorry for the good kids who came to school to learn but were harassed by the thugs and jocks. I was ready to leave, but just didn't have the guts."

"Well, if you are happy then I am happy for you. What are you going to do? Find a job?"

"Nah, I have a small inheritance from my folk's estate and plan to live off the grid and prepare for the apocalypse. What do you think about Wyoming?"

"If you like hunting, fishing, and bears, it's a great place. It would also be a great place to get away from the "Walking, Starving Dead" when the shit does hit the fan."

"Ayup, that's what I thought, too. Can you help me get caught up on surviving an EMP or CME? I'm already signed up for some survival and first aid courses."

"I'd be glad to. I can show you my homemade Faraday cages and give you plans for several different ones."

"What about a Faraday Cage big enough for a truck?"

"Not a problem. It's the same concept, but bigger and costs more. You just need a metal skin totally around the vehicle. A metal pole barn with no windows and a metal floor should work."

"When can we meet?"

"I'll come down to your house next Saturday. Have a six pack of Blue Moon for me."

"Done."

The next month sped by as I took short classes on first aid, solar installation, off grid living, survival cooking, sanitation, water purification...whew, I took a lot in, but I learned more than I could have ever imagined.

I decided that I really would make some big changes. I called a realtor and put my home up for sale.

The realtor inspected my parent's home and said, "Matt, your folks put a fortune into this house, and I won't be able to get nearly what they have in it back when it's sold. I mean, it's a 6,000 square foot modern home with a pool, guesthouse, and five acres in the high dollar section of Smyrna. I know the home has a lot of upgrades, but in this market, I don't think it will bring more than $700,000, and that's if you give me six months to sell it."

"What can you get if you have to sell it in two months?"

"I would guess around a hundred thousand less."

"Sell it in two months."

"My commission is 6%."

"Get it sold now."

"The house is in great shape. It will sell quickly at the reduced price."

"I also want to sell my dad's shop. Do you know anyone in commercial sales?"

"Yes, our Nashville office can handle the sale. May I assume a quick sale?"

"Yes, ma'am, I'll get my brother on board with the sale and be ready to discuss it with your broker."

"I have a friend in that division; his name is Fred Cabot. He'll call you this afternoon. What do you think the business is worth?"

"I turned down a million and a half a year ago from Nation Auto Repair. Wait, I think I should call them first. Sorry, but why pay a realtor if I can get a quick sale myself."

"I understand."

***

I called the general manager of the local Nation Auto Repair, and he put me in touch with the VP of Acquisitions.

"Mr. Jones, so you want to pursue selling to us now?"

"Well, I have a realtor who says they can get me $1.9 million less the $115,000 realtor fee. I'll take $1.8 and screw the realtor."

"Just a minute; I have to make a call."

As he spoke with the Executive VP for Acquisitions, I got a distinct feeling I was buying a used car. When he hung up he looked down and to the left, a sure sign he was lying, and with those hound dog eyes said, Matt, my boss says he is definitely interested in purchasing your shop, but our top price is $1.6 mill."

"Well," I said, "I understand. I'm sorry to waste your time, as well as mine. It's good that I have another appointment at 2:00 pm. If he can't meet my price, well, I guess I'll just hold onto the property, and consider renting it out."

I stood, offered my hand and said, "Thanks, again, have a nice day," and turned to leave.

His sad expression turned sincerely sad as he said, "Matt, sit down, maybe I can get him to raise our offer. Let me call him back. Please, have a seat."

I remained standing and said, "I'm not here to negotiate a selling price. $1.8 mill is the price. As I said, I have another appointment in about an hour and a half. If your boss can meet my price, please feel free to give me a call. I'll present it to my next appointment. Who knows, he may raise the bid.

Good day, sir," I said as I turned to the door.

"Matt, Matt, please, come on back. Tell ya' what I'll do, I'll give him a jingle right now and get his final offer. If he agrees to your price, can we conclude the deal, now? You can call and cancel your next appointment."

He stepped out of the room for five minutes, came back with a big smile on his face, and said, "It's a deal. Come by next Wednesday morning with a clear title, and we'll have the money wired directly to your bank just as soon as our lawyers Okay the title."

I thought to myself, yep, I'd smile all the way to the bank.

We shook hands, and I left to have lunch and then find my brother. Buddy had been pestering me to sell the shop since the day he found out we inherited it.

He and his wife were alcoholic yuppies living far beyond their means. The shop brought in $75,000 a year for each of us and would for many years, but his wife wanted a nicer house and a membership at the country club. I fought the sale for two years, but now I was ready to sell. I would take the money and buy my Bugout home in Wyoming.

I sat in the restaurant searching my iPad for land for sale in Wyoming. I searched several websites. You can buy a lot of land in Wyoming for half a million dollars, and I would have over a million in the bank after all bills were paid and I relocated.

On a whim, I called Buddy, and he answered, "Little brother, how's it hanging?"

"I am great. Hey, I need to talk with you. Can you come over to Chili's now?"

21

"I'm busy. Now if you've finally come to your senses and want to sell the shop, I'll be there in ten minutes."

"Get off your secretary and be here in five."

Buddy walked into the restaurant, and several of the waitresses came over and gave him a hug. He kissed them all on the cheek, ordered a pitcher of Margaritas, and came over to my table.

"Little brother, I'm glad you came to your senses. Did killing that punk help you decide?"

I punched him in the gut as hard as I could; he doubled over, sat down, and when he could breathe again, said, "I should whip your ass, but I need the money. Perhaps I'll whip your ass after the sale."

"Don't you ever say anything like that to me again, bro. Besides, you'll have to find me. I'm leaving town. I'm flying to Hawaii and Nashville can kiss my ass."

"Okay, okay, I'm sorry. That was a stupid thing to say. How much will we make?"

"We split $1.7 million after realtor fees."

"Holy shit, I thought the place was only worth $1.5. Kiss the realtor for me."

"He wouldn't like that. Now, I'll set up a meeting with our lawyer in the morning. Make sure you are there. You will sign whatever he tells you to sign and then next Wednesday I'll give you a check for $850,000. You have to handle any taxes, capital gains, etc. Check with your accountant."

"Hey, I'm a big boy. I can handle my money."

"Yeah, I guess you can."

"Give me a call and your contact information when you get settled. Marge and I'd like to have a relative to visit in Hawaii."

"I'll bet you would."

I shook his hand and left.

***

"Matt, I have the paperwork ready. Where's Buddy?"

"Relax; don't get your panties in a wad. He's getting a ton of money and will be on time."

"Does he know that you are the realtor?"

"Hell no, I worked hard to sell the property while he sat at every bar in town."

"You could have taken him to the cleaners, but I see you charged the standard 6%. All legal and kosher in my book."

Buddy barged in barely on time and said, "Where's my money."

Our lawyer answered, "Buddy sign here, here and there. That's all. Your money will be wired directly to your account by this time tomorrow."

"Great, come on little brother, let's go celebrate."

"No thanks, I have work to do," I said as I gave him a hug.

I never saw or spoke to him again.

The house sold three weeks later for $625,000, and I pocketed $587,500 plus another $150,000 from the sale of the furnishings, paintings, and vehicles. I was flush with 1.7 million cash and itching to find a new home so that I could get away from the reporters, critics, and people in general. I wanted just to be left alone.

Be careful what you wish for, cause ya' just might get it.

***

Smyrna, Tennessee

I made appointments with three different realtors that covered the entire state between them. I planned to give each one two days to show me their properties and then the following week I'd make a decision. I gave each one the following list of what I wanted:

- A medium size log house with a fireplace and a well
- At least five acres of tillable land
- A pond
- A metal garage at least 40x60
- 50 to 100 acres
- No one living nearby
- A river or lake nearby.
- A stream on the property
- No towns within 5 miles

All of them wanted more detail about the house, and my family. We settled on a minimum of two bedrooms and two baths. I gave them a limit of $600,000-$700,000. They each sent six listings and asked me to choose three to speed up my visit and make it as productive as possible.

I gave them a week to find suitable listings and flew out to Casper, which was closest to the first listings. I had three flights and had to change planes once to get to Casper.

I always enjoyed looking down at the land, houses, and farms below when I flew, but this time the scenery had more significance since I could be living on a piece of that ground below. There was still snow on the high peaks, and the white blanket made a stark contrast with the rocky terrain and trees.

Hatch Realty and Ann Baxter's properties looked good on paper, but none of them was a fit for my needs. What I didn't tell the realtors was that I hired a helicopter to shuttle me around for the week. I wanted to see the properties from the air. Yes, I did the Google Earth search, but nothing replaces a real time flyover. Four houses had been built in the 13 months since Google had last mapped the area. These four properties had neighbors less than two miles away and were too accessible.

I was through looking at the houses by 10:00 am on the second day and instructed the pilot to fly me to Pinedale, which was 180 miles away.

Pinedale, WY

We landed at the Pinedale airport, I looked over at the pilot and said, "Roger, I will rent two cars and need you to take my bags over to the Lakeside Lodge, check us in, and then I won't need you until breakfast at 5:00 am.

Our first listing is at 11:00 and I want you to fly us over all three before we pick up the realtor at 10:00. I hate surprises, so we'll do a little scouting ahead of time. Here's some money. Go try to enjoy yourself tonight."

"Sir, you already pay for everything."

"Please, take it. It will make me feel better. I'm going to drive into Pinedale and walk around to see if I like the place."

"Okay and thanks. Remember not to exert yourself too much until you get used to the altitude."

Damn, that's why I was tired and breathing harder than normal. We were at 7,000 feet above sea level. The air is definitely thin up this high.

The clerk at the counter said, "Mr. Jones we only have one of your cars here at the airport. You can take one, and I'll have someone give you a ride to our main office in Pinedale for the other car."

"That's not a problem. Roger, take the car, and I'll go to Pinedale."

Roger left and headed to the lodge. I was waiting for a ride when several people came into the lobby from an inbound flight.

The clerk looked up and said, "Patty, glad to see you back home. Sorry about your mom. How are the folks back in Colorado?"

I looked over to the woman approaching the desk and saw an attractive redhead wearing jeans, a Levi jacket, and cowboy boots. She had a Stetson hat on top of her long red hair.

"Carl, I'm glad to get home and away from my family. It was crazy. Everyone was fighting over mom's house and possessions.

Oh, I'm sorry, who is your friend?"

"This is Matt Jones; he is interested in making Pinedale his home if he can find a homestead that suits him. Hey, he needs a ride to our office. Could he hitch a ride into town with you? It would save me a trip."

She replied, "Hi Matt, I'm Patty Gale, and I run the Gale General Store and Hardware Shop in Pinedale."

"Pleased to meet you, but I don't want to impose."

"Nonsense, grab your gear and follow me to my truck."

"Thanks, I'm ready to go. I sent my gear on to the Lakeside Lodge with my friend."

She had 1967 short narrow bed Ford pickup that appeared to be in excellent condition.

"I like your truck. Is it your husband's hobby?"

"No, it was my dad's and I restored it after he passed four years ago. My husband is a city boy who does not like to get his hands dirty.

I like working with my hands. I did all of the work myself except for the local body shop that painted it for me. How do you like the Black Cherry color?"

"I like it a lot. I have a black 1949 FI that I inherited from my father. The bodywork and interior, I had restored. I swapped out the old flat head for a 460 with a C6 tranny and a heavy-duty rear end. It's set up with none of the fancy electronics; just a carb and a distributor with points."

Patty started laughing, and I was turning red-faced when she said, "This is quite a coincidence, I'm also a prepper. I don't think the world is going to end, but snow storms, earthquakes and you know, shit happens. I am working to prepare for any opportunities to excel that may come along."

"I didn't say I was a prepper. I just like the old way of doing things."

"Really? I think you are a prepper who wants to get away from people and be ready for when TSHTF. But that's your business and none of mine."

That made me chuckle. I felt better and replied, "I'm looking for a modest home with 50 to 100 acres that I can get away from the rat race and not be bothered by people. Do you know of any places for sale like that? Carson Realty is showing me three properties tomorrow."

"Is one of them the Williamson place?"

"I don't know. I just have the addresses. Here are the three listings."

She pulled into a parking space at a gas station and looked them over.

"No, it's not here. The third one might do for you, but I'll bet the first two will not be to your liking. They are mansions with rocky property, but great views of the mountains. You know those places are selling for around half a million to three-quarters of a million dollars don't you?"

"Yes, that was the range I told Carson."

"I think Mary Williamson is ready to sell her place and it would be perfect. It's about eight miles north of town. Her husband was a scientist for NASA and a hardcore prepper. They built their home to his specifications and spent a fortune getting it prepared for the upcoming apocalypse."

"You sound sure an apocalypse is coming. I don't know that I want a place that everyone in town knows about. A Bugout location should be a secret."

"Mr. Williamson was positive that TEOTWAWKI (The End of the World as we know it) was always just around the corner. The house's upgrades are a secret. I know because Mary is like my sister. I supplied most of the material and delivered it myself to the construction crews. The crew that installed the survival upgrades flew in from North Carolina. Mary's husband figured that if the SHTF, North Carolina was too far away for the crew to show up on his front door.

It's a beautiful log house with a basement blasted into the rock and has a large safe room. There are a large metal barn and seven acres suitable for farming. She also has horses, mules, cattle, chickens, and a gaggle of geese.

Her dad read that the Roman Legions kept geese as sentries. He loved to say, "Hey, ya can't sneak up on a goose."

Oh, shoot, I forgot she owns about 125 acres. Now, most of the acreage is rocky mountainsides and ravines, but excellent hunting and fishing."

"It sounds too good to be true. Why are you being so helpful?"

"I want to help my friend, and I also believe that someone like you will pay top dollar for her place. Many others would not appreciate some of the, uh, upgrades.

I'll talk with her today, call you back, and let you know if she is interested. If she is, you can save some money on the realtor fee. By the way, I don't like John Carson. He is an egotistical bastard."

"Okay, sounds good, and thanks."

I got out at the car rental office and gave her my phone number.

I got my car and headed out to find a place to eat lunch. I found a diner next door to Gale's General Store and ate lunch there. I thought about going into the store, but thought she might think I was a stalker.

I walked around town for a couple of hours, but I stood out like a sore thumb dressed in my slacks, golf shirt and windbreaker, so I walked into Gale's General Store and bought some clothes that were more appropriate for the area.

"Howdy, whatcha....oh, Hello, what can I do for you," said the man behind the counter?

"I need a pair of jeans, a denim long sleeve shirt, and a Levi Jacket. Oh, and a pair of good boots."

"Yeah, you do kinda look like a city dude. We can take care of you. Let's see; you are a 34 waist by 30-inch inseam and a large shirt and jacket."

"Yes, but make it an extra-large jacket. I like plenty of room. I'd like the pre-worn look clothes if you have them."

Smiling, the clerk said, "Sure thing, Partner, coming right up. I'd recommend some of these wool hiking socks to help break in the boots. We don't want you to get blisters on your first day here. Go through the red door, and the fitting room is on the left."

I walked through the red door and saw Patty. I started to say hello, and she placed her finger over her lips and whispered, "You never met me. I'll explain tomorrow."

She called about two hours later and said that the Williamson house could be for sale if the price were right. Patty said that we could look at it the day after tomorrow at 2:00 pm. I told her to meet me at the airport at 1:00.

***

Don't give up yet. I promise, the end of the world is coming, but for now, I have to tell about how I got to know Patty and Mary and how shit happened. Besides, how many wannabe authors survived "The Flare?" This might be your only chance to read about one of the most significant occurrences in human history.

★

The Alpha Omega trio did not follow the rogue star. They formed a line and began falling away from the galactic core. Away, and toward an M-Class star on the outer edge of this spiral galaxy. It is a small yellow star.

Chapter 2

The Williamson Homestead

8 miles from Pinedale, WY

John Carson was a pompous ass just as Patty had warned me. Two of the three properties were not even close to the specifications I gave him.

The first day was a total waste, but the third property was a close fit to my seemingly unorthodox quest but was $750,000, which was more than I want to spend since I planned to spend another $200,000 to install the necessary security and prepping features. The extra cost was in six bedrooms and five baths.

"Matt this house is perfect for you. It has 25 acres, a large house, and a large barn."

"If it were $450,000, I'd be interested. What part of my instructions did you fail to understand? I feel like you wasted my time and you are now trying to pressure me into a property that is overpriced for what I want. Man, I live alone. I need a 1,500-2,000 square foot house and 100 acres. Thanks, but I'll pass. I love the area, but these aren't for me."

"Matt, I know the area, and you won't find any property better suited to your needs. Call me if you change your mind."

We dropped him off at the airport, and I asked Roger to fly me around the area to familiarize myself with the countryside the north side of Pinedale.

We spent a couple of hours checking out lakes and even stopped at an outfitters store to ask about the area. The owner had the normal hunting, fishing and backpacking equipment and supplies, but I was pleasantly surprised to see a large section of survival gear and food. We had supper at the diner in town, then went to a bar on the road north of Pinedale, and spent a couple of hours drinking and shooting the shit with some good old local boys.

I was talking with the owner of a dude ranch when there was a commotion at the back of the room. I heard glass break, men yelling, and then a fight broke out. Two big bouncers ended the fight quickly enough.

"George, get your sorry ass out of here and don't come back until you can act like a man. The next time you put your hands on my wife's ass, I will kick yours so hard you'll taste my shoe strings. Now get the hell out of here you damn drunk."

The bouncers took him out the front door, took his car keys, and told him to walk home. I saw his face as they dragged him out of the bar. It was George Gale, Patty's husband.

***

Patty arrived on time, and I asked her if it was okay if we took the helicopter over to the Williamson place so I could see it from the air.

"It's okay with me, but I'd better call Mary, so she doesn't try to shoot us down."

I laughed, but Patty interrupted and said, "I'm not kidding. She takes her privacy seriously."

She called Mrs. Williamson and received permission for us to fly over the ranch. I had Roger fly around for half an hour until I saw the entire property. The house was half a mile off a dirt road and in the middle of the acreage. Most of the land was rocky foothills about eight miles northeast of Pinedale.

It was great hunting property and had several lakes and streams with the house in the middle of the 20 or so acres of flat land. We landed the chopper on the front lawn about 50 yards from the house. Mrs. Williamson waved to us from the front porch.

As Patty and I were walking to the house she said, "Sorry about the other day, but my husband is very jealous, and I didn't want him to get the wrong impression."

"Not a problem. I'm just happy that you took the time to show me this property."

"I'm glad to help."

I didn't tell her about seeing her husband being thrown out of the bar. I didn't want to embarrass her.

Patty introduced us, and I shook Mary's hand before we went into the house and sat in the great room. She was not what I expected at all. I thought she would be a nice old grandma type with her hair rolled up in a bun. Instead, I saw a nice looking woman about 40 years old and rather attractive.

The log house was not what I expected either. It was 2,500 square feet with an open floor plan and cathedral ceilings that had the exposed support logs showing. It was beautiful.

"Matt, my husband and I built our home after he quit NASA. He had several patents on improvements to some type of oil drilling equipment, so money wasn't an issue. I was one of his students twenty years ago. My husband thought that the world was only a short time from an all out nuclear war and was obsessed with being prepared to survive. I played along with his strange hobby as long as I got what I wanted in my house. I'll tell you a little about the construction and features before we take a tour."

"That would be nice."

"There is a five thousand gallon water tank under the house, a bomb shelter supplied with food, water, radios and other supplies designed to support four people for three months without leaving the shelter. The bomb shelter, as well as the barn, is EMP proof, as are all of the vehicles on the property. We have two pickups, a tractor with a bucket, two ATVs, a golf cart, and a large two-ton truck in the barn. All are EMP proof. There are two fuel tanks under the barn. There are a 5,000-gallon gas tank and two 2,500-gallon diesel tanks, one for the generator and one for the trucks.

I'll keep the Chevy pickup. There is a small warehouse in the basement with enough food to keep four people alive for over a year. There is a large steel safe full of ammunition and guns of all types in the bomb shelter."

"Are the guns included in the sale?"

"Yes, I never liked guns much. I keep a .357 magnum in my purse, but never had a need for any of those fancy military or hunting weapons."

The bomb shelter was in the basement, and I would have never found it in a year of looking. Two hidden mechanical latches allowed you to pull a five-inch thick steel door outward to allow entrance.

Mary made me go back up the stairs so she could keep their location secret until after I bought the place. The bomb shelter was a small house with two bedrooms, small living room, a large warehouse of food and supplies, and a bathroom. The gunroom had hidden mechanical latches to gain entrance.

We ducked into the gun room, which also had large safe type door with a combination lock just inside the entrance. I saw twenty long guns and shelves full of pistols and ammunition. I picked up a Barret .50 Cal BMG and looked through the scope. I was in hog heaven. There were several Bushmasters, M&P15s, AR10s, 2 Remington Model 700s and a host of other rifles and shotguns. I especially liked the Keltec KSG bullpup that held 14 rounds of 12 gauge shells.

Barely able to contain myself, I said, "I like what I see. I'd planned to buy many of the same guns."

Smiling, she said, "Really? Well, I'm not much of a gun person, but I know my husband only bought the best. We have a 1,000-yard target range down by the smallest lake. The property has two lakes, three ponds, and two year round quick flowing creeks on the property.

Shoot, I could go on for hours. Oh, yes, we have solar heating, solar cells on the roof, wind turbines for electricity and a geothermal heating system, and every critical energy source or heat source has a second backup."

I was speechless...well, for a second or two, before I said, "Very impressive. So far, it all looks good."

I finally asked, "Why are you selling your home?"

"I'm alone and can't keep the place up without my husband to help. I want to move into town and take it easy. I want to enjoy reading by the fireplace instead of tending to the horses, mules, goats, chickens, and assorted other animals that my husband acquired over the years. I know you want to know what I am asking for the place and I think $700,000 is a fair asking price."

"Ma'am, from what I've heard and seen so far, I agree."

"Will you be bringing your family out in the near future?"

"I only have two Springer Spaniels, no wife or kids. I was a public school teacher who finally burned out trying to teach kids who did not want to learn, thanks to a no responsibility society.

That was at the same time; my wife decided she liked her boss at the real estate office better than me. I was, apparently, too boring, and not rich enough. I did: however, inherit some money from my parents and decided to get away and prepare for the inevitable demise of a society that doesn't deserve to survive. I'm sorry, I didn't mean to say those things, and I don't have much of an exciting story to tell."

"Matt, I looked you up on the internet and found that you have a very exciting story to tell, you are a real hero. You saved that teacher from certain death, and then got the shaft from the school board."

Somewhat embarrassed, I replied, "Hardly a hero, it all happened so fast.

Please, I'm sincerely asking you to keep all of that ancient history to yourself. I want to live quietly, and in peace. I didn't even tell my drunken brother where I moved."

She looked a bit embarrassed herself and said, "I'll keep your secret, but you should know we have some great women out here who would love to date a real man like yourself."

"I don't want to sound unappreciative, but I'm not ready for that yet."

"Okay, I get it, and I am sorry. I didn't mean to pry into your business."

"No, really, it's okay; I didn't take it that way. I can tell that you have a good heart, besides all you gals love to be matchmakers but for right now, I just want to be alone for a while with my dogs and the great outdoors."

Thinking back on that encounter, I think Patty was blushing the whole time…could be wrong, but…maybe.

We spent the next two hours taking a tour of the place with Mary. I found that everything I had planned to do to make my new home apocalypse-proof had already been done and more.

Her husband had even installed a sluice run across one of the creeks and installed an electric turbine to produce electricity. This property was producing enough electricity to power a small village. The power plant was also enclosed in a Faraday cage, and the small lake, which was spring fed had clear, but danged cold water fit for swimming.

I took a short break from the women, and, over a tall glass of sweet tea, I looked at my planned list of improvements and realized that Mr. Williamson had already made or installed everything on my extensive list. Obviously, great minds *do* think alike.

He had even installed a top-notch wireless security system with cameras and a gated entry to the house.

He had also installed a series of old telephone poles and repurposed them as fence posts with inch thick cables running through each of them at both chest and knee height. Hell, it would take a tank to ram its way onto the property. I only had to make just a few additions, and this property would become perfect for my needs.

I asked Mrs. Williamson to meet privately with me. We sat down and talked about the property.

"I think your place is worth the $700,000 and won't try to talk you down, but I do have some questions and reservations."

"Shoot."

"Can I talk you into giving me some training on the home's features?"

"I'd be glad to. If you commit to the purchase, we can work out a schedule for next week."

"All right, agreed, of course. With luck, we can get that done this week. Since this is a cash sale, a survey is not required. I'm comfortable with the stated boundaries. I think we could close this week.

Oh, I almost forgot, are there fish in the lakes and streams?"

"Yes, my husband fished several times a week and always brought trout, bass, and bream to our table. He said they were full of fish. Of course, no one else was allowed to fish or hunt on our property."

"Will you be giving Patty a fee for bringing us together? If not, I want to reward her myself," she asked.

"I planned to give her $20,000."

"Good and I'll add another $20,000 to match yours. Now, what do you know about her husband?"

Deciding to be brutally honest, I said, "I saw him at a bar last night. I found him to be a pitiful piece of crap, a drunken, worthless shit.

I don't want him to know about the property."

A solemn look drained Mary's face of color as she said, "Yes, that sounds like a regular night for him, and yes, you are right about keeping him in the dark. He would spill his guts after a few drinks."

"I would appreciate it if you were to give her my money also and tell her it's payment for services rendered, and don't take no for an answer. Let's give it to her in cash to help her hide the money from her husband and the stinkin' Feds. I get the feeling she might need a safety net one of these days."

"Matt, I have exactly the same thought. Don't worry; I'll take care of it."

"If you'll get your lawyer to draw up the papers, I'll have the money wired to your bank at closing. Which bank do you use?"

"Wells Fargo."

"Good, I'll start my own account there this afternoon. Oh, do you want a deposit?"

Smiling, she said, "No, I wasn't trying to sell the house so no loss if you walk. I do need 30 days to move out, and that is not negotiable. Agreed?"

"Not a problem, as long as I can start moving my stuff into the garage and the barn immediately."

"Sure, that's fine with me. I plan to stay around here and will probably move into a hotel until I find a nice little home."

"You can stay here until you find a place. I'm eager to get moved out here, not eager to kick you out. Why waste the money on a hotel?"

"I might take you up on that, so don't offer unless you mean it."

"I do mean it. It will also give us an overlap on anything I need to know about the property.

So, do I have my Shangri-La?"

Smiling, but serious, she said, "Absolutely, as soon as I have the dough in my account. You do have the money, right?"

Laughing now, I said, "Yeah, I think I might be able to scrape up the cash. Seriously, it's a done deal from my side."

We shook hands, and then I took Patty back to the airport.

"Can I buy lunch?"

"No, my husband will be looking for me."

"Patty thanks for putting me in contact with Mary. I promise you that I'll never forget your help. You'll also be receiving a nice reward for helping us with the sale."

"Oh no, I can't take your money."

"The hell you can't, and yes you will. I'd much rather a nice person like you gets paid than a twerp like Carson. You earned it. Mary will handle it when we close."

She blushed and said, "Well, okay, thanks, I can use the money. My trip back home nearly broke the bank, and my inheritance is tied up in court for several months to make sure my mom's bills are paid."

As she walked away, I thought, *damn, too bad she's married.* Then I mentally slapped myself for even having those thoughts after just escaping from Jane. That woman made me distrust all members of the female persuasion. I know that line of thinking isn't rational, but it is what it is. I just wanted to get into my new home, make a few new friends, and hide out until whatever happened, happened.

We were able to get the house inspection done in 2 days, and two days later, on Friday. Man, oh man, things sure run at a different pace in beautiful Wyoming. Of course, we didn't let the man see any of the secret rooms or survival features.

I was unbelievably happy. Then I calmed down, did my usual thing, and put a list together of stuff I wanted to do, and things I needed to purchase.

After working on my list, I suddenly realized that, even though I still had a considerable nest egg, I also had no income. Ouch. Therefore, I put a budget together that had me eating a quarter of the time on my stock of food so I would keep most of it from spoiling. I would fish and trap another quarter and purchase the rest from the General store.

I figured that if I could stick to my new plan, I wouldn't go broke for about 20 years...after that...hmmm. Oh well, I'd worry about that 20 years from now.

Still, I decided to purchase 100 pounds of pre-1964 silver coins as a hedge, to make my nest egg good for 15 years. I told myself that silver would have to increase in value, and if the worst happened, I thought that a silver quarter would always buy a loaf of bread.

I also planned to inventory my survival supplies and food. Mary's husband had a perpetual inventory system that he kept on clipboards hanging from the doors to the supplies. I told myself that I would try to keep that system up to date.

"Did I mention that I was happy?"

***

The Wrangler Café

Pine St, Pinedale, Wyoming

The dawn sky had been a bright crimson red and had turned nearly black as the sun rose and fought to penetrate the storm's clouds. The weather front brought a wind driven rain. Happily, the late morning forecast promised clearing skies with calming winds.

Mary switched her gaze from the wet street and clearing skies to Patty as she sipped her tea during their luncheon at The Wrangler Cafe and said, "I like that Matt. He's gonna make some woman a great husband."

"Yes, he seems to be one of the near extinct good ones. Not that I'd know from any of my experiences. Are you going to play cupid and fix him up with one of our single gals in town?"

"Something like that. There has to be a special woman out there for him. He needs time to heal, and I do believe that time heals all wounds."

"Yes, I guess it does. At least I hope it does. Oh, I'm sorry; I didn't mean to say that."

"I know honey, but if you ever need to talk, well, you know where I am.

Now, I have a small satchel with some cash in it for you that express both Matt's and my appreciation for your help in selling the house and property. Keep it close *and* hidden from everyone else. Do you understand?" Mary asked as she handed the bag to Patty."

"Matt told me about this, and when I told him I couldn't take any money for doing you a favor, he said that I could and I would. Still, I can't take this much just for introducing you two."

"Not to be repetitive, but yes, you can, and yes, you will! I only put in half, and Matt put the other half in for you. He is very thankful that you warned him about Carson and helped him find my place. You saved him hundreds of thousands of dollars."

"He does seem to be a straightforward and honest man. Kinda' cute, too."

"He spoke highly of you as well."

"Don't try to push him at me. I'm happily married."

"Bull shit. I'm your friend, so don't even think about lying to me. I've seen the black eyes and bruises. No woman falls down that much. Hell girl, everyone in town knows George is banned from all but two bars in town for picking fights when he gets sloppy drunk. Now you listen to me. You keep this money hidden, and not in a bank that will create a paper trail. Don't you dare let George blow it on booze and women."

Patty started crying, and Mary went around the table to comfort her.

"I didn't know that people knew he was seeing Jean."

"The snake hits on every woman in town when he's had a snoot full. He does most of his whoring around away from home, but everyone knows everyone else in a small community. Sorry, but you need to kick his ass out. The store is yours, and you can make a good living from it once he stops robbing you blind."

"I hate the thought of divorce and always felt I could change him. It's taken a long time, but now I know that won't happen. You're right; I have to stand up and stop being a doormat. I'll do it. I'll see a lawyer next week."

"That a girl. Maybe you'll find a nice man who needs a good woman like you."

"Mary, you old dog. You want to fix me up with the new rich guy."

"I'm only a few years older than you. Matt's not rich. He inherited enough money to buy my place and live a simple life off the grid. He's also single, has two dogs and no kids. I like him."

"Then you date him."

"Smart ass."

***

The next 30 days flew by as I traveled back and forth between Pinedale and Smyrna. Mary insisted that I stay at my new home during the transition. I quickly fell in love with the place, as did Gus and Tina, my dogs. They spent a great part of

43

the day romping around the property chasing squirrels and rabbits and being chased by the geese.

In my spare time, I had my, soon to be ex-garage convert my 1949 FI to four wheel drive, sold my car and bought a used Jeep Rubicon. I had the garage convert the ignition and fuel injection to EMP proof pre 1974 type systems. Then I had them shipped to Pinedale, Wyoming. Sounds good to say that, yep, I think I'm gonna like my new hometown.

A moving company took only one truckload to move my belongings from Smyrna to Pinedale. Most of the furniture stayed with the house, but I kept my dad's personal mechanic's tools, woodworking machines, and gun collection.

I also purchased a large amount of gold and silver coins and had them shipped to my new homestead. The coins were placed in a safe in the gun room inside of the bomb shelter. Pardon the pun, but you can't be too safe in post-apocalyptic America with your gold and silver. I would also place most of my barter goods in the bomb shelter.

I started calling my new home, 'The Jones Homestead.' It just sounded good to me, and I was the only one I had to please these days.

I closed out my bank account in Smyrna and transferred all of my money to the Wells Fargo branch in Pinedale.

I spent several hours nearly every night researching on the internet to figure out the best trade goods I should purchase to replace paper money when it became worthless. Food, whiskey, ammunition, guns, medical supplies, feminine hygiene products, especially toilet paper, and birth control items were high on the list along with silver and gold.

I ordered large quantities of all of the above except for guns through the internet and had them delivered to Patty's store so she could deliver them to the homestead. I tried to pay her for delivering the supplies, but she wouldn't hear of it. No one, but Patty and her husband knew there were large quantities of supplies since she made several deliveries to out of town customers each week. Patty knowing was one thing, but I was not happy about that rat bastard husband of hers knowing anything about me at all.

The truth is that I was like a kid in a candy store. I only bought what I needed to survive, but think about it; it's all stuff that's fun for the most part. Guns, knives, axes, water distillation devices, supplies for my Bugout bag, backpacks, animal traps, survival food and the list, goes on and on. A hundred thousand dollars can buy you a lot of shit.

I still had over $800,000 in the bank. I would put aside enough to pay taxes just in case the apocalypse doesn't happen before April 15 next year. I was happy, happy, happy.

Well, I was happy until I met one more time with my buddy Sam Nolin the next Saturday to update him and say goodbye. We met for supper at the Outback in Murfreesboro, and I filled him in on my progress.

"Well, you certainly have accomplished a great deal over the past two months. Your new home sounds perfect. Now, what do you do if twenty armed men attack and take it away from you?"

I stammered and cussed before answering, "I'd fight back and kill the bastards."

"Yeah, sure, one man against twenty? Do you think you could win that battle? They could take turns sleeping while half attack your home every hour of the day until you fall asleep."

"Shit, I hadn't thought about that. I don't want more people at my place to share in the security. What the hell do I do?"

"Well, keep your place a secret for starters. Plan on being run out of your home. Hide supplies in several locations away from the house. I would suggest using plastic drums to store food, water, guns, and ammunition. The things you need to survive. You might build a couple of small cabins on your property far away from the house for shelter during those cold ass winters, and Matt, the winters in Wyoming are freakin' cold."

"Boy did you burst my bubble. I lose my house forever and live like a cave man."

"No. You regroup and fight a guerilla war against those bastards and retake your home after you pick them off one at a time."

"Look, I'm not Rambo. I'd just try to live off the land."

"No, you'll do what you need to do to survive, and keep what is yours. Take some more survival, first aid, and marksmanship courses. Be prepared for any and everything.

Oh, make sure you have several suppressors and learn to use a compound bow. Learn to kill silently. A quiet shot from half a mile away gives you time to escape. An arrow is a silent death. You could kill a dozen men one at a time and never alarm the rest."

I was confused about something he had said, "Suppressor, don't you mean silencer? Don't silencers just go pfft when you shoot?"

Shaking his head, Sam said, "Jeez Matt, that's 007 movie crap. Now listen and listen good. The word is suppressor because there is no such thing as a silencer. There is still a loud but suppressed bang, and think about it, when that slide slams a new round into the chamber it makes noise, so get that movie crap out of your head. Guns are noisy…period. Now, that's why you need to learn to use a bow; remember what I said, arrows are silent killers. Kill quietly, and it will scare the dog crap out of those thievin' bastards. Got it?"

I was embarrassed, and ashamed that I hadn't realized these things before, but said, "All right, good advice. Now I will be Rambo."

"Take the courses far away from your home. The guy training you could be the guy coming to take it away from you.

Don't tell anyone where it is. You have already told me too much my friend. Even your friends will kill you to get food for their starving children."

"I will take your warnings to heart and do my best to use your advice."

"Matt, one last thing; I have a friend at NASA who gave me a heads up that both NASA and the Military expect major solar storms at any time. You will soon see radio and cell phone reception become spotty and have interference.

The grid will definitely go down in some areas around the world. The Aroura Borealis will reach much further south. The big Carrington event could happen before winter."

"Oh shit! Why aren't they warning the public?"

"Right, oh shit! They think there is nothing the public can do to get prepared and want to avoid panic. The panic could be worse than the actual event."

"Thank God for your friend."

"I'd take the courses and then get home, stop traveling by air no later than 90 days from now and then stick close to home until it passes. Don't be in a plane when the Coronal Mass Ejection hits the earth. Only some military planes can survive a major solar flare."

"Thanks, that's great advice, and for setting me straight on suppressors. I just can't believe that I hadn't realized that a gun wouldn't go pfft."

Chuckling, Sam said, "Atta boy, Matt, now here is one last topic. I know you've noticed the infrastructure of our country has been left to rot for years, we pulled our military from overseas and are fighting a major war against crime and drugs in South America."

"Yes, but what do those have to do with prepping?'

"I don't know, but I think the government has some secret project that is the largest ever conducted. Don't count on them for any help and they may even become our biggest threat to survival."

"Thanks, Sam. You have probably saved my life, and I'll probably never see you again. Sam, take this as a token of thanks for saving my life. Open it when you get home."

I handed him the small box with $50,000 cash and said, "Goodbye my old friend."

As I was leaving, he said, "Be careful."

***

I found several survival schools in the Atlanta and Dallas areas and signed up to take courses over the next two months. Then I found the local Red Cross manager and signed up for First Responder training.

I learned about survival medicine, edible wild plants, snares, booby traps, shelter building, surviving without weapons, knife fighting, and a host of other skills. I took several more courses during late summer and early fall. This caused me to stay longer than I had planned. I almost wished the shit would hurry up and hit the fan so I could use the training.

Then I came to my senses and decided when I got home I would start living as though the fit had hit the Shan. This made me very proud to know I could use my newly gained skills to prepare me for when it happened.

Yep, be careful what you ask for.

When I flew back to Pinedale, Mary was kind enough to pick me up at the airport. As I came out of the terminal, the Wyoming cold hit me like a hammer to my kneecaps. I thought, oh crap, I didn't expect it to be this cold in mid-fall. There, it was; the Wyoming cold and it was going to get much colder with a lot

48

of snow. Snow was already ass deep to a tall Indian at elevations only 500 feet above my little oasis.

Tennessee was never as cold as it was about to get in Pinedale.

She asked about my trip back east and said, "I'm so happy you are back, something is going on. I don't know exactly what but TV and radio signals have gotten very bad since yesterday, and the internet went down this morning.

The news is filled with new wars being fought around the globe. Russia, China, and Iran were running amuck conquering territories around them. The surprise this morning was that suddenly Russia attacked India in a massive invasion preceded with a nuclear exchange. The Indians lost.

The Chinese launched a massive invasion of Southeast Asia, the Philippines, and Sumatra at the same time. The world was going crazy. I was just glad we weren't fighting.

That quickly changed when news of our victories against the drug gangs in South America turned vicious. Our President went on TV, said that several of the South American governments were in collusion with the gangs, and had to be replaced. The USA would watch over them until they could hold free elections. The world was going crazy."

Stunned nearly beyond words, I said, "What? Are you serious? All this happened since yesterday?"

"What the fuck is going on, Matt?"

I was glad I was dropping out and had moved to Wyoming.

✪✪✪

49

⭐

The cold depths of space held the atmospheres of these three wandering nomads frozen for billions of years until, dead ahead, a faint pinhead of light began beckoning the trio on a collision course with a yellow sun billions of miles away.

Chapter 3

The Jones Homestead

The place was finally mine, and all of my possessions had been delivered. I had been gone for eight weeks when I walked up the four steps to the house.

"Matt, you look like you haven't eaten for a week. You look like Rambo coming up the steps with that pistol, knife, and ammo belt."

"I've been taking some courses in living in the mountains. I learned how to trap, hunt, skin, and tan pelts. I'm not Jim

Bridger, but I can survive in the woods. Keep all of that to yourself."

"Of course I will."

"Matt, if the shit hits the fan and I showed up on your doorstep, would I be welcome?"

I gave her a hug and replied, "Mary, you will always be welcome here but please don't bring half the town."

"Thanks and I'd never do that."

"I need to fill you in on the real reason my husband quit NASA and built this place."

"I thought he retired."

"No, he was part of a team that discovered something horrible was going to happen and he quit to prepare this place so we could survive.

Only a handful of scientists, military, and government officials know about the pending apocalypse, and half don't believe the worst will happen."

"What is the cause of the alarm?"

"In two months the sun enters the highest solar activity phase in the last 10,000 years. If we get hit with a CME during this period, it will make the Carrington event pale in comparison."

"But that wouldn't cause an apocalypse; it would ruin satellites, disrupt the grid, and create havoc with GPS systems. The governments of the world would just shut all power generating stations, transformers, and communications down during the event. It would only take months to recover."

"That's true if it wasn't for Alpha Omega I, II, and III."

"What the heck are they?"

"Astronomers think they are part of a young solar system that didn't form properly or part of an older one where their sun went Nova. The bottom line is that they are going to hit the sun during this peak period of solar activity."

"Mary, of course, that sounds really bad, but the sun is so large that it wouldn't even notice the impact."

She took on a sullen appearance and retorted, "Matt, you could not be more wrong. The Sun will definitely notice, and it will cause an enormous Coronal Mass Ejection that will fry all electronics and will potentially be an E.L.E. (Extinction Level Event) on the side of the earth that is hit."

Now I felt her dread, and became ashen-faced as I asked, "When is this supposed to happen?

"The solar activity has already started and will get much worse over the next two months.

The first collision will occur in 59 days, the second three days later, and the last and worst 29 days after that."

As she continued, her voice began to develop a vibrato effect in her effort to hold back the tears that threatened to overwhelm her. "The problem is that these planets are hundreds of times larger than the earth. The second one is the smallest, and it is massive.

I can't remember the composition of the planets, but the largest has a core of molten iron but is surrounded with frozen Hydrogen thousands of miles thick.

The first two stir up the shit, and the third's impact causes large ejections of plasma that may entirely circle the sun and send an E.L.E. our way.

A direct CME hit wipes out all life and leaves the Earth a scorched ball. A near miss just ends life for those caught on the receiving end of this horror," sobbed Mary, now unable to hold back her tears.

I slumped back into my chair and said, "Damn, I don't know how to process this information. I need a day or two to clear the shit from my brain and think about this."

"The good news is my husband's astronomer friends are certain that we will only get a close miss by the largest CME, loss of all unshielded electronics and back to the wild, wild west, oil lamps, and for most people, just one horsepower, if they can get a horse."

"Wait a minute. Will the Faraday cages work?"

"Yes, well, in theory, God Willing and the crick don't rise. That's why your bomb shelter, barn, and garage were built to withstand any Solar Flare or EMP attack. I know, the construction doesn't look it, but every building on the homestead is a steel building. The logs are just façade.

"And the government isn't telling anyone?" I asked, my depression turning to anger, near rage.

"No. That pissed Frank off and helped him decide to quit. The government has been stockpiling electronic gear and manufacturing replacement transformers for two years, but Frank told me that they would only go to the major cities on both coasts while we sit in the dark, for decades, maybe forever. The government has not told any other country. They feel this gives us an advantage in the post-apocalypse. The government doesn't know that the scientists leaked the info to the Brits and Israelis."

"I'm sorry, but I can't wrap my head around this. Let's get back together and determine what we have to accomplish in the next 59 days. Does Patty know?"

"Only you and I know."

"Let's not tell her or anyone else. We just charge ahead getting ready."

"I agree. One favor please."

"Shoot."

"Can Patty and I stay with you in the bomb shelter when the last collision occurs?"

"Of course you will! Look I just gotta ask. Why did you sell the place if you knew this was coming?"

"My husband was dead, and I didn't care about living. I already liked Patty, but during the sale, I got to know her much better and then I met you.

I really haven't spent much time with anyone in town because Frank and I stayed at the homestead. Now I know you two and feel as though you are my friends. I want you two to survive."

"Is your middle name Cupid?"

"Maybe, time will tell."

Mary moved into the guest room and still cooked for us every day. She wasn't a gourmet chef, but she cooked good down home food that stuck to your ribs.

I killed a deer my first day back, we had deer steaks and made the rest into deer jerky and sausage. I was very proud of my first kill on my own land. I tanned the hide and hung it in the great room. I have to tell you that butchering and tanning are difficult, messy jobs. I did get used to it, though.

I was supposed to travel back to Atlanta one more time that week to finish my training, but since that option had dried up, I relished exploring my property and seeking places to locate my caches of survival supplies. I purchased twenty plastic 55-gallon drums from Patty and used them to bury my caches. I had to bury most of them with rocks since you couldn't dig more than a couple of feet without hitting rocks. I tried to conceal three a day and soon had them all hidden.

I made a map along with some markings on trees and rocks to help me find them should the need arise.

I tried to shake the impending doom from my mind and concentrate on what we needed to do to increase our chances of survival. It was rough, hard work, and I was pleased with the reflection in the mirror. There was no more excess weight; that had been replaced with muscle. I noticed that my face seemed more...I don't know...hard, almost like it had become carved in granite.

Both Mary and Patty complemented me on the change. They said that my face looked chiseled. Yeah, it felt good.

Yes, I guess I am bragging since I want you to know that I dropped over 50 pounds during my training. I was never what you would call a lard ass, but I was a bit chubby at five foot ten and 240 pounds. Okay, screw it. I was fat. Get over it. I did. Maybe that's why the bitch left me. Like Jimmy Buffet said, "Hell, it could be my fault..."

The most significant find during my wanderings around the property was a cave about half a mile up the mountainside. I was looking for another place to hide a cache when I stumbled upon the cave. I was riding the ATV with the drum strapped on the back when I needed to stop and take a whiz.

I was about 500 feet up a ravine when I stopped the ATV. I heard a noise and saw a bear coming towards me from some bushes on the side of the ravine. I shouldered my rifle and waited to see if it was going to attack. I knew the .338 Lapua would bring the bear down, but I didn't want to kill such a magnificent animal unless forced to do it.

The damn bear saw me, was startled and ran at me. At the last minute, it rose on its hind legs and swiped at me. I shot it in the chest, and the large killer Lapua round dropped that bear like a stone. It was beautiful, and I was proud that I handled myself so well in a pinch but sorry for the bear.

I think that was the moment I realized that I was actually seeing a new me. I wasn't quaking in fear, I felt exhilarated and strong.

Later I wondered why the bear was out, and about in late fall. She should have been hibernating. I never did find out, and no one else had any suggestions, either.

I looked over to the side of the ravine and wondered where the bear had come from. I kept my rifle ready and walked through the scrubs to find an opening into the hillside. The opening was about four feet high and led into a very dark chamber.

I went back to the ATV, fetched my flashlight, and entered the cave cautiously. The opening led to a tunnel that kept increasing in height until I could stand upright about twenty feet in, then it opened up into a large room.

The room had a ten-foot ceiling and was about 15 feet wide by thirty feet long. I was expecting to see human skeletons, gold, and Spanish swords and armor. What I actually found were boulders, small animal skeletons, a dirt floor, and a place where there had been many fires over the centuries, though there hadn't been a fire in many years.

I did see a place on one wall where someone had made scratches as though they were tracking how many days had passed.

This place was perfect for my bugout location if I was chased out of my house.

I scouted the entire cave and found it only had one opening large enough to get through but appeared to have a tiny crack that opened to show daylight on one side. I made a sketch of the cave and started planning what to stock it with and how to keep it hidden.

I started by hauling the drum into the cave by slowly pushing the drum into the mouth of the cave. After about 10 feet, I turned the drum and rolled in on into the cave.

I tied the bear to the ATV and pulled it further up the ravine, cut off a hindquarter, and the loins, and then drove past the cave pulling some brush behind me to wipe out the tire tracks. I kept brushing my path until I was several hundred feet past the mouth of the ravine.

I drove back to the house while my mind was thinking about how to make the cave my primary bugout location.

I made a mental list of my needs and quickly decided to leave the other caches alone and to purchase more supplies for the cave. I also came up with some ideas to hide the mouth of the cave in case someone wandered into the brush as I did. I suddenly remembered to buy pallets of dog food when Gus and Tina greeted me at the door.

I decided not to tell anyone, including Mary, about my find. Loose lips could get my newly buff ass killed. So, anyway I drove into town that afternoon, parked in front of the General Store and went in to meet with Patty and her husband to order my supplies.

I saw Patty at the back of the store and Mary was behind the counter waiting on a customer. That explained why she had to rush out this morning and left me with a cold bowl of cereal.

I said, "When did you start working here?"

"I'm just helping out until Patty can hire a clerk."

"I'm here to order a few things. Have a great day. I'll see you later."

I walked to the back of the store and said, "Hey Patty, can I talk to you in private?"

"Of course, come on into my office. Hey, you look better each time I see you."

"Yeah, well, I've been eating better, and the ranch takes a lot of work. I grew up on a farm, but must have forgotten how much work it takes."

I followed her to the other corner and entered the office behind her. I must admit that I did enjoy the view. There's just nothin' as fine as a pretty gal in boots, boot jeans, and a cowboy hat; yeah, she even made that flannel shirt look good. No slapping myself now, it must be all the physical change.

"Patty, I want to order a lot of supplies from you, and I don't want anyone to know about the order. Of course, George will know, but no one else. Can you do that?"

"I guess you don't get much news out there, but I would have thought Mary would have told you that George and I separated last week and I have filed for a divorce."

"I'm sorry for you and no, I didn't hear about it. No, wait, that's not even close to true. I didn't like him from the first time I ever saw him. You definitely deserve better. I hope I haven't offended you."

Blushing, Patty said, "No, of course, you didn't offend me. I'd have been offended if you defended the rat bastard. So there."

"Well anyway, I need to purchase the items on this list from you. I'll purchase the ammo online if you don't have it in stock."

"There are a couple of items that I'm not familiar with, but I can get everything else on the list and can deliver it in a week or two, but are you sure you want it delivered? Why don't I have it delivered to Cheyenne, and we can go and pick it up there. We can use my truck. That way, no one will know."

I put on my serious face and asked, "Can you speed up on the delivery. I'd like to get everything as quickly as possible, like yesterday."

A concerned look overcame her face, and she said, "Well, sure, but it's going to be much more expensive. I'll get the order out today, and we'll be able to pick it up, let's see, this is Monday, no problem we should have everything ready by Wednesday afternoon. Does that work for you?

I thought you had enough for 10 people to survive for a long time."

"Just chalk it up to paranoia, and yes, Wednesday is fine. The food is all long shelf life items, and the rest will keep for 25 years. I never want to be starving in the snow when the lights go out due to a failure of the grid. I'll bet you are asking about the 200-gallon steel tank. I can get it elsewhere, but thought I'd give you a chance at all of my future purchases."

"Thanks, I'll get a price on one and get back to you before I order it. I've ordered a couple before, but this is the first one with a large hinged opening."

"I'm in a hurry. Go ahead and order it. I know it will cost more, but it will be worth the money."

"Damn, I forgot to tell you that I also need one of those heavy garden wagons that you have on display outside. The big black one; I'll take it with me. Oh, and have everything packaged in heavy duty boxes. I'll pay extra for that, but I need it. Make sure none is over 50 pounds. Sorry for the extra work."

"You are the customer, and you pay your bills, so you get what you want.

Okay, what is going on?"

Not replying to her question I simply asked, "How did you talk a rich lady into being your clerk?"

Understanding that I did not wish to say more, she said with a smile, "I promised to throw George's ass out if she'd cover his job for a few weeks."

"Are you okay, did he make a scene?"

Very proud of herself, and almost laughing she said, "Well, he started to, but Mary's 357 magnum calmed him right down. I haven't seen him since. When he left, he was so scared

59

that I thought I saw a dark spot on his crotch. Damn, but it feels good to be free of that worthless sack of shit."

I laughed, shook her hand, and headed up to see Mary.

"Hey have you mentioned to Patty about the warnings about the upcoming solar event?"

"Yes, and we have both been quietly stocking food and other supplies at her house. I think I found a place that is about a half mile from Patty's place. I made an offer this morning and should know by lunch. I won't tell her about Alpha Omega III, but I wanted to give her a sense of urgency."

"Take back the offer and stay with me until this catastrophe is over. You might not need a place."

"That's a great idea. I'll give it some thought. Thanks."

She wasn't convincing on stopping the purchase.

"Assuming we aren't all fried, I hate to be Mr. Gloom and Doom, but she should know that within two to three days after TSHTF her store will be looted and nothing will be left. They might even go to her house thinking that the store owner would have food squirreled away at home."

"Good advice. Would you mind if I invite her to supper tomorrow so we can give her some brief training on being prepared?"

"No, not at all, just so long as we keep it between us three.

Oh, and back off the house thing. You are staying at the ranch. No, don't say it. I need the both of you. Now, you two just figure out how to make it happen. Nuff said!"

***

Unfortunately, I got a chance to use my new skills later that night. I had supper at the diner after leaving the General Store. I had a great meal then apple pie with ice cream.

I figured that I'd better eat ice cream while I could since it would be damn hard to make after TSHTF. I finished eating, paid my bill and left to walk to my truck, which was parked across the street by the Barber Shop. It was dark outside, and several streetlights were out. I stopped, bent down to open my door, and felt a crack and pain in my shoulder. I fell to the ground dazed and saw a man hovering above me."

"I missed your head, but I won't miss you this time. I'll teach you to mess with Patty, you son of a bitch."

I moved my hands in front of my face and caught his foot. I yanked it toward me while lifting my body. The man fell to the ground as I kicked him in the side then in the balls. He tried to get up, and I kicked him again to the side, bent over, and grabbed his wrist.

I twisted his wrist I felt the navicular bone break which caused an incredibly intense pain and asked, "George what makes you think I'm messing with Patty" You are drunk and the town clown. Get away from me before you make me mad, and I kill your sorry ass."

He scrambled to his feet and ran away. My head and shoulder hurt like hell, but I was otherwise unharmed. I was amazed that my training kicked in and I was able to defeat this attacker. Okay, I know he was a drunk, a bully, and a coward. Oh, what the hell, he'll be dead soon anyway, and with a cast on his wrist I don't think I'll be seeing him anytime soon.

This incident reminded me of something my combat instructor said, "Don't be afraid to break a bone or kill an attacker. If someone is trying to kill you, just put them out of action for quite a while, giving them time to rethink their actions. If he returns for more, kill him, you don't want to spend your life looking over your shoulder more than you have to after the collapse.

When he first drilled that into me, I thought it was macho crap. Now, I knew it was not, and I would follow that advice. If someone comes after me, they will be dead. Damn, I felt strong, not arrogant because I knew there were lots of guys out there that could end me, but if they didn't, well, too bad for them. Oh, he also said, 'Never fight fair.'"

I heard a commotion behind me and turned to see Gary and Betty Allen running up to my side.

"Matt are you okay. One of our customers saw George slipping up behind you and told Gary. It was all over before we could help you."

"Thanks, but I think Georgie learned his lesson about attacking strangers."

"Come back into the restaurant and have a cup of coffee while we call the police."

"No, I think he will leave me alone, and I don't want to cause Patty any problems. Besides, he'll be at the hospital getting a cast put on his arm."

"Okay, it's your life, but that asshole isn't done with you yet. I don't know how you got on his bad side, but he won't drop it."

Smiling a sinister smile, I said, "Actually, I think he will.

Thanks, but I'm okay."

Gary and Betty owned the Mountain Hideout Restaurant next to Patty's general store. They were in their early forties and a good-looking couple. They had two kids and a thriving business in a great place to live.

I had the radio on as I drove back home and heard the announcement that NASA is forecasting an unusually high incidence of solar activity in the weeks to come.

I noticed there were static and a few blank spots in the dialog. This was what Sam told me to expect. I wondered if Sam knows about Alpha Omega. Now I was waiting for the Northern Lights to move further south and the big Coronal Mass Ejection.

When I got home, I asked Mary to look at the back of my head and shoulder.

She examined me and said, "What happened. You have a scrape on your head and a hell of a bruise developing on your shoulder."

"A jealous husband thought I was messing with his wife."

"That damned George. I knew he would be trouble."

"Look, I took care of Georgie. He'll be in a cast for 16 weeks, so don't tell Patty. She has enough worries."

Smiling… she asked, "What did you do to that boy?"

"Oh, nuthin' much, just snapped the navicular bone in his wrist. It is also the most difficult bone in the body to heal. No big deal."

"Yeah, well you just be careful and watch your back. He still might get uppity."

And there it was again, watch your back; look over your shoulder. Okay, now I really get it.

✪

Now, entering the solar system known as Sol, the trio plunged toward the warming point of light, which grew in intensity, and caused their atmospheres to begin to thaw.

Alpha Omega III's huge atmosphere of methane, long frozen in the interstellar cold, could now be seen with the naked eye as a comet like tail, which ran before it like the mane of a wild Mustang.

Chapter 4

Preparing

The Ranch

Wyoming

When Patty arrived at 6:00 Mary giggled and said, "Perfect timing, sweetie, you're just in time to have a Bloody Mary with Mary. Supper will be on the table in just a few minutes."

I set the table, carved the roast, and chilled some wine for our after supper conversation.

Patty was dressed in her usual cowgirl gear, jeans, long sleeve shirt, Levi vest, and Stetson hat. I noticed that she had perfume on and it smelled great. She also had on more jewelry than normal, and her jeans seemed a bit tighter.

She had a pistol in a shoulder holster that made a bulge below her right breast. I wasn't looking at her breasts, but the extra bulge did catch one's eye.

Mary told me a couple weeks back about running George off. Since then Patty started carrying a gun.

"Supper is ready. Dig in."

We ate, talked, and wolfed down a cherry pie for dessert. Then we retired to the great room where Patty started the conversation.

"At first I didn't give much thought to this solar flare stuff, but everyone has noticed the static on our TVs, phones, and radios. The local, state and federal officials are downplaying any long-term effects, but I just do *not* trust 'em. So, having said that, Matt, what do we need to do?"

"I replied, "All right, first and foremost, don't tell anyone else what we're doing. Don't misunderstand, I mean tell no one.

Prepare yourself emotionally that your store will be looted right after the lights go out. Credit cards won't work, and banks will be closed. People will rush to the stores as they do before a big storm is going to hit.

Everyone with a pacemaker will die during the event, airplanes will fall from the sky, and the grid will go down. There will be no electricity to power anything. Nothing electronic will work, phones, cars, and computers will all fail.

After three days, there will be no food in any stores, and the food warehouses become targets. Gangs of thieves, thugs, and drug addicts will band together to control food, drugs, and water.

Within days, people will be breaking into houses to steal food. Two weeks later, they will kill horses, dogs, and any other animal to eat. Your friends will kill you over a scrap of bread to feed their kids.

Those who don't freeze from this damnable Wyoming winter will run out of their medications. People on anti-depressants will go crazy, and others will die. All medication supplies will run out during the next year. Diabetics, heart patients and anyone being kept alive with modern drugs will die. During this same period, mass starvation will kill most of the people on Earth."

"Will anyone survive?"

"Yep, Mary, Patty, and Matt, 'cause they are ready."

"Cute, Matt, and yeah that's good news."

"There will, of course, be others. The outdoor types will hunt, fish and scavenge for food. They will survive longer than the city people who will all be dead in 90 to 120 days. Some will even make it all the way.

Your job is to stock food, water, and other supplies away and then survive until the others die off.

This may sound harsh, but there will not be enough food for everyone and a friend before the event will cut your throat for a biscuit if their child is starving after the lights go out."

Patty shook her head and replied, "I've heard most of what you just said, but I guess the reality is now smacking me in the face. I feel so alone."

Rather harshly, I said, "Good grief, Mary, didn't I make myself clear yesterday? You two are moving your butts in here, and quickly. No nonsense, your place is too close to the road, and that makes you a nice target especially for slave traders. Of course, if you want to become drugged out whores being traded around from gang to gang until you die, I guess I can't force you to come here.

From a bit of a selfish side, the fact is I need the help. I can't run this place and protect it 24/7. Damn it, you are helping me as much as I am you.

So, yes, start stockpiling items such as food, whiskey, ammunition, guns, medical supplies, feminine hygiene products and birth control items along with silver and gold to trade for items we may find we need later.

Now, did I convince you sufficiently of my sincerity, so that you'll shake a leg and get moved in here?"

Patty snickered and replied, "Mary, we both know he's right. Besides, he's such a big strong man. I'm sure he can protect us poor damsels in distress."

"Funny girls, real funny, but in my experience, the female is always the deadlier of the species.

Now, a few words of warning; purchase the small cheap half pints of whiskey and never let anyone see more than a small amount of any trade goods. You will become a target if people start to see you as a store.

We will only trade if we have to, and never let anyone follow you home. Have your guns ready at all times. Buy the gold and silver in other towns."

"What guns do we need?"

"A Shotgun, Carbine, and a pistol. I'd go with a 12 gauge pump, Keltek Sub 2000 and a full-size 9mm Glock."

Mary replied, "I like my .357."

"That is a great gun, but it only holds six bullets, you know, those pesky lead thingys that come out of the pointy end of the gun, sorry, I couldn't resist. Anyway, the Glock 17 holds 17 rounds in the magazine, and one in the chamber. You can easily carry three more magazines and reload quickly. The .357 is harder to load and is terrible to load up in the dark.

The three extra magazines are to be carried until things fall apart. After that, you will up the mags to six, on the belt, and one in the bullet launcher."

"Point taken; I'll buy the guns tomorrow."

Patty spoke up, "Mary, we have all of those at the store except the Keltek.

Matt, I have four AR 9mm carbines that take the Glock 17 -9mm magazines. Will those work?"

"Yes, they're definitely a better combat gun, but the Keltek is a fine weapon out to around 100 yards, and it will fold in half and fit into your Bugout bag. Oh, and the fact that it only weighs about 5 pounds fully loaded, is definitely a benefit. Unfortunately, the front sight on the Keltek is a piece of crap. It's plastic and will move, but the M&P15 front sight fits perfectly, and is completely stable."

"I'll order two, just to keep them in our Bugout bags and have the ARs for daily use when the grid goes down."

"Patty, order seven of the Glock 17 thirty-one round magazines for each of us."

"I will. Mary, get the rest out of the case tomorrow. Matt, can you give us some lessons on the guns. We can both shoot pistols and hunting rifles, but the AR and Glock are new to us."

"I'd be glad to. Bring them and some ammunition out tomorrow, and we'll go to my range and familiarize both of you with your new guns."

Patty interrupted, "Oh, sorry Matt, but the supplies won't be to Cheyenne for pickup until Friday, at the earliest. Everything is slowing down."

"Damn, oh, well, we'll have to make do. Okay, let's hope for Friday. We'll leave around 6:00 a.m."

Mary's face made it plain she approved of the two of us going to Cheyenne together to pick up the order. Made me feel all prickly, dang her.

The girls had me thinking about how much I should hedge towards the end of the world vs. living after there is *no* end of the world.

The answer appeared to be purchasing several hundred thousand dollars' worth of silver, gold, and platinum along with a shit load of good quality wine, whiskey, and high dollar guns.

This placed us in a position of having what we needed to survive TEOTWAWKI in a bit of luxury or selling off the collection to survive in the regular old boring world.

It took a lot of effort to hide the purchase and not let the world know we were sitting on half a million dollars' worth of goodies besides my million dollars' worth of house, bomb shelter, and other survival crap.

I actually woke up dreaming that I was on the news as the biggest fool in history. I was on a reality show for spending my inheritance on doomsday prepping.

However, since you are reading my story about how I survived the early days of The Flare, I guess the fools are dead and gone while I survived. The jokes on them and I look pretty smart. Hell yes!

***

Pinedale, Wyoming

"Mary, I'm very glad Matt showed up when he did. The TV and radio were both off and on all day. The government put out a statement telling us to be calm, a few minutes before you finished your bath. The shit is going to hit the fan soon.

I'm ordering enough Wise survival food for both of us and tomorrow I'll get us all the can goods I can take from the store without alerting anyone. I'm also ordering enough seeds to plant a hundred gardens."

"I like that. Good thinking, now we need to concentrate our efforts to move to Matt's."

"I will move to Matt's, but I plan to hide supplies here as well. My place has a water well, basement, pond and is at the back of my property out of sight. I'm afraid that Matt is definitely right about two women alone with a lot of food being a big target, but it can't hurt to have a fallback hideout."

"I am truly thankful that Matt insists we come to his place, and I think this weekend is as good a time as any. If the CME hits on Monday, then this weekend is best."

"The only reason Matt might throw us out is if there isn't enough food. Therefore, we will stage enough food there to feed the three of us for a year.

Triple the order of survival food and order 500 pounds of dried beans and another 500 pounds of rice. Also, order spices, salt, and sugar. We'll pay our own way with food, cooking, and companionship."

Patty blushed but didn't take the bait.

"Sounds good to me. Let's ask what he thinks of our plan tomorrow on the range."

"Good idea. Oh, certain, soon to be ex-jealous husband attacked Matt the other night. He kicked George's ass and sent him packing."

"Shit. I thought George was harmless. I need to apologize to Matt."

"Oh, no, you don't need to do any such thing, "Let sleeping dogs lie. He doesn't want you to know. I only told you because I want you to take any threats from George seriously."

"I will."

"Okay."

"Let's order everything air freight into the airport and pick them up there, that way we can take them straight out to the Ranch without being seen, and we'll have them much earlier than regular freight."

"Oh, yes, good idea on the airfreight. I'm getting a little nervous that we won't be ready."

"Oh Patty, we both need to be at the Ranch in the bunker with Matt when The Flare hits. This solar flare will be the most powerful in history. There will be x-rays and the possibility of a high dose of radiation when the CME hits or passes by the Earth."

***

The Ranch

Pinedale, Wyoming

I woke up late, was worried that I was late for something, and then remembered that I was retired and it was Saturday. Mary stayed in town to work on their prepping project, so I made a pot of coffee, cooked some bacon and eggs, and had a late breakfast.

The girls were due at the ranch about 1:30, and I wanted to take a quick tour around my property before they arrived.

I was trying to become familiar with what was normal. I could use the ATV to travel the edge of my property on three sides, but the back 10 acres where the cave was located had to be walked, or covered by horseback.

There was little chance of someone coming down the mountain, so I only drove to the mouth of the several ravines and canyons and used binoculars to check the back end of my property.

There was one old dirt road that cut my property in half, and I always checked it for fresh tracks. I enjoyed taking Gus and Tina for a ride. All I had to say was, "Go Bye Bye" and they ran to the ATV. They were well trained and obeyed my commands.

Tina would lie down next to me and watch while Gus sat up and was always alert for a squirrel or rabbit. He would whimper when he saw one as though he was asking for permission.

If I had time, I'd let him chase the unlucky rabbit. Squirrels were just too quickly up a tree, or into their burrow. He usually brought the animals he caught back to me, and I released the mainly unharmed but slobbered on animal back to the woods. The dead or injured ones would become dinner.

I had never seen any signs of trespassing until today. I followed the tracks a few hundred yards on foot and saw a red Jeep parked by an old cabin. Hell, I didn't even know the cabin was on my property. It was an old hunting cabin built like an old barn. The wood siding was vertical as on a barn but had narrow wood strips covering the joints. A dingy green metal roof topped off the structure, and a stone chimney was on the north side.

I had my M&P15 and Glock ready as I snuck up on the cabin. The door was open, and I heard strange sounds coming from the cabin. It took me a minute to realize what the sounds were.

I yelled, "Come on out with your hands up."

A voice replied, "Don't shoot. We're coming out."

A young man and girl came out of the cabin with very red faces and half-naked bodies. Gus growled fiercely and scared the two half to death.

"You can put your hands down, but don't move or Gus will rip you to shreds. What are you doing on my property?"

He was rocking from side to side. She was red faced and scared. He said, "We were just exploring the woods and stopped to rest."

"Yeah, I heard you resting when I got here. You look about 18, and she looks about 15 or 16. You do know you could be charged with statutory rape of a minor, or child molestation. Tell me why I shouldn't report this trespassing?"

The girl stammered out, "I'm 18, and he is my boyfriend."

"Bull shit. Now get out of here and don't come back or I'll get the sheriff involved."

"I promise we won't ever come back."

"Go, git, now!"

They ran to the jeep and fled back down the trail. I explored the cabin and the area around it and found that there were signs this wasn't the first time people had come to the cabin. There were beer cans, whiskey bottles, and used condoms around the cabin. I had to get this stopped ASAP.

After they were out of sight, I went back to the edge of my property where the road entered. I discovered that I could cut three or four trees down and stop any normal vehicle from coming in by the road. I could do the same thing at the other entrance.

I would also post no trespassing signs on a cable across the entrance. I thought I should probably burn the cabin down since everyone in town had probably brought their girlfriend there at one time or the other.

I wondered why Mr. Williamson hadn't blocked the road but later found his chain across both openings had been cut. I would place a couple of trail cameras and trip wires to alert me back at the house. I would stop this crap.

***

The women arrived a little after 1:00 pm and brought lunch from the diner. I was starving since the events at the cabin made me late getting back to the house.

"Hello. Is that lunch?"

"Hello, Matt. Yes, we brought some burger baskets from the diner. Betty and Gary told me to say Hi to you. Hi!"

"I'm glad you brought lunch. I was late getting back from my tour of the property. Did you know there is an old cabin in the back northwest side of the property?"

"Yes, and I had forgotten about it since it was in pretty bad shape and we never went back there. Frank had to block the road with a chain to keep the teenagers from parking back there."

"I ran into a couple in the cabin this morning. They were very busy and didn't hear me approach. I think I scared the crap out of them. The boy was driving a red Jeep."

Patty spoke up, "The boy had black hair, was about six feet tall and very muscular."

"That's him. Do you know him?"

"Yes, he is Sheriff Alton's boy."

"Well, the sheriff is about to become a grandfather if his son and that young blonde girl keep this up."

"That's the Merrill girl, and she's only 15. Bob has warned Robby several times about messing around with her."

"Well anyway, I'm going to block the road and perhaps burn the cabin down to help keep these trespassers off my property."

"Frank put chains across the road. How did they drive in?"

"Someone cut the chain. I'm going to drop several trees across the road and perhaps use the tractor to pile some dirt up across the road."

"You might want to re-think that. The road is the only way to get a larger vehicle out the back way in an emergency. Frank knew he could unlock the chain or cut it in a pinch."

"Damn, I hadn't thought about that. Thanks for keeping me from making a big mistake."

"Burn the cabin and the kids will stop trespassing."

Shooting Range

The Ranch

We ate our French fries, burgers, and cokes, and then went to the range to shoot.

Patty lowered her tailgate and placed a blanket on it before laying the guns down. I saw a large amount of ammunition behind the guns along with thirty to forty boxes that appeared to contain more guns.

Both were good shots with the pistol and 9mm AR. They were a bit scared of the 12 gauges but shot them enough to be familiar with their operation.

I had them shoot from behind cover, reload and advance to cover and repeat. I put them through the paces for several hours. They were getting better by the minute. The last thing I had them do is shoot at the dueling target tree. The winner was the shooter who got all six steel targets on the opponent's side. They both won twice before I called an end to the shooting for the day.

"Ladies, I can grill some deer steaks or take you into town to the diner for supper. Your choice."

"We would rather eat with you out here. Patty and I will prepare the sides while you grill.

Before we leave the range, come over to Patty's truck. We brought ammunition and extra guns.

The solar activity seems to be rapidly increasing, just as you warned, and we both think the big one is just around the corner."

Patty spoke up, "We'll try to get most of the stock out of the store. Whatever we can't get out can be picked over by the survivors. Hopefully, those who get the leftovers find something useful."

I must admit that I had second thoughts since I was suddenly filled with concern about the reality of being responsible for these two lives. Then I thought that's definitely a win-win. I really wanted to be alone, but the possibility of having partners was growing by the day. Besides, I had my man cave. Yeah, it was the absolute right and proper thing to do.

"I have to say one more time, tell no one about the house, property, or survival supplies, and there *cannot* be anyone else coming out here with you. No kids, no relatives, nobody, period.

I don't care if they are dying or will be killed by thugs. We can't take in everyone, or soon they will over run us and take our food and shelter."

Patty replied first, "I agree. I know I will feel bad, but this is our survival. The others have had the same warnings and haven't done anything to prepare for the apocalypse."

"Okay, bring your supplies out here, and we'll unload them in the barn until we can get them down to the bomb shelter."

I was deep in thought as I checked the steaks on the grill, when Mary said, "Patty, I'll make the sides while you fix us some stiff drinks. I know I could use one."

I broke free from my thoughts enough to reply. "Make mine a Bulleit and Coke. Make it a double."

I made a mental note to have Mary order 10 cases of Bulleit Bourbon. The money wouldn't really matter when the lights went out. I needed to stock up on some luxuries along with necessities. My mind was going a hundred miles an hour trying to think of things that would make post-apocalyptic life easier.

"Please order 10 cases of Bulleit, 10 cases of Jose Cuervo Tequila, 10 cases of Vodka, and 20 cases Of Bloody Mary mixer. Add 20 cases of Blue Moon beer. We also need to order some board games and games like bean bag toss."

Patty shouted back, "I never thought of that, but we do need something to pass the time."

"I believe we will be consumed just trying to survive for the first six months to a year; after that, we will have long winters to contend with."

We finished supper and retired to the great room to discuss our survival plans when Mary said, "Matt, please turn the TV and radio on. I want to know how strong the reception is today."

The radio was sketchy, and the satellite reception for the TV was poor at best. I looked outside at the satellite dish and noticed it was not getting dark outside. I stepped out on the patio, looked to the north where I saw a beautiful display that rivaled Fourth of July fireworks.

"Holy shit, come on out, you ain't gonna believe this shit."

✪

Now inside the orbit of Mercury the Alpha Omega III Planet, as large as Jupiter followed the other two planets tracking directly into the heart of Sol, gaining speed as that star's gravity inevitably pulled her toward their union.

Chapter 5

Aurora Borealis

The Ranch

Fortunately, the flare missed and caused only minor damage. Television and radio signals returned to normal, and most of the world went back to pre-scare living. People went to work, watched football, played, vacationed, spent too much for Christmas gifts, and fussed about how the government got everyone all riled up for nothing.

World attention was drawn away from the solar flare scare and pivoted to the three, previously unknown comets, which were readily seen by the naked eye.

These huge and beautiful comets, traveling in line was believed to have fallen from the outer reaches of our solar system. They rapidly passed by and continued on their inward leg around the sun.

Of course, very few knew that these were not comets at all, but a trio of rogue planets on a collision course with Sol...T-32 days...

***

At the ranch, things continued to come together as our end times preps continued. We knew, and we did our best to be ready.

We were very busy over this two-month period, placing the girl's caches, my 200-gallon drum, purchasing, and stocking, a vast quantity of supplies, marksmanship training and watching the sky for the change we knew must come.

The Northern Lights could barely be seen above the northern horizon. Then just a week ago, they began dancing around until the northern sky was filled and continued to extend further south each night.

The Borealis became so bright the stars could no longer be seen. The moon became a pale shadow of reflective brilliance. There were several times when they intensified as the solar activity grew in magnitude.

The news media, somewhat cowed after the scare reported that the change was due to the normal ebb and flow of flare cycles of the Sun.

Conspiracy theorists raised the alarm and made claims government was hiding the truth about an upcoming disaster from the public.

Government talking heads responded by giving yadda yadda canned speeches about the Sun's cycle of intensity, and the clamor began to fade.

For once, the conspiracy theorists were correct, but they had no idea how right they were until it was too late.

Riots began when the computerized payments of Social Security and Welfare checks came to a screeching halt because of a malfunction of the computer system that tracked all payments.

Numerous government offices around the country were ransacked, and stores were looted.

***

The 59 days leading up to the solar collision passed all too quickly. I knew that light took eight minutes to travel from the sun to our eyes here on Earth and was scared shitless that this was an Extinction Level Event…an E.L.E.

We had finished eating and watched the sun above the western horizon. The collision was due any minute according to Frank's notes. How scientists can pin down when two big assed bodies are going to hit down to a minute is far beyond me, and I was a science teacher.

The bunker was prepared for quick access. I did not trust scientists to be able to tell how big the boom was going to be.

I wondered if the Dinosaurs suffered from a similar fate. Of course, we didn't want the collision, but like watching a slow motion train wreck, we simply could not stop looking. We had to see the collision.

Patty said, "The radio and TV are on, and I have my Kindle hooked to the internet. We'll soon know what effects the solar flare has on communications."

All other electronic devices not in the shelter or barn were unplugged and turned off, even though the surge would not arrive for a couple of days following the assault on our sun. All vehicles were in the barn and shielded.

"I replied, "Most of the charged particles take a day or two to travel from the sun to the Earth, so don't be surprised if we only see a small flash of light today."

The eastern sky was dancing and shimmering with greens, purples and indigo colors as the sun began to set in the west. We changed our focus to the western sky and watched the sun fall below the horizon.

Suddenly a brilliant light flashed from the sun that hurt my eyes and lit up the sky brighter than high noon. All three of us snapped our eyes shut in an instant. We lost vision for a few seconds, and our eyesight maintained a fright filled, blurry glow for several minutes.

Patty was stunned, but finally screamed, "What the fuck was that? Pardon my French, but that was more than any solar flare that I've heard of."

"That was Alpha Omega I."

"Oh dear God!"

"It's the first of the three planets that will hit the Sun. The next is in three days and the last 29 days later."

"So we have 32 days before we find out if we live like cavemen or get fried like shrimp on the barby?"

I spoke up, "Frank was right about the first planet hitting the Sun and even had the time down to the minute. I prefer to think his astronomer friends will be right about the impact of Alpha Omega II and III."

I told my companions, with more gusto than I felt, "We are prepared, and we will survive. It won't be easy, so we have to suck it up and do what it takes to handle the immense challenges after The Flare."

I took Patty in my arms, hugged her, and said, "You are going to be okay. The world will change, and we will adapt."

This seemed to calm her down. We sat and talked over drinks. I tried to change the topic several times, but the conversation always shifted back to the elephant about to hit the Sun. (You know – "elephant in the room.")

We watched as the light dissipated, but the deepening sky remained much brighter than before. The Sun ducked below the horizon, and again, we had the full effect of the Northern Lights.

The Ranch

Today our cell phone, radio, and TV reception went to hell. They were all out for hours at a time and filled with static when they worked.

We suffered a power outage caused by damaged transformers and found that several of our electronic devices were dead.

We had numerous discussions during the next 72 hours while waiting on the next collision. Most centered on how to help Mary and Patty's friends without hurting ourselves.

We decided that Patty would have a 50% off credit card only sale on the types of survival food and gear that would be needed after the Flare. They both knew that credit cards would soon be worthless, so this was a way for Patty to help the community.

She made sure she had very few guns and ammo on display and limited the purchase to one gun and two boxes of ammo to make sure no one person hogged the weapons and ammo.

Yes, it was somewhat hypocritical of us, since we had enough guns and ammo to equip a small army. Tough shit! I trusted us; I did not trust the rest of the world.

The Wyoming winter weather certainly did not improve as snow fell, and cold intensified.

We'd spent a fortune in the days leading up to the first collision and couldn't think of another item we would need after The Flare.

People were afraid after the first collision and swamped the store, buying everything that wasn't nailed down. Because of the 50% sale, Patty's store was the first to have only empty shelving. Mary felt this factoid might mean Patty's store would not be destroyed.

***

The Ranch

The anticipated second collision would occur at noon according to the notes Frank left for Mary. As before, we gathered behind the house and waited to see what this event would produce. This time we all had sunglasses and a piece of welder's glass to look through to keep our eyes from being damaged.

The actual collision as seen through the sunglasses and welder's glass resulted in a large visible swirl of flaming material that appeared to reach out and break away from the Sun. The sun was so bright that this was missed by anyone not using eye protection.

The skies held no clouds, and the sun reflected off the snow covered ground, creating a dazzlingly brilliant glare, which became even brighter, painfully brighter.

Five people on the streets, who happened to be looking toward the sun, were blinded by the flare. Those remaining citizens grew alarmed when the sun got brighter for a few minutes before returning to normal. Several of them stormed the mayor and sheriff's offices to get an answer to this terrifying event.

"Matt the Sun just gave birth to a smaller Sun."

"That's a cloud of plasma, and it's heading our way. I doubt that it will hit us, but the cloud will be a million miles across by the time it gets here. This will cause electronics to fail, and the grid may go down."

"Will planes fall?"

"Damn good question. The government should ground the planes, again, like they did back during the first flare."

Patty replied, "I'm driving over to the airport and warning Mr. Simpson. We have several friends that fly."

"Whoa! What will you tell him?"

"I don't know, come with me, and we'll think of something on the way."

It was a fifteen-minute drive, and we decided that Patty would tell Mr. Simpson that she had watched one of those doomsday prepping shows and it warned about solar flares causing planes to crash. We arrived as one plane was taxiing to take off.

We walked into the small concourse and went to the administrator's office.

"Mr. Simpson. Hello."

"Hi, Patty. Long time no see. Who is your friend?"

"This is Matt Jones, he bought the Williamson place."

Smiling, Simpson said, "Well, hello Matt, it's a pleasure to meet you.

Patty is this a social call, or do you need to charter a plane?"

"Actually, we'd like to make a suggestion. I'm sorry to interrupt, but since we just had a major solar flare don't you think you should close the airport and ground the planes."

"What solar flare?" asked Simpson, "Oh yeah, that's right, I did notice it got a lot brighter outside at noon, but I haven't heard anything about a solar flare."

Patty said, "I noticed it getting bright, looked up at the sun with my sunglasses and saw the flare. Maybe nothing, but I watch all of those doomsday prepping shows, and one mentioned that a solar flare or EMP blast could cause planes to crash."

"Solar flares won't wreck electronics unless it is more powerful than ever recorded. Do you know something I don't?"

"No, of course not, I'm sorry to alarm you, but I wouldn't fly for the next several days if I were you."

He laughed and said, "Patty, why, I'd get laughed out of town or hung if I closed the airport. We rely on tourists to fly in and spend their money on hotels, fishing, and hunting."

"Okay, I'm sorry that I disturbed you. I guess you know better than I do about this stuff.

Well, we've got errands to run, see ya' soon, bye."

We left and drove home in silence. I had much to think about from what Mr. Simpson had said. There were dozens of serious hunters and outdoorsmen vacationing in the immediate area and hundreds around the state.

My mind wandered to the impact these people could have on our survival. They would be stranded here without food or supplies they would need for long-term survival. A group of these men could be a serious problem.

Mary handed us a beer as we walked into the kitchen and said, "Let me guess. They looked at you like you were crazy."

"Yeah, that pretty much sums it up all right. I hope nothing happens, but every science fiction book I have read on solar flares and EMP blasts have planes falling out of the sky like rain. They also have people with pacemakers dropping like flies."

"Well since Mr. Simpson has a pacemaker, I guess flying may not be what kills him."

I replied, "Damn, that's right. Planes will start falling tomorrow; pacemakers will stop, and many cars will crash. Most will make it through this flare, but all will fry with the next one."

The radio and TV were on but with very spotty reception. During a brief moment of clarity on the TV, we heard the announcer say, "Stay calm. The Sun experienced a...............which is normal ....elect.........Go on about your....................We will have a more detailed.............."

"Those bastards in DC are still downplaying the danger from the collisions."

I spoke up and said, "We need to stay very low key now. No one will believe us, and we certainly don't want them remembering that we said it was going to happen after The Flare.

Don't do anything to draw attention to us. I'm not going into town or seeing anyone but you two from now on."

Patty looked at me as though I was a pariah and said, "I know you are right, but can we stand back and let these people die?"

"The short answer is, yes we can. We have to, or we will be flooded with people stealing our food and supplies. You have to get over it and realize that 80% of the world will die in the next six months regardless of what we do. This is why I planned to slip in here quietly and live alone through the end of the world, as we know it. Loose lips will get us killed."

"I know that you are right, but it sounds so cruel and selfish."

"It may be cruel, and it may be selfish, but I am going to survive, and if you follow the plan, you will survive also. Tell the world, and we all die. Sorry to sound so mean, but that is the truth."

Mary spoke up and said, "Patty you are a very nice person, and you feel for people. This could get all three of us killed.

Honestly, honey, I hesitated on allowing you to join us because of your big heart. Normally it is a wonderful thing, but now you have to look out for yourself, and us.

We are since we started this project, a family that will survive because all of us were prepping before we knew the end of our world was coming.

Of course, we'll shed a tear for those who refused to prepare for a disaster, and then we will slap ourselves and do what we have to do to survive."

Mary's blunt talk forced Patty to wake up and get back with our program. She never was a weak link again.

***

"Roger tower. Approaching at 9,000 and runway is in sight. Will........"

Mr. Simpson heard the clerk scream, and there was an explosion about a mile from the airport.

"What happened?"

"The flight from Denver lost altitude and crashed onto Highway 191."

"Call Pinedale and get their emergency crews out here. I'll take the firetruck out to the crash site with Ralph."

"I've tried to call on the land line and my cell, no signal. I'll try the radio."

Mr. Simpson tried to start the fire engine to no avail. He and Ralph grabbed several fire extinguishers and took his pickup out to the crash. There was nothing to do since the plane had hit the ground nose first and disintegrated killing everyone aboard.

He looked up, saw a fireball, and then smoke coming from Half Moon Mountain. It had taken a few seconds before he realized that another plane had just crashed into the side of the mountain. He tried his cell phone, and there were no bars and no service.

"Ralph, another plane crashed. What the hell is going on?"

"Maybe that crazy lady was right about the solar flares."

"No, the government would have warned us."

***

The Northern Lights were the brightest and most active in recorded history. There was no darkness, but it wasn't quite daylight, either.

You could drive your car without the lights, or read a book without a lamp. The entire sky over Wyoming was filled with ever changing scenes consisting of vivid green, violet, red, yellow, and blue. Some patterns appeared to be green rain falling on the Earth while others consisted of swirls of solid or multiple colors. I was fixated on them.

Mary watched the display and said, "I wonder how many planes have fallen from the sky?"

"I don't know, and I guess we'll never know. I don't think we'll have normal radio communication for many months, hell, maybe not in our lifetime. After the last collision, we'll get the walkie talkies, short wave, and cell phones out of storage and check for signals without giving away our position."

"I agree. I hate to just hunker down and wait for most people to perish while we survive; however, I do want to be among the remaining survivors."

"Me, too. Do you think we can count on Patty to keep her word about not telling people about our plans?"

"I believe we can, but we must always be on guard. Doomsday has to be straining on nerves and mental processes. Trust, but verify."

"It's been ten days since the second collision; is there anything we should be doing? I feel like we are just marking time until Alpha Omega III hits the Sun."

✪

Alpha Omega III's atmosphere began to boil as she continued her trans-stellar quest to mate with Sol. Now, with a tail stretching 10 million miles, her long journey was finally nearing completion. Alpha Omega III would join with this small star in an orgasmic explosion of light and plasma, thrusting outward in all directions.

Chapter 6

The Last 10 Days

The Ranch

I gave much thought to the question concerning what we should be doing before Alpha Omega III slammed into our sun. We met every day in the kitchen to discuss our goals and preparations.

I no longer went into town for any reason. My friends; however spent a few hours each day in Pinedale. Life in town seemed to have shifted into high gear as people made their own frenzied preparations for the end of days. They also noticed that several hunters, unable to acquire transportation home had begun to congregate at the Corral Bar and Grill to discuss and evaluate their next move in the event an incoming C.M.E. really would prove to be civilization's end.

On the thirteenth day before Alpha Omega III's scheduled impact, I asked Patty and Mary to pick up the best steaks, seafood and wine money could buy in Pinedale.

I grilled three 16 oz. Filet Mignon to medium rare perfection along with skewers of shrimp, scallops, and lobster mixed in with onion, bell pepper, squash, and served a $7,000 bottle of 1997 Domaine de la Romanee Conti, which, of course, was not available in Wyoming. These folks were far too smart to spend so much for so little. In a frivolous orgy of spending, I had purchased it, along with some others. Come on, it was TEOTWAWKI.

Mary brought a homemade banana pudding that was the best dessert that ever passed between my lips. Patty made her famous potato salad. We ate until we were stuffed and retired to the glassed in the deck at the back of the house to enjoy the light show and drink more of the outlandishly expensive 1997 Romanee-Conti wine.

"Well ladies I thought, and then thought some more, and finally I have come up with the very last thing that we need to do before the world ends."

"Pray tell what your mind came up with?"

"There is *nothing* more that we have to do. Therefore we enjoy life each day until we have to button up in the bomb shelter and hunker down until all of those damn charged particles either fry our asses or pass us by."

"So what do you intend to do?"

I replied, "Drink some of the finest 24-year-old single malt Scotland has ever produced, read War and Peace, hunt and fish.

Come to think of it, I guess I'll wait until spring for the fishing part. It is winter, in Wyoming, ya' know."

Mary giggled, and said, "You are wise beyond your ears, I mean years. From this day forward, you shall be known as 'The Sage of the Ranch."

Laughing now myself, I replied, "Thank you, I humbly accept this great honor. Do I need to take a knee or something to make it official?"

"Smart ass…"

Mary chimed in, "I will pass the time quietly thinking about Frank, take a couple of hikes into the mountains, and sip a few glasses of wine while I gorge myself on great food. Who gives a shit if I gain a pound or two at the end of the world?"

Patty didn't say anything even though we stared at her.

I spoke up and said, "Well Patty?"

"I am going to ride my horses. Drink more wine than I should and cry way too much. Hell, let's face it, other than hunting, fishing and sightseeing there's not a whole lot to do out here."

I added, "Every day I become more and more pleased with the conversion of the Den into a theater. That, coupled with the thousands of movies, and TV series vids just might get us through the PTSD we are already displaying, because it's not like we can go see a Broadway play or take a cruise to the Bahamas."

"Good point. I must agree that our bucket list has turned a bit vanilla."

I suddenly came up with a great idea, "Let's each plan one surprise event for all of us to enjoy before the collision."

They liked my idea and we agreed to have our plan ready by the next day. Mary drew the short straw and had to be the first to get our events off the drawing board, and out of the chute, Patty was next and I had the grand finale two days before the end.

The whiskey and wine were flowing a bit too freely when Patty said, "We need to have a name for the end of the world. TSHTF, TEOTWAWKI, or The Event all sound too scientific or too clumbershum. Lesh juss call it The Flare. Saying "The Flare" will mean the exact point in time when shit will shit the fan; the Sun sent shit at us, and the world fell apart."

I can't really write the words as bad as she slurred them, but you get the point. We were all three sheets to the wind when "The Flare" was adopted as a point in history. It was now the appropriate nomenclature to describe the worst disaster in the world's history. It has the same significance as AD or BC in the history of humans on Earth.

I decided that after The Flare, I would spend time playing with the old Gregorian calendar and figure a better way to calculate the months, 31 days here, 30 there, and of course good old February.

Yeah, yeah, I know. None of us could pronounce nomenclature; it came out as "normen clapshure.

Mary also reminded us that the dinosaurs were wiped out by an asteroid might argue with us about the worst disaster in the world until Patty put that to bed with her final statement of the night before passing out.

She replied eloquently, "Fluck the dinoslhaurs."

"Okay, it was hilarious at the time, to three drunks."

***

Mary took us on a sightseeing tour of the mountains and stopped beside a mountain stream that was so cold it took your breath away, and so beautiful that it helped restore our faith in God's handiwork. That gave me the idea to store my extra beer in the stream behind the house. I would have cold beer forever, or at least until it ran out. We hiked for several hours before hiking back to the house for supper. We had a great time together and went to bed early.

The next day Patty instructed us to meet up at the corral at 7:00 am the following morning. We arrived to see three horses saddled up and ready to go. As before we each had a canvas bag with our lunch strapped to the back of our horse.

Patty led the way, and we took off at an easy pace. I must admit I did appreciate the warmth of my mare's flanks, and the vision of the cold breath exiting her nostrils thrilled me in some deep place. Yep, it was a wonderful idea.

She took us on several trails through the foothills of the nearby mountains stopping to look at the scenery, and a multitude of wild animals.

We stopped at noon for lunch beside a mountain pond and ate our sandwiches sitting on a log beside the frozen pond. I was glad for the rest, or should I admit that my butt was overjoyed to be off the horse, and yes, the next day my butt was sore, and my inner thighs were somewhat chaffed.

The trip was great, but my ass was dragging by the time we got back to home and had supper.

Now, it was my turn to deliver a well-executed event that each of us would remember for the rest of our lives; however, long, or short that might be.

It took me three days to set up my survival course. It had numerous events to test our skills, and we had fun competing in the events.

The first three events tested our rifle, pistol, and compound bow expertise. The next three tested our knowledge of various survival skills, and the last two were designed to be fun.

The first was climbing a rope net to the top and coming down the other side. The last event took some serious planning, as it required each of us to swing on a rope over a mud pit. I used the mini-excavator on the rear of one of the tractors to dig the six by eight by two-foot deep pit in the big barn. I placed heaters on each side of the pit so make the area warm and toasty. Well, come on, you know that frozen mud is no fun, at all.

At first, the girls balked and wanted no part of swinging over the mud, but when I cackled like a chicken, they agreed. What they didn't know was that I had greased their ropes. I thought that was hilarious, them, eh, not so much. Honest, I didn't mean for it to turn out to be mud wrestling, but the girls both slipped off their ropes and into the mud.

Patty looked at Mary and said, "So, he wants to play rough, huh? Get him!" So, they dragged my ass into the mud with them.

They sat on me with my face, under the mud for what seemed an eternity before letting me up. We were throwing mud, splashing muddy water and pushing each other down into the two-foot deep slop.

At that point, it was them against me, and they nearly drowned me in the mud before I cried, uncle.

Anyway, we had a great time, and I would remember the smiles on the girl's faces for the rest of my life, mainly because of how their white teeth shone through the mud on their faces.

✪

Chapter 7

Collision

"Ladies and Gentlemen, the President of the United States!"

"My fellow Americans, I know that many of you have heard rumors about an object careening through space that will hit the sun in the next few days.

It is with a deep sadness that I must tell you that the rumors are true. A trio of rogue planets has invaded our solar system. The first two smaller planets have already been consumed by our sun. It is the consensus of the scientific community that these collisions are responsible for the increased sunspot activity of the past week.

The third and largest planet, Alpha Omega III will impact with the sun in a few days. I want to assure you that our scientists have assured me that we are in no danger from that collision. The sun is huge in size compared to the object striking it later this month. Unfortunately, the resulting solar flares will most certainly interrupt satellite communications such as radio and television.

The worst-case scenario is that it will cause temporary power outages as some of our electrical grid receives a surge of charged particles as the flare passes by the Earth.

I am, therefore ordering all power generation stations to shut down 24 hours before the flare approaches Earth to reduce the damage to our electrical grid.

The power will be turned back on as soon as the flare passes the Earth. This will take approximately another 48 hours.

Our Director of the Department of Homeland Security will follow me and give you instructions on what you can do to get through this minor crisis with the least negative impact on your lives. Thank you, and I know that we shall come through this together."

"Thank you, Mr. President, for your encouragement, and leadership now we will hear from the Director of DHS, Secretary Jeffery Bullship."

"Ladies and Gentlemen I will only cover the bullet points on what you need to do to prepare yourselves for this temporary inconvenience. The details will be broadcast on your local TV and Radio stations, conditions permitting.

- Stock enough water for three days.
- Have enough prepared food in your home for three days.
- Have candles ready when the power goes out.
- Stay home during the power outage. All businesses and unnecessary travel will also be shut down by Executive order. Only hospitals,

police stations, and other essential workplaces will remain open.

- Do not panic and run to the store to buy a month's worth of food. Most of you already have a week's worth of food in your pantries.

- Stay tuned to your local emergency broadcast channels for further instructions.

Thanks for your understanding and your compliance with these directives. Remember, we shall get through this together.

This has been a public service announcement."

Numerous reporters began screaming questions at the retreating Secretary,

His last words were, "I'm sorry, but due to calendar restraints, there will be no Q&A period just as I stated before the press conference. Have a nice day."

***

The last 10 days before "The Flare" passed just way too damn quick to suit me.

In some ways, it seems truly funny, no, not ha ha funny, that I came here to be alone and found two friends that I truly enjoy being with every day.

Mary has been a perfect addition to our little tribe and very interesting, but I must admit, I found myself falling for Patty and thinking about her every day.

She was beautiful, smart, and sexy in an outdoorsy sort of way. I couldn't tell if she thought of me in the same way because she was so private with her emotions and thoughts.

I urged both to stay at the ranch several days before The Flare to make sure they were safe in case Frank's friends were off a bit in their calculations. In truth as I really had no idea how life would be after TF, so I really wanted to spend more time with Patty before the insanity, or rather before The Fit Hit the Shan.

On Tuesday afternoon, Mary gave me a hug and went into the kitchen to prepare spaghetti and meatballs for supper. I took her a glass of red wine while Patty poured our glasses of Blue Moon with a dash of orange juice. I know, I know, man up and don't fruit the beer. Who cares, I might not know much, but I do know what I like.

"Patty, I'm very glad you two decided to stay here with me until after the collision."

"Me too, anyway, I knew you would be scared and needed someone to hold your hand. So don't worry, it'll be all right, Patty's got you."

She took my hand in hers and held it.

"Oh, my but you are so perceptive, but yeah, I guess that is it. Seriously, this is a terrifying time for all of mankind. We have already seen a large part of our electronics fail after the first two smaller collisions and the largest of the three, Alpha Omega III will be worse. Well yeah, I guess I am worried.

Life will never be the same again. I expect to live like Jim Bridger, except with an old Ford pickup. That is until the gas runs out or spoils."

"Thanks for having us out here and we do know that without you pushing us to prepare we would probably be in dire straits in a month. Thanks."

She bent over and kissed me on the forehead.

"Supper's ready."

***

We listened to the live broadcast of the President's static filled address to the country together that night and found it to be a load of crap.

"What just happened? A reporter asked about a series of invasions of several of Equatorial African countries by several European powers. Russia has massively invaded the Mid-East."

He did not get an answer.

"That broadcast was meant to keep everyone from panicking. You do know it was pure BS, right?"

Both girls looked solemnly at me and in unison said, "Really, ya think?"

***

There hadn't been a delivery of produce into Pinedale for two days. The last grocery truck arrived a day ago and would be the last one if our worst fears were proven correct.

The transportation network was falling apart as the electronics continued to fail. Many more planes fell out of the sky, cars crashed, people with pacemakers died, and the grid had many blackouts.

The government finally started warning that the upcoming solar event would likely be far worse than was, at first anticipated, but most people couldn't receive the broadcasts, so the alert went mostly unheard. That left at least half of the American people in the dark. All but emergency and military flights were grounded.

The solar activity between collisions was already more potent than the famous Carrington Event, and worsening each day.

***

Most of what I'm telling you though occurred away from Pinedale and took years to spread around the world, and half of that is suspect regarding accuracy.

The rumor that genuinely pissed the survivors off was that the President, Congress, and their friends were hiding in a large EMP proof bunker with enough food for a hundred years.

The truth was that bunker was actually in Brazil directly below their new offices. Yes, Brazil was the first to be annexed by the U.S.

***

Frank's notes indicated that the third and final collision should take place at 5:27 am on a Thursday. We decided to sleep in Wednesday and take more naps during the day so we could stay up all night to try to catch a glimpse of Alpha Omega III as it approached for its dance of death with the sun.

The notes said that it should be the brightest object in the night sky with a comet like tail of 10,000,000 miles.

Frank also predicted that the Borealis Lights over the northern tier states would make it impossible to see until the last couple of nights before impact. We watched for it each night in the western sky just before dawn each day but did not see it until just a few hours before the collision.

He also noted that the astronomers predicted that the Coronal Mass Ejection would take approximately two days to arrive in Earth's inhabited space. The plasma and charged particles would have the effects of a small sun passing close to the Earth.

A direct hit or even a close pass to the Earth would scour the planet's surface and cleanse it of all life. We thanked God; the prediction was that the plasma cloud would miss the Earth by a million miles and only result in devastation of our grid and all unshielded electronics.

A new question began to circulate via ham radio. How the collision might affect the Sun's output of energy and light to the Solar System.

The governmental prediction was that the Sun's loss of mass would be negligible statistically; however, Frank warned that the survivors should be prepared for colder overall temperatures, for the next ten thousand, or so years.

Mary told us that she had asked Frank about this, and he replied that since the sun's output may be diminished during the remaining winter months, and carry over into the following year, the ice sheets of the world would grow, and reflect more of the sun's heat back into space. This would result in even more ice forming, and we could find ourselves in a new Ice Age.

Mary didn't tell us that part until the night before the collision.

***

I had my strongest field glasses trained to the sky and could only see the never ending display of color exploding in the sky in sheets and swirls.

Mary handed us a glass of wine and said, "I need to mention one thing that I just found in Frank's notes. He had a special section that covers his teams forecast on what the Sun and the Earth may be like after the collision. It is not good."

"How bad is it?"

"They think the ejected material will miss the Earth as you know and the Earth and most people survive without electronics, well initially.

Most people will starve or kill each other later. The problem is they forecasted that the Sun will lose enough mass to cause it to go into a period of lower solar activity and increased sun spots."

Patty said, "Why do I think that won't be good?"

I was thinking at 90 miles an hour when I blurted out, "We are screwed. It will cause the temperature on the Earth to drop. We will have longer and more severe winters. Why didn't Frank build his shelter at the equator or at least much farther south?"

"He doesn't say. Please don't blame him for what's about to happen. Matt, you came to Wyoming and bought property here without receiving the warning from my husband. I told you after the sale. Patty, you were here and didn't know to try to head south. We are all here, and now we have to make the best of the situation."

"Damn, you're right. Patty and I would be here anyway. You are the only one who could have been in a warmer climate."

"I'll never know, but my guess is that this was where he always wanted to live and took a chance that it wouldn't happen."

I took a big drink, raised my glass, and saluted Frank, "Here's to the man who probably saved our sorry asses just to have us freeze those sorry butts off."

"Salute."

Mary spotted Alpha Omega just before 4:00 am and pointed it out to us.

"There it is. Can you see that long white streak in the green just above the northeastern horizon?"

"I saw it immediately, but Patty took a minute to find it in the sea of exploding colors."

"It's so tiny. How could something that small put a dent in our Sun?"

"It's actually the size of Jupiter."

"You are the science guy, so why does Alpha Omega have a tail like a comet?"

I said, "Well, the atmosphere of Alpha Omega has been frozen for about a gazillion years, and as it nears the sun the atmosphere is thawing out and boiling off. Man, I'll bet that tail is at least ten million miles long. Wow!

Oh, shit, this is starting to get way, too real here. Up until right now, this has just been something that might happen, may not happen, and then probably will happen. Oh shit, it's going to happen."

Tears came to Patty's eyes as I took her in my arms and held her to try to make her feel safe.

"We are going to be okay. We are prepared and can survive anything this world throws at us. Please don't cry."

"I believe you. I really do, but I can't shake this sense of dread for the human race. Millions of people will start dying in a few hours," Patty said as she pulled away from me.

"Yes, you are right, they will, in fact in just a few weeks that number will jump into the billions. Our job is to hunker down, hide, and let the death and destruction pass us by. We won't come out into the world until most of the looting, death, and disease are over. This winter will kill off all but the best prepared."

I pulled her closer, kissed her, and said, "Patty, I have to tell you that I want you to stay with me and become part of my life. I have come to love you, Patty."

She kissed me and said, "Thanks, this will save our lives."

Huh…wait…what? Did she just say *thanks*? Oh, crap.

We continued watching the sky until there came a faint glow from the sun rising over the mountains. We lost sight of Alpha Omega III about the same time due to the glow from the sun. I looked at my watch and saw it was 5:28 am. The collision had happened, and the light from it would arrive in seven minutes.

"Grab your welder's glass, but be prepared to look away. This could be much brighter than the Sun."

We were counting down until the eight minutes had just passed before we finally saw a burst of light over the horizon; the whole landscape became a brilliant white and then…darkness.

Mary yelled, "The Sun is gone. The collision destroyed the Sun."

"Calm down. It's just your eyes recovering from the blast of light; our vision will come back in a minute."

It took several minutes for us to be able to see without white spots. The sun was peeking above the mountain, but we could see wild swirls jetting out from it and a bright mass just above.

"Look! That's the mass ejection forecasted by the astronomers. Now we need to pray it heads away from our Earth. We have two days before that shit gets here.

Expect no radio reception for weeks, all electronics to be fried, and most vehicles to die, and of course, the grid will be dead for years."

"Matt, why will it take years to get the power back online?"

"The short answer is that the large transformers all over the Earth that reduce the power from the main generators to the transformers that distribute the power to subdivisions and factories will be fried along with the small ones. The small ones can be manufactured quickly. However, the U.S. doesn't even manufacture the large ones anymore. They are all produced in Korea and China. Just tooling up to make them will take years. Then the military and major cities will get them at first. Wyoming will be last in line with all of the low population mountain states."

"Shit."

"Right, shit."

We all took short naps, and I was very disappointed that Patty went to the spare bedroom instead of napping with me. Yes, I had noticed that she didn't tell me that she loved me when I told her. My feelings were hurt, and I began to wonder if I was just being used. I woke up to hear rattling pots and pans in the kitchen.

"Mary, I'm starving. My stomach doesn't know it's the end of the world."

"How does a western omelet with bacon and toast sound?"

"Great. I'm hungry.

I noticed a new sound coming from the back of the house and downstairs. That's a new sound. What is it?"

"The power failed an hour ago, and the emergency generator kicked in. We will have to ration our power use to save diesel if the wind and solar don't produce enough. I wonder how things are going in town. "

"It scares me to think that I might not have met the two of you. If I hadn't had that chance meeting with Patty, I wouldn't have met either of you. I actually came here to be alone, what an idiot I was. Being alone is the last thing I want. Even though I still have a bad taste in my mouth about a lot of people back in Tennessee."

106

She laughed and said, "Did kissing Patty leave a good taste in your mouth?"

"I don't know. She didn't like it as much as I hoped she would. She appears to be distracted and doesn't have time for me. Until now, I didn't think I would ever want a relationship again. I mean, I knew someone would eventually come along. I just didn't think I'd fall for someone who didn't fall for me."

"Yes, she's been a little quiet lately, but I really think she likes you."

We heard Patty coming down the stairs and changed the subject to a trip into town.

Patty said, "I really want to see how things are going in town. It will be the last time we will ever have to see a large group of people again. I also want to stop by my house to bring more supplies here. We'll be safe today and tomorrow. I don't think any of us should venture out after that other than to check out the property. We should also start rotating on guard duty."

"I was going to bring that up tomorrow. I took down all of my cameras and sensors so they wouldn't be damaged by The Flare. We won't have the luxury of the early warning they provide until I get them back up next week."

Mary replied, "Perhaps we need to block off the roads and place traps until then."

I added, "I think you are right. Our Bugout location is up in the hills west of here. I need to take you there, so you'll know where to go if something happens to me. We also need to take some spare clothes, bedding, and extra food up there."

"Where is this place? Frank and I walked the entire property several times. Did you build something?"

"No. Mother Nature made a cave over millions of years of water flowing through the rocks. A small stream still flows through the cave."

"That's great. I was afraid you were going to try to get us all in the 200-gallon tank."

We all laughed at that and moved on to their trip to Pinedale.

They strapped on their pistols, retrieved their carbines, and walked out to the barn to drive Mary's Chevy pickup over to the town. I watched them drive away until they disappeared and got ready for a trip around my property.

I placed several cartons of MREs, two sleeping bags and some canned goods in the back of the Kawasaki Mule and headed out to travel my fence line around the property. Of course, I had a 9mm Glock, M&P15 and my carbine snug in my Bugout bag.

It was only about a mile and a half around the front three sides of my property, but I took my time to watch for signs of intrusion and took several hours. There were no signs that anyone had been on the property, so I drove straight to the old cabin. I parked a couple hundred yards away and walked up to the cabin. No one was there, and I saw no fresh signs of any partying. My message apparently got around to the local teens.

I drove on over to the ravine, parked a short distance from the cave and took the supplies in and stored them. The entrance hadn't been disturbed, so I headed on back to the house after thoroughly wiping my tracks away. I approached the house carefully to practice this habit for the future.

The house was just as I left it and I busied myself preparing supper for the girls. They had done most of the cooking, and I wanted them to take a hot bath, relax, and let me serve them when they returned in a couple of hours.

They had promised to return before dark, which gave me plenty of time to prepare the meal. Fried pork chops, corn on the cob, mashed potatoes and green beans along with their favorite wine. I took a shower and then started preparing the vegetables while the chops marinated in my special wine based sauce.

***

The girl's trip into town didn't go as expected. They had to turn around and head to Patty's house when they saw a gunfight in progress at a roadblock at the edge of town.

Mary turned the truck around and said, "I guess we'll have to cancel until Matt can go with us. I don't want to get involved in that mess."

She drove along the back road to Patty's house when they saw a kid on a snowmobile in a driveway. The kid waved and quickly rode towards them and the road. They drove on not thinking much about the kid who was soon out of sight. A few minutes later, they turned down Mary's driveway and parked in her garage so they could load the truck without prying eyes wondering what they were up to and discovering what was in the truck.

They loaded all the remaining food, clothes, weapons, and personal items that would fit in the back of the pickup. The truck had a camper shell so their stuff would be hidden during the trip home. They didn't look outside, or they would have seen the kid peer in through the garage door window closely watching them load the truck.

***

He rode quickly home and told his dad and the men who were visiting, the woman who lived three houses down on the right had a lot of food.

They still had plenty of food, but the store was empty as were the restaurants. They had kicked, scratched, and beaten their neighbors to get their cart full of food out to the truck only to find the truck wouldn't start. They had to push the damned cart the five miles back to their place. Then the hunters arrived and provided fresh meat.

"Charles, we won't hurt the women, but we need their truck and half of the food. It should be easy taking them away from two women."

They got their ATVs out of the garage and sped off to Patty's house and arrived an hour after the women.

"Jeb, let's watch and make sure there are no others around. I don't want to be sucked into an ambush."

They watched for about an hour until they saw the garage door rise and charged towards the vehicle backing out of the garage.

***

Mary lifted the garage door with the manual pull rope, looked around outside and said, "Patty, let's head on back to the ranch. This took longer than I thought. It will be getting dark in a couple of hours, and I want to get home and fix supper."

"I guess I'll have to start calling it home. It was your home, so it comes easily to you."

"What's going on between you and Matt? I saw you two kissing. I know he likes you."

"He told me he loves me."

"Great, what did you say to him?"

"Thanks."

110

Mary started backing the car out of the garage when she answered, "What? I thought you cared for him. I know he wants you."

"George wants me, but mainly in his bed. I don't know this guy. He is divorced and hasn't dated in months. I wonder if he wants me because I am a woman and near him. I really like him, but it's too early to say, love."

"You got him wrong. This is a good man. He...."

Mary didn't finish the sentence because her door was yanked open and a gun was pushed into her face. She reacted by pushing the gas pedal to the floor. The tires squealed, gunfire erupted, the side window shattered, and Mary felt intense pain in her side. Patty drew her sidearm and returned fire as Mary whipped the wheel around, slid sideways, shifted to drive, and spun the tires as the truck sped away.

Patty was scared to death but reacted quickly as her training took over. She pointed, aimed, and squeezed the trigger at the closest threat. She fired twice striking him twice and then turned to the man by the garage door. She was reaching out the window as the truck sped away and fired several times before he fell. She heard the window shatter behind her and felt the glass pieces impact her neck and face, but did not feel the bullet as it entered her back.

Mary saw the closest man get shot in the chest as Patty returned fire. Several bullets blew out the back window as she sped away. Patty kept shooting, and then slumped over in the seat.

"Patty! Patty! Damn it, girl, wake up."

She pulled over, painfully leaned to Patty's side. She opened the door, rolled Patty forward so she could check out the wound. Patty had been shot below the shoulder, and the bullet went through the muscle on the outside of the ribs. Mary tore her shirt and made two wads to put pressure on the wounds. She tied the two wads in place with torn strips from Patty's T-Shirt.

She didn't look at her wound and drove towards home before crashing into a tree a half mile before the turnoff to the ranch.

***

I knew they were running late, but wasn't worried at first because they were armed and the road between here and Mary's place only had a few people. All of them knew Patty and most knew Mary so there shouldn't be any problem.

I busied myself setting the table and waited for their return. It got dark, and I knew something must have happened. I tried to stay busy while thinking that nothing could have happened when I suddenly grabbed my guns, hopped in my truck and headed to Patty's place.

The Northern Lights were dancing across the sky, and I almost didn't notice, as it had become an everyday event.

It only took 15 minutes to get to Patty's place, and I found two dead men and a shot up house. The bodies were being hefted by several women. I guess they were taking them home.

I spun the truck around and sped back into the dark towards home. I thought that they must have taken a back road and I missed them on the way. I was flying low when I saw the reflectors off in the woods. I jammed on the brakes and slid past the spot. I backed up, drove down into the woods, and parked behind Mary's truck.

They were both slumped down in the seat. I used my flashlight to check on them and saw they were both wounded. I picked Patty up and placed her in the bed of my truck then returned, picked Mary up and placed her beside Patty.

I quickly checked them out and saw that neither was bleeding profusely. Mary had a chest wound so I took a baggie and taped it to her chest with duct tape to help seal it until I could get her home. Patty's wound was through and through and didn't look like it entered the chest cavity, so I hurried them back home.

Mary had the worst wound, so I worked on her first. I gave her a strong pain pill so I could do what I had to do.

My training included taking care of gunshot wounds, but the instructor made it clear that death was likely from any wound to the chest cavity. She had been shot in the side, and the bullet exited her back missing any vital organs. Infection would likely be her worst enemy.

I cleaned and swabbed both holes with antiseptic and then stitched both wounds before starting an IV with antibiotics. I did everything I had learned and could find in the manual, now it was up to God and Mary to decide if she would live.

I was so busy trying to save Mary that I was surprised when Patty mumbled. I washed my hands, put surgical gloves on, and examined her. I removed what was left of her T-Shirt and bra so I could get to the wounds and swabbed her with antiseptic. As I thought, the bullet entered the flesh outside the rib cage under her left arm and exited the side of her chest.

The bullet probably scraped her ribs, but I wasn't going to perform any surgery. The best thing for her was for me to swab the wounds with antiseptic sew them up and start an intravenous antibiotic, just as I had done for Mary. Compared to the gunshot wounds, picking the glass out of Patty was a tedious affair.

I slipped a pain pill under her tongue and double-checked the medical book to make sure I had done all I could.

I cleaned her up and placed her arm in a sling from the medical supplies. Then I covered each of them with medical scrubs and blankets. I added a 5% glucose IV to both women, then reread my medical books to make sure I hadn't missed anything.

I had already done more than I thought I'd ever be called upon to do. I was scared shitless.

I tucked both under their covers and brought my supper back to the great room where they were laying on the two couches. I finished eating and brought an air mattress into the room so I would be close to them during the night.

I would have to rely on Tina and Gus to bark if strangers came around. The dogs didn't bark that night, and I was able to sleep for two hours at a stretch. Staying up for 48 hours sounded easy two days ago, but it surely did suck now.

It was even worse when the alarm went off every two hours so I could check on the girls.

✪

The billion-year odyssey of the Alpha Omega trio concluded in a colossal, fiery display of ejected plasma, cast outward into the Cosmos.

In a final act of kindness, Earth lay only indirectly in the crosshairs. The planet Earth would continue. However, humankind's continuance was, and may still be, in doubt: only The Earth Abides.

Chapter 8

Coronal Mass Ejection

I guess you noticed that I changed from handwritten to typed text, which has to be much easier to read than my awkward attempts at cursive writing. Even my best effort smeared a bit. Now I have to go back and type the first seven chapters. Crap!

You have waited patiently, and now this is where TSHTF, or TFTDM (The Flare that devastated mankind).

***

I woke up to Patty talking fitfully in her sleep.

"No George! Stop!"

Then there was silence before I heard her yell, "Go! Go! They're shooting."

It was early morning, and I'd had enough sleep to get by, but not enough to stop yawning every few minutes.

I checked on Mary and saw no change in her at all, so I returned to Patty. I could stare at her face the rest of my life and hoped I would. Suddenly her eyes opened, and she stared up, into my eyes.

She blinked several times before uttering, "Where am I? Where is Mary? What happened, my side hurts like hell?"

"One question at a time young lady. Y'all got into a gunfight with two men. You killed them, but they wounded both of you. Still, they lost; you won. Your wound isn't too serious, but Mary's may be life threatening."

She lunged upward and hugged me as she cried, "Darling, please help Mary," as she screamed in agony.

"I will, but right now, please, lie back, and rest. I will take good care of both of you, but she is in God's hands. Her wound is severe."

I left her and checked on Mary who needed fresh IVs. I made the change and swapped out Patty's antibiotic IV, then fixed breakfast, and warmed up some chicken noodle soup for Patty. I hated to wake her, but she needed to eat.

I shouldn't have worried as just the smell of the soup brought her eyes open. I helped prop her up on two pillows and fed her a spoonful at a time until she ate her fill.

"You're a good nurse."

I looked over at Mary and replied, "Right now I hope I'm a great doctor."

Patty shook her head in acknowledgment, closed her eyes and almost instantly fell back to sleep.

An hour later, she awoke again, and asked, "Does the Doctor have a bed pan?"

"Oh shit."

She began to laugh, but the pain it caused shut down any attempt at levity. She said, "No, just pee. Help me to the bathroom."

When I tried to return her to the couch, she balked and wanted to sit in the recliner next to her friend. I helped to get her seated, moved her IV, and then placed a blanket over her.

She looked under the blanket and said, "Nice T-Shirt ya' got here, Doc, now where did you put my shirt and bra?"

"Your shirt is in the garbage, and your bra is soaking to get the blood out. I'm afraid it might not come clean. I'll try bleach."

"Matt, thanks for taking such good, care of us. Mary told me you were one of the good guys. She was right, you are."

"Thank you. I don't think anyone has ever said something as nice as that to me. It means a lot."

I hadn't turned the heat on, and the air was cool. She sat there and watched Mary for the next several hours with the blanket up to her neck. I knew it was going to get much colder before this was over.

Just before lunch, I asked, "Patty are you all right with me taking a run up the road to make sure those people aren't looking for us. I also need to bring the truck back. It will only take an hour or two tops.

"Yes, just leave a couple of Glocks with the 31 round magazines and please get back quickly."

This experience had immeasurably matured Patty. I felt much better about her survival prospects. No longer was she the fearful, cry for the masses, little girl.

She had morphed into a woman worthy of bringing humankind back from the abyss. I felt an incredible pride and tenderness for this lovely and determined woman.

After feeding Patty another bowl of soup, I checked on Mary. She was still asleep and resting peacefully. I checked her IVs and then tended to Patty. I again took her to the bathroom and then returned her to Mary's side.

Patty looked down at the bag on the side of Mary's couch and said, "Catheter?"

"Yes."

Patty managed a weak smile and said, "If she asks, tell her I installed it."

"Yeah, thanks, I was wondering how to handle that."

"She won't ask, but you know, just in case.

My face turned red, and all I could say was, "Yeah, okay, gotcha'. Here is a bottle of water and a chocolate bar in case you want them while I'm gone."

I kissed her on the forehead and left.

I had planned to ride a bicycle to where the truck had careened off the road, but the snow, which seemed as though it would never thaw, lay heavy on the road forcing me to don my snowshoes and trudge on down the road.

What I saw actually frightened me; tracks in the snow, tire tracks, and no way to hide them.

I found the truck still deep in the woods. The only way anyone would have spotted it was to approach from behind in the dark with the lights on. The reflectors shine very well on the back of the truck. I would remember this and tape over the ones on all of our vehicles.

I started the truck and then checked it for any damage. The truck had numerous bullet holes but was not mechanically damaged, so I stowed the snowshoes inside the camper, placed my Keltek carbine and Glock on the seat next to me and the truck fired right up.

I put the truck in four-wheel drive and backed cautiously out of the woods and onto the Highway.

I drove slowly back to Patty's house, passing a house where several people waved at me. I waved back and went on. I pulled the truck off in the woods, hid it a quarter of a mile from her driveway, and walked up to the house from the woods.

I was only about 100 feet from the back of the house when I heard two men drive past in an old Chevy car.

They went up the road a short ways then drove back and pulled into Patty's driveway. They got out of the car and walked around the house as if looking for Mary's truck.

"I know that bitch came back here. Come on let's go in the house. They may have hidden the truck. We'll make them wish they were dead instead of my brothers."

It was clear these men didn't know that both women were wounded and they wanted blood.

I moved a little closer to the main door beside the garage and waited for them to come out. I only waited 10 minutes, and both walked out cursing.

"Those bitches took everything worth having. We will track them down and kill them."

"But after we have some fun."

"Oh hell yes, ya' know I'll bet it'll be more fun for us than those two murderin' bitches."

I had a bead on the mouthy one, squeezed the trigger, and a red cloud blew out the back of his head with bits of his skull and brain matter. I quickly re-aimed and placed two bullets into the chest of the second man.

I walked up to them and saw that the man with the sucking chest wound was not dead...yet. He was fighting desperately to get a breath, and trying to speak as he coughed blood. His eyes were pleading when I calmly shot him in the forehead without a second thought.

The snow in which the two men lay had turned crimson before the bodies cooled, and their hearts stopped pumping.

I stripped them of their weapons and ammo before searching their car for anything of use. I didn't find anything useful, so I opened the hood, took the distributor cap and spark plug wires.

I thought about torching the car, but I just could not bring myself to harm a car that might save a good person's life one day.

I took a different route home to avoid the house where the people waved at me. I would deal with them later.

Killing the two men began preying on my mind during the trip back home. I kept second-guessing myself, wondering if it had really been necessary to kill them. I drove home, got out of the truck, and promptly vomited as I fell to my knees. Even though I had come to know that, they had to be scratched from the rolls of humanity, for everyone's safety.

I was not a murderer, and that was absolutely what I did not want to become. I stood there frozen, standing in the dry, blowing snow, my hands on the truck as I realized that there were way too many bad people out in this, not so Brave New World. People would kill me, or the girls, for a scrap of food. I realized beyond question that I had to deep six this moral issue and do whatever it would take to survive. Yeah, whatever it takes to survive.

Sheeple, or Sheepdog? To be one of the sheeple I had to place my safety in the hands of others. No, that would just not do at all.

I decided then, and there to be the new face of law and order. I was born to be the sheepdog, a vigilante.

This moment proved to be an epiphany for me that would be a driving force in my life.

No, there would be no more vomiting or second-guess the killing of evil men. It became crystal clear to me, try to hurt any innocent person around me, you die.

Looking back at this moment I think the glare from snow brought everything into sharp clarity. It had a precipitous impact upon my evolution, or mutation, depending upon perspective.

The snow was a foot deep, and I had no way to hide the tracks.

"Patty, I'm home! The trip went well. I brought the truck back, and the supplies were still in it."

"Thank God the rest of that bunch didn't find the truck. Did you see any of them?"

I thought about not telling her about the fight, but I decided that I would never lie to those I cared for.

"Two more men from the house about a quarter of a mile this side of your house came to greet me. The short story was that they intended to rob and kill me, then do the same to you, and worse. I saw them first and ambushed them."

She looked thoughtful for a second before saying, "I'm glad you did it. People like that must not be the ones to inherit the Earth.

I knew that kid followed us to my house. We should have known he wasn't running around in the snow. The kid was their lookout."

"Patty, I have to go back to determine if they are a threat to us. We have killed four of their men, and there could be more looking to settle the score.

I'll take one of the sniper rifles with a suppressor. My plan is to sneak up and determine if they are a threat. If they are, I will end that threat. If no threats, I'll get my ass back up here."

I considered; threats and tracks in the snow.

"When do you have to go?"

"Now, I hate to leave you alone again, but I want to neutralize any threats before they show up at our doorstep. Besides, we are blind until I can reinstall our surveillance cameras and sensors, and that's not good."

Patty asked, "Why not just put them back up now? The Flare is passed, isn't it?"

"No, you were only out for the night. The Flare should hit tomorrow sometime. Even then we can't put them right back up because we don't know if there will be more CMEs resulting from the shock to the sun. I think it'll be best to wait at least a month before we set them back out."

"Yeah, I understand. Look, she is still out, so take me to the bathroom one more time, place some snacks by my chair and I'll be okay."

"I want to place another bag of antibiotics by your chair. Can you manage to change it out when the other goes dry? I'll change Mary's IV now."

I helped her to the bathroom again, got the IV restarted, placed the snacks, and water by her chair, thus fulfilling my nursing duties. I tried to kiss her on the mouth as I left, but she moved, and I ended up by kissing her forehead.

"Matt, I'm not ready for a relationship, yet."

"Okay, I understand. Thanks for being up front with me. I'm really sorry if I caused you distress, but please let me know if you do become ready."

"Yes, Matt, I'm good with that. Thanks for being so understanding."

Oh, I was so understanding, yeah right; I was hurt and mad when I left.

***

I went to the gun safe to retrieve an AR 10 that I had set up as a sniper rifle. I knew I might have long-range shots, and the AR makes a fine close quarter weapon, too.

I changed into camo's and selected body armor from the gun room. I needed to take more precaution when preparing to exchange gunfire with thugs. I did not want to get a bullet in the gut and die a slow, painful death.

Concerned about nightfall, I left the house about 2:30, drove towards the potential enemy, and again parked off the road a quarter mile from the suspect house.

I carefully walked deep into the woods and circled around to the back of the house. As I moved closer, I wondered if I could shoot any of the women who might be a danger to our survival. Frankly, I was surprised I had so calmly killed the two assholes without even hesitating. Killing them was like killing a copperhead before it could bite you. There was a rush of adrenaline, and then relief. I resolved never to be bitten by snakes.

No one was outside, so I snuck in closer to the house. I heard talking from the side window and moved close enough to listen in on the conversation, again tracks. My presence would not go unnoticed. No matter what I did, I could not hide those damnable tracks.

***

"Charlie, you know those men were bad. They would have eventually turned on us when the food ran out. We don't even know where they came from."

"Marge, I was fooled. I have to say I felt good at first when I felt we would have safety in numbers, what with everyone else gone. They had guns, and I thought they would help protect us, and it was a good idea to scavenge from the empty houses. That is 'til they got killed running Patty off."

"Patty was a good person. I hope she made it safely to where ever she headed. I just wish someone hadn't sabotaged our car."

***

I listened in long enough to be sure these people were not a threat and then quietly walked upon the snow to the front door, drew my pistol and wrapped it against the door.

"Charlie..."

"Shut up Marge, quick hide in the potato bin, now, damn it, move!"

Marge ran to the bin, climbed in, and closed the lid while Charlie made his way to the door.

Standing beside the door, Charlie asked, "Who's there? I got a gun."

After hearing the conversation, I smiled knowing he had no firearm. I said, "Charlie, open this door now before I kick it in and put a bullet in you! Now, Charlie, now!"

Fearing the unknown voice might carry out his threat, Charlie slowly opened the door and found himself peering down the barrel of Matt's AR-10.

"Please, sir, don't shoot!"

I said, "If I open the door, and someone is waiting to attack me, you will die first."

Opening the door, Charlie said, "Sir, no one is here with me, I swear."

I entered, visually searched the room, and asked, "Where is Marge? Get her in here."

Please, we have nothing for you to steal. Please don't kill us, well, just please, let us be.

Wait, how do you know our names?"

"I said; get her in here, now!" Quaking in fear, Charlie said, "Marge, get in here, quick."

"All right, Charlie, sit down and relax just a little! If you play your cards right, you *will* get out of this without anything bad happening to either of you. Am I clear?"

"Oh, yes sir. We understand. We won't cause no problem, thank you. How kin we be a'helpin' you, sir?"

Marge slowly came into the room and nearly fainted when she saw my AR.

"Oh, God, are you going to kill us?"

I pointed for her to sit beside Charlie.

After she was seated, I sat across from them and lowered my rifle.

"As I said, I am not here to do you any harm. I know your names because I overheard your conversation a few minutes ago, and overhearing it saved your life."

I showed them my stethoscope, and said, "If you had said the wrong thing, you would both be dead by now."

"Thank you, thank you, but what do you want from us?"

I smiled at him and said, "Right to the chase, very good Charlie.

Okay, here's what I demand, notice I did not say request. I will return the distributor and wiring so you can get on the road.

If you stay here, you will freeze, or starve, or become slaves. You must leave here by dawn tomorrow…not one minute later, and you must never return. Clear?"

Both said in unison, "Oh, bless you, sir. Leaving here is all we want to do, and tomorrow at dawn definitely works for us. Where do you think we should go?"

"Head south, old buddy head south…and be quick about it."

"Yes, sir, we will."

I left four things for them in the car, a note telling them where I hid a pistol, a case of MREs from the truck, and a hose.

Yeah, I know, I'm just an old softie. They didn't have a Preacher's chance in hell, even with the pistol.

No sheepdogs here. I had no doubt they preferred to be in the center of the flock. Still, I had to give them a small, all be it a very small chance to make it.

***

I arrived back at home, put away the truck and equipment, and went into the great room to see how Patty and Mary were doing. I saw them still asleep, so I pulled a chair up beside Mary and held her hand while I watched her sleep. I noticed she was becoming restless and hoped it was a good sign that she would wake up soon. Patty squirmed in the chair for an hour before waking and seemed very happy to see me.

"Matt, how long have you been back?"

"Oh, about an hour I guess. You were sleeping, and you need your rest, so I didn't wake you."

"Matt, I want to tell..."

"I think you have said it all. What do you want for supper?"

"Okay. Wait, I forgot. What did you find out about the people down the road?"

"They are good people, but entirely too weak to have much of a chance in this new reality.

The bad guys wandered into the area last week and promised to provide security if the people would share their food. There wasn't enough food, so they started raiding the area and had the bad luck to run into you two."

"I'm glad. I hate killing over food and property."

Suddenly a very weak voice said, "What the hell are you two talking about and who beat the crap outta' me?"

Mary was still in bad shape and needed constant attention, but with luck, it seemed the worst might just be over. The drugs had beaten any infection, and now it appeared she just needed lots of time to heal.

Patty replied, "What do you remember?"

"I remember we were going to your house to get our stuff and then nothing."

Patty filled in the gaps and pretty much took over caring for Mary as they both healed. I still had the chore of transporting them to the restroom and a while later to the supper table. We decided that supper was the one time that we should all be seated around the table.

The radio buzzed with the special emergency alert signal. The static caused us to hear only about half of what was said, but it scared the crap out of us.

"Ladies and…sklxxt…the…sklxxt… of the United States of America."

"…sklxxt…the CME will reach us early…sklxxt…the …sklxxt…the morning. Stay in…sklxxt…sklxxt… You will be safe. I want to assure…sklxxt…the…sklxxt…The DHS and FEMA…sklxxt… This is the last communi…sklxxt… the power on. I repeat…sklxxt…"

"We can't take questions at this…"

"Mr. President, Reuters has reported that the USA has invaded…sklxxt…invaded India and Indo…sklxxt…and Russia…sklxxt…the…Mid…sklxxt…and Africa."

"The President has a pressing…sklxxt…taking questions."

The reporters all yelled at once.

"It has been reported that there are three planets that collided with the sun; is that true?"

The Press Secretary must have continued to follow the Presidential party.

"There are numerous reports…sklxxt…that the major…sklxxt…are invading the equatorial regions of the world in a simultaneous attack. What the hell is going on? Is it the end of the world?"

There were no answers to the many questions.

***

What we didn't know at the time was that there was a clamor in the room as the reporter's phones constantly vibrated with messages from their offices.

All communications from the room to the outside world were immediately cut and those reporters were arrested and detained.

***

I turned the radio off and said, "This is confusing and alarming. The government continues to downplay the upcoming disaster, and now we have reports of massive invasions of other countries by several world powers, and I'll bet those invaders are from northern climes. That possibility did not bode well for us."

We discussed the reporter's questions, but we didn't connect the dots between Franks warning, and the invasion of countries in warmer climates.

***

I sulked by myself in the gun safe for several hours wondering how I had gone from hating women to falling in love with one who could care less about me. Honestly, I reacted like a brat who didn't get his way. I planned to be polite to Patty, but run her off at the first time I could when I knew she would be safe. Yeah, that will teach her.

I decided to take a better inventory of my arsenal while I was hiding from Patty. I had placed several guns and ammunition in all of the caches and the cave but felt I needed to add a few selected weapons to the cave. I would keep the .338

Lapua in the house gun safe but would move the Barrett .50 cal to the cave along with plenty of ammunition. I found a mixture of several different rounds. There were ball, tracer, and armor piercing rounds. All of them could wreak havoc on anything short of a tank, but I liked the idea of being able to kill a truck at half a mile using the .50 cal armor piercing rounds from a mountain hiding spot.

I also selected a Ruger American .17 HMR for small game hunting and picking off intruders when I wanted to save the larger caliber ammo. Frank had 5,000 rounds of .17 ammo. I was busy keeping my mind off Patty when it dawned on me that the CME was due to hit or pass by in the next 5-10 hours. I locked up and headed upstairs to join the girls.

***

"Patty I heard the last bit of your conversation, and it appears you two aren't hitting it off as I hoped. What's wrong?"

"Oh, he's fallen for me, and his feelings are hurt because I don't feel the same way about him?"

"I can't see why you didn't fall for him. He's good looking, a kind, and wonderful person and has a great home."

"I don't know. I like him, but I think George made me leery of all men. George started out a nice guy then changed over the years as he failed at one business after another. He resented my success. George never valued hard work and always drank a bit too much."

"He drinks, but he never drinks to excess. If I were a few years younger, he would be my man. I know the heart wants what the heart wants, but you won't find a better man."

"Go for it. You are a very beautiful woman, and no one would guess you are in your forties."

"Hell girl, I'm 42, Matt is about 35, and I want a man a little closer to my age so we can grow old together. No, I'll leave him for the young fillies like you."

***

I woke to the sound of my alarm at 2:30 and remembered that the outer fringes of plasma cloud should be hitting the Earth at any time now. I prayed that we only received the dissipated particles and not the concentrated core. I went into the great room and woke the girls.

"Ladies, it's 2:40 and the Northern Lights have kicked into high gear. There is a very bright and very large cloud traveling away from the Sun, but away from us, that has lit up the sky. My guess is that the CME is approaching fast, which is good for us because it should pass with the U.S. faced away from its path.

I really don't want any harm to come to any other country, but the worst part of the hit on the Earth is going to be China, Russia, and the Middle East. I just hope the Israelis have taken precaution because that part of the world is going to be hit very hard. I could care less about the others."

"Can you help me outside so I can watch it pass by," asked Mary?"

"Yes, I'll help Patty out to the back deck and then come back for you."

"I can make it on my own. Please help Mary."

"Okay Mary, let's get you up and outside."

Mary was a trim 130 pounds and easy to assist through the kitchen and out to the deck. I helped her into a chair beside Patty and then went in to make some coffee.

"Look, it's a weird green daylight out here. The sky is like a soup made of iridescent colors. That huge blob of green light is passing by as the Earth turns us away from it. That's why we just see the glow and not the cloud."

I returned, heard Mary's comment, and added, "That's right if we were hit by the main body of the cloud we probably would be dead in a few hours. The Earth is blocking the worst radiation and charged particles from hitting us."

***

The outer fringe of the CME plasma cloud bombarded Europe, Russia, China, and the Middle East. The plasma interacted with the Earth's magnetosphere creating an enormous electrical surge that fed into the world's electrical grids.

Power generation stations with copper windings in the generators melted along with blown transformers, and melted transmission wires. Most electronics suffered fused components and were ruined.

The side of the Earth away from the plasma suffered the same type of damage but to a much lesser extent. Electronics were fried, but most copper wires did not completely melt down. The grid was down, but only because of blown electronics and transformers. Most people on the receiving side of Earth took a massive dose of radiation. Many died within a week, and no one really knew what cancers and mutational changes to the human genome would come.

Cars, trucks, jets, ATVs and any vehicle made with electronics controlling their ignition or fuel system failed and would not run again unless those systems were replaced. Overheated electronics and wires caused millions of fires, which resulted in large swaths of cities being burned to the ground.

The entire Earth was now back to horse and camel transportation except for the people who had pre-1975 vehicles without electronics, or military vehicles that had been hardened against EMP blasts.

Fire trucks would not be available to help put out fires even if the fire hydrants could provide water. Police cars were dead. The police that stayed on the job had to walk or ride a horse to chase down those who considered this disaster to be an opportunity to be looters, or rather, undocumented shoppers.

Men and women with pacemakers died that day, and millions of others began the downward spiral to death as their medications ran out. Insulin, blood pressure medicine, and antibiotics were no longer manufactured or any other medications. People would soon start dying from infected cuts and decayed teeth.

There was no ready source of clean drinking water so disease would spread rapidly. Mankind would lose 80 percent of its population in a few short months, perhaps, and probably more. I could not comprehend just then what a world of 7,000,000,000 would be like with only seven hundred million, at best.

It would be a few days before the major riots began to finish the destruction of the modern large cities. Grocery stores only had three days of goods at most, and trucks weren't delivering from the warehouses. The warehouses would become battlegrounds as survivors fought and died for the scraps of a civilization thrust, in the blink of an eye, into the dustbin of history.

***

We watched the sky perform light shows that boggled our minds with electric blues, greens, yellows, and reds. There was still a bright green glow around the entire Earth from the charged particles striking Earth's protective atmosphere.

Mary aptly described the light show, "Matt, it's almost like one of those 65 inch plasma TVs puked its guts out over the entire sky. It's a riot of colors."

"Yes, no need for LSD tonight, the colors, the colors!"

Patty and I had a good laugh as Mary looked at us with a wry grin.

We continued to watch in awe until well after dawn when Mary asked, "Anyone hungry besides me?"

"I could eat," I replied."

"You can always eat, but yeah, me too. I'm also hungry, and I'll take the hint that I should get up and fix breakfast. How do deer sausage, scrambled eggs, and toast sound?"

I quickly replied, "No Patty, I'll take care of y'all until you are both well. Of course, I'll expect some great meals after that."

Mary replied, "That's a deal. Patty, you'd better keep an eye on him and make sure he doesn't poison us."

She replied, "Don't worry, I'll keep a close eye on him and give him some cooking classes to boot."

***

"I know you want to stay away from town, but don't you think we should know what's going on there."

"It's going to become very dangerous there in the next few days. I want to stay away from people as much as possible, but I agree on keeping an eye on what is happening in the area is important. I'm just not sure how to go about it safely. You two know best that people can be dangerous."

"Damn skippy, we've both learned a lesson from our trip to my house."

"How many people know about this place?"

"None in town know about the prepping. Most in town know that Mary and Frank built a nice place up here and think Frank retired from NASA."

"I guess they also know I bought the place and probably think I live up here alone."

We talked about our options at dinner on several occasions.

"Where did George end up when you threw him out?"

"He was staying at the Great Divide Boarding House and found a job as a janitor at a bar on the edge of town."

"I think we can safely say that George will come looking for you and about a third of the town will come out here looking for food. I think we should take the chance and only wait a week to install our cameras and sensors. Until then we need to post a guard every night."

"I can stand watch, but Mary won't be able to for a couple of months."

"I agree with you being a lookout, but really, where. It's way too cold for any of us to be on guard outside I think it's best if we post you just beside the window looking onto the front porch with an AR while I sleep on a cot close by.

I also think that we made a mistake in just the three of us trying to secure this place. I've inventoried the rations, and we could have added another three people, and still have food for a year. Crap, crap, crap, what have I done?"

"Matt," said Patty, "what you did is make it possible for us to survive. Yeah, I guess we have made a serious mistake concerning people and survivors. Well, the bottom line is that we have to put on our big girl panties, well, not you and step up. You wear whatever it is you guys wear."

Her outburst left us all chuckling for a few seconds before reality kicked back in.

"Okay, what do we really do?"

"Next week we'll post Mary in front of the monitors so she can handle the electronic surveillance."

"I like those Ideas, but won't she doze off and miss intruders."

"The sensors include movement and sound. The monitoring station has an audible alarm that has a volume adjustment. It would wake her up. I also have two remote monitoring handsets that you and I will carry at all times. They are connected by a signal from the main station and have the same video and sound capability."

Later that night when it was my turn for guard duty I crawled out of my sleeping bag and noticed a chill in the air. I went to sleep with only my mosquito net above me and woke up deep in my sleeping bag, and now I needed a jacket for guard duty.

Patty noticed I was shivering and said, "It's colder than I ever remember for January. Hell, we've got three more months of winter. Is this caused by the CME?"

"It's too early to tell, but yeah, I think so. Let's just hope it's only a small drop in the average temperature. I don't know much about climatology, but those Global Warming politicians were very upset at a fraction of a degree change upward in temperature. We can't control the sun, so we have to improvise and roll with the flow. Let's begin planning for the worst case."

"How will we know what the worst case is?"

"We won't, but I'd suggest starting at an average day in the Artic."

"Hell, I'd rather die."

"That possibility may also be in the cards."

She replied, "Well, thank you very much, Mr. Gloom and Doom," as she threw her dirty socks at me.

"Seriously we need a plan to bugout to a warmer climate."

"What, wait, huh? Bug out? Are you nuts?"

★

Chapter 9

Pinedale, Wyoming – After "The Flare."

Obviously, I wasn't in Pinedale when the shit hit the fan, or as the girls say after The Flare, so most of this is not firsthand knowledge. What you are about to read is from what the residents told me, or I saw later.

The town stayed calm until the last collision because Sheriff Bob Alton said it had to stay calm. Sheriff Bob, as he was called, listened to the radio and TV announcements and knew bad times were coming. He had 10 deputies to cover the whole county and placed them on 12-hour shifts 6 days a week until things calmed down.

Sheriff Bob was a big, slow-moving man, but his mind was constantly evaluating his surroundings and thinking ahead of any possible trouble.

He had been a Lieutenant in the Army Military Police and had been extensively trained for multiple contingencies including nuclear warfare.

He immediately saw the solar flare situation to be similar to a nuclear EMP blast and began planning for the worst case.

He placed extra flashlights, walkie-talkies, radios, emergency weather radios and batteries for all in steel garbage cans, lined with rubber insulation, and lined steel lids, in his garage.

He and his wife begin stocking piling food by sending her to several nearby towns to make large purchases of non-perishable foods from Cosco and Sam's Club. She paid cash and made sure no one knew where she lived. She also purchased survival gear and ammunition at every store and outfitter within a hundred miles.

She stocked hundreds of pounds of beans, rice, sugar, and salt along with several closets full of can goods.

Sheriff Bob had a small spring fed lake on his property, so he wasn't worried about water. He took several 50-gallon plastic drums, cut them in half and built a pretty good water purification system.

He placed, washed, and purified sand in one-half drum with a cheese cloth filter over it. That drum flowed into another filled with charcoal that flowed into another with purified sand. The water from the last drum flowed into a 50-gallon plastic drum and then was treated with bleach to finish the purification. He wasn't sure he needed the charcoal, but it made him feel good that it would take out most carcinogens.

For transportation Sheriff, Bob had an old 1962 Chevy truck and two mules that he used to travel through the high country when he went trout fishing.

Sheriff Bob gave the town's people warnings to stock up on food and to be prepared for the worst.

"Bob, why do we need to prepare for a solar flare?"

"Because it could block communications and fry the electronics in everything. That's the worst case. If that happens, it could be weeks before food can be transported in from the warehouses. I'd prepare just like you would for a long winter storm."

He knew this was watered down, and downright misleading, but he knew telling people the truth that they would not have electricity for the rest of their lives, was not in anyone's interest. Well, he knew that was just silly because panic was the last thing anyone needed.

Most of the people did purchase more food than usual, but as Bob knew, it would never be enough to survive the upcoming disaster.

***

Patty was at my place when panic spread around Pinedale three days after the first CME. She had left her assistant manager in charge of the store and left on two weeks' vacation before The Flare.

The week before The Flare, the following exchange took place.

"Patty, should you be leaving with this solar flare stuff keeping everyone on edge?"

"I haven't really been feeling well, and Mary and I plan to sit this thing out. Things should be okay, but if there's trouble don't get hurt over someone stealing a can of beans.

Just hold the 50% sale and when the shelves are bare, put a sign on the window, leave the door to the store open and go home.

If credit the card readers go down, tell folks that they can pay for everything as soon as the craziness is over."

"But Patty, if you're going to just give everything away, why not put out a free for the taking sign and leave it open?"

"Yes, we could do that, but if we did, the place would be wrecked. When this nonsense is over, I'd like to restock, not rebuild."

"I gotta' tell you, Patty, I'm scared. Could I buy some food now on credit? You can take it out of my check later."

Patty wrote a quick note, "You have been with me for a long time, loyal, and a good friend. Here, take this voucher for you to receive a gift certificate for $2,000 worth of anything in the store. That way you can't be accused of stealing. If you take more, just sign for it on the IOU log book.

Oh, and do the same for Bruce."

"Patty, thank you, this really means a lot to me."

The assistant manager loaded up her van and took the supplies home with a big smile on her face. It was only a few days later that all hell broke loose at the store.

She was late to work on the morning after the Alpha Omega III collided with the sun. Her car wouldn't start, and the TV and radio were dead. She knew Patty depended on her to open the store, so she saddled her son's horse and rode into town.

She hobbled her horse in the vacant lot behind the store and placed a bucket of water at the corner of the fence in hopes the horse wouldn't kick it over. She planned to check on it every couple of hours.

She walked around to the front of the store, and there was a crowd waiting to get in along with the part time cashier.

"Wilma, you're late. Patty always opened the store on time."

"Bruce, my van was dead this morning, and I had to ride my son's mare in today."

She noticed there were several horse and wagons tied to the trees in front of the store and one old pickup.

There was a round of "My car was dead, too," from the crowd.

She opened the doors and let them in while the cashier turned the lights on and prepared to man the cash register. The first few hours were busy, and then there was a surge at mid-morning after everyone realized that all TVs, radios and most vehicles were dead. Then the line backed up and out the front door.

Wilma told the crowd, "I'm placing a one cart maximum on all purchases so we can make sure everyone gets some food."

"This pissed off the people in the store and made the people waiting in line happy."

George pushed two carts, side by side, to the cashier and demanded to be let out without paying.

"I own the store, and I'm taking this food. Don't try to stop me."

Wilma walked over to him and replied, "You don't own the store and Patty kicked your drunken ass out. You are not going to steal this food."

George punched her and tried to push the carts through the door, but one was stuck. Several of the men grabbed George and threw him out into the street.

George was drunk, and the rough treatment made him a bit wobbly.

"He yelled, "I'll kill all of you sumbitches and my cheating wife."

He left heading back to his room where he retrieved his .38 revolver. He grabbed a bottle of scotch from the kitchen table and went back to the store. He walked in waving the pistol, and everyone scurried to get out of his way.

Wilma saw him and said, "George, put the gun down. You're not going to shoot anyone over a can of beans."

He pointed the gun at her, pulled the trigger, and smiled as she fell to the floor with a red stain spreading on her chest.

George filled a cart and calmly pushed it out the door and down the street. He never looked back.

The cashier said, "Go get the Sheriff. I'm closing the store."

The people panicked and started taking what they wanted. Fights broke out, and more shots were fired. The cashier high tailed it home with a ham and a turkey under his arms. The store was now a battlefield of scared and desperate people. The store was empty, and five bodies lay on the floor by the time the first deputy arrived. All of the guns and ammo from the display cases had been looted, but the gun safe was still secure.

***

George waited until dark to go back to the store. He was still worried that he would be seen since dark wasn't dark anymore due to those damn lights in the sky. He had guessed correctly and found the store looted except for the gun safe and the hidden storage room.

He knew the combination to the gun safe and had the safe open in short order. He found a bag to load with ammunition and shouldered three M&P15s and two Ruger 9mm pistols. He was ready to take the war to his cheating wife and her rat bastard lover.

He then found the hidden latch to the storage room and as he hoped, found food, liquor and more ammunition and guns. He loaded up a shopping cart and took it out to the horse and buggy that he had stolen earlier that night.

He took the arms and ammunition to Patty's house, passed out, and didn't wake up until mid-morning.

***

Sheriff Bob surveyed the damage at the store and allowed the kinfolk to take their loved one's home to be buried.

"Sheriff, how soon will you have the man who killed my brother Billy in jail?"

"There are no witnesses, and I doubt that we'll find anyone to testify. I'll try to find someone who saw the riot, but don't count on any arrests. This was a riot, and everyone was guilty of something."

"Screw you. If you don't handle this, we will."

"Good luck, now understand me real clear, you little shit, if you cuss me again, I'll put your sorry ass in jail for a day or two, until you heal up. We clear on this, I mean, real clear."

Having never heard Sheriff Bob speak to anyone like that, he was cowed and said, "Yes sir, I'm real sorry. I didn't mean to be a wiseass. It won't happen again. Hell, I know you'll do your best, but if I find him first, I'll…."

"LeRoy, don't you be tellin' me what you gonna' do. You do what you gotta' do, but you ain't gotta' be tellin' me. You got me?"

"I got you, Sheriff."

"Atta' boy. Please tell your ma how sorry I am about Billy. I hope she understands why I won't be able to come out for the burial."

"Don't worry, Sheriff, I'll make her understand, but right now she's a grievin'. Bye."

"Bob the safe was locked yesterday. This morning it was wide open and empty. Look over here. There's a hidden storage room that had a lot of ammunition, food and several guns. Whoever the thief was, he dropped more than he stole.

I think George came back and stole the guns. I went to his room several times yesterday and this morning, and he didn't go back there," said the deputy.

"I agree. I need to find Patty and this Jones fellow and warn them about George. After shooting Wilma, he's probably gunning for both of them. Jealousy is a powerful evil. Take the rest of the guns, ammo, and food over to the jail and lock them up in a cell. If y'all need any for your family, just take 'em.

Bo, you take my horse out to Patty's house to warn her about this and check for George. I'll take my old truck out to the Williamson place and warn Jones."

Bob knew the riots and killing would ravage the town and just three lawmen would only get themselves killed trying to stop the mad men and women.

Half of Pinedale's people died over the next two weeks and another quarter died over the next month. Most of the remaining folks left when the temperature continued to drop, and the food began to run out. The rest simply froze.

***

The next morning George rounded up all of his drinking buddies who were just a step away from starving and doled out food to them. His plan was to form a small army to take the Williamson place and any other ranch that had food. He would kill Jones and take his wife back.

George looked at his friends and said, "My wife purchased tons of food, ammo, and guns for that Jones fellow who bought the Williamson place. He didn't pay for it, so it belongs to me. If you help me get rid of him, I'll share the food, weapons, and ammo with you. Everything, well, everything except Patty. Y'all can have Mary."

There was murmuring, and an open discussion before several of the men said, "Hell yes. We'll join you."

George passed around several bottles of whiskey, and soon all of the men wanted to join in on the raid on the Williamson place. The men were half-drunk and spoiling for a fight. Their fear was beginning to morph into something new, power, no law, nothing to stand in the way of having whatever, or whomever they wanted.

"That Matt Jones kidnapped my wife and spread rumors that she threw me out. I have to rescue her and get those supplies for all of us. Starting right now, we are the law, and the law is what I say it is."

All of the drunks agreed to meet at Patty's house at 4:00 am the next morning and march over to the Williamson place.

"We'll kill anyone who gets in our way and have plenty of food," said George."

***

146

It was damned cold; still, Deputy Bo loved the outdoors, and he was well prepared for the elements. He could feel the heat from the horse's flanks warming the inside of his thighs.

He finally saw the house up ahead and hoped George had slept it off by now.

He'd known George since high school, and they had been friends then. Now he felt George was more of a nuisance than a friend.

When George wasn't drinking or gambling, he was a nice enough guy, and he had fond memories of camping and boating on the local lakes with him.

George dismounted in the driveway and walked up to the house.

He knocked on the door and said in a firm voice, "George, it's me, Bo. Come on out and say hi to your old buddy."

Suddenly the door exploded in front of the deputy, and the double aught buckshot tore through his chest. George kicked the door open and shot the deputy in the head with the shotgun.

"That will teach you to come after me, lawman."

***

Sheriff Bob arrived at the gate to the Williamson place and found it chained and locked. He looked in his toolbox, found a bolt cutter, and cut the chain to gain entrance. He opened the gate and drove up to the house making sure he honked a couple of times to make sure Matt knew he had company coming.

He stopped a few feet from the front steps to the house and got out of his truck.

He heard a voice say, "Sheriff, I have a gun on you. Take your pistol from your holster with your left hand, lay it on the steps, and move away."

The Sheriff complied with the orders, saw Matt carefully pick up the pistol, put it in his belt, and walk towards him.

"Why did you trespass on my property and what do you want?"

Before the Sheriff could answer, Patty ran down the steps hugged the sheriff and said, "Matt, Bob is a good friend, and he means us no harm. Put that gun down."

"Patty, let him answer my questions first," Matt said as he somewhat lowered the AR.

"Sorry for cutting your chain, but I came to warn you that George killed Wilma, took food, liquor, guns and ammo and says he is coming here to get Patty and kill you. I came to warn you."

I still didn't trust the Sheriff or anyone for that matter, but I handed his pistol back to him and asked him to come on in, out of the cold for some hot coffee.

"Patty would you please get the Sheriff and me some coffee?"

"Of course, I'd be glad to.

Bob, how do you like your coffee?"

Smiling now, Bob said, "You know me, and my sweet tooth, Patty, black with 3 sugars. Wait, hold the sugar if you're short. I guess I just gotta' learn to drink it black, at least for however long coffee lasts."

The Sheriff then told us what had happened in town at the store.

Patty screamed, "No!" and began to cry. She said, "Oh my God, Wilma, no! She burrowed her head against my neck and sobbed. Patty was furious about George killing Wilma and threatening us. She said, "We'll be ready for him, and we'll bury him and anyone who comes with him."

I helped Patty to her bed. Patty protested, saying she was all right, but I can be forceful if necessary. I convinced Patty to go upstairs.

"Sheriff, I surely do want to thank you for bringing us this warning.

We'll be ready for him, but if he tries to harm anyone, he'll get buried where he falls.

Patty and Mary have already been shot by men who tried to steal from them. They killed the men, but both were wounded. Patty's wound was not serious, but Mary is still recovering."

"Were the men from around here?"

"No. They may have been on a hunting trip and decided to take over this area. They are all dead now."

"How many were there?"

"Four. Patty and Mary killed two. I killed the other two when I went to find them when they didn't return here from a trip to Patty's home."

"Did you have to kill them? I could have arrested them."

"It was kill or be killed. Bob, do you have the ability to feed a hundred killers? As people begin starving, they will kill to feed their families. We don't have much, and we will not share what little we do have with people who wouldn't prepare for bad times."

"Yeah, you are right, Hell, I'm in the same fix. I've been a prepper most of my life. I'll probably lay down my badge and hunker down until the herd thins its self out."

"That was our plan. Bob, but please hear me. The weather is going to get much colder than any time in Wyoming's recorded history. As soon as Mary gets better, we figure to head south to a warmer climate."

"What makes you think this?"

"Mary's husband was a NASA scientist, and they knew about the three planets possibly colliding with the sun. He told her that the sun would lose enough mass to cool it down a bit which would result in Global Cooling."

"How cold will it get?"

"He was worried that it could be a new Ice Age."

"Oh shit!"

"Yes, oh shit. The problem is the longer we delay, the harder the trip south could be. More snow will fall with every storm that comes through, and it will not melt until July. Let me rephrase that; some of the snow will melt, and it will start snowing again no later than early September, possibly even August. In 25 years, there will be a half mile thick glacier right on this spot, and it will stretch all the way down into northern Arizona.

It's going to happen, Bob. It really is.

If Alpha Omega III had arrived in spring, instead of winter, we might have been able to make it here, as there would be less snow to melt, but with it arriving in mid-winter, there will be deep snows that will not melt in the now colder summer months.

This snowfall will cause more and more of the sun's heat to be radiated back into space. It's gonna' get real cold. There will be practically no life from the Central Highlands of Arizona to the North Pole and the same in the southern hemisphere.

That has to be why the industrialized countries have invaded the equatorial countries.

In an absolute worst-case scenario, the entire planet could become a snowball for hundreds of thousands of years. It has happened before, and only volcanic eruptions began the snow melt."

"Matt, are you sure you know what you're talking about? This is hard to believe.

I've always figured to hunker down for about 90 days and let the bulk of the people, and the craziness dies off before trying to travel. As you said, even those who were the good guys will kill to feed their families. Only the real mountain people and a few people like us will survive here over the winter, and then we'll be killing each other to get food.

Okay, I'm convinced; I'm going home and preparing to travel south as soon as possible. Why don't you and the girls go with us?"

"I wish we could, but Mary needs a couple more weeks of rest before it will be safe for her to travel. Is there anything you need that we can help with?"

"I have food, weapons, and ammo. My old truck is a two wheel drive. Do you have an extra 4x4?"

"Yes, but I'll have to check with the girls. They both have one, and I have one. I hope we'll only need two."

Mary was willing to give her 4x4 to the Sheriff, so he drove it back to the police station, fueled it up, and piled weapons and ammo in the bed. He told the dispatcher he was resigning, told her to get home, pack up and head south. He also told her to tell the two deputies to go home, pack up their families, and do the same thing.

Sheriff Bob felt guilty deserting his post, but he rightfully knew that his family was more important to him than what was about to be left of this town.

***

"So George is coming here to kill you and take me back in his loving arms. He'll have to bring a damned army. I should have shot that little weasel the last time he hit me."

"Patty, you know him the best. How much of a threat can he be?"

"Not much by himself, 'cause he has no guts, so I'd bet he has talked some of his drunken friends to join him in this crusade. They'll be drunk when they arrive and should be easy to defeat."

Mary replied, "I'd prepare for the worst. Matt, will the remote cameras and sensors work now?"

"The ones across the front of the property are hard wired. They will work as good as new. The ones around the sides and back will broadcast, but there will be interference and contact will be broken at best. I'll place them, and then we can finish making our plans.

I'll chain and lock the gate while I'm out."

Patty spoke up, "They will come from a town or my house. Both routes result in them coming in from the west. They will attack in the morning as soon as George can get them sober enough to fight.

Hell, they may stay up all night and stagger in to be slaughtered, so expect anything."

I loaded the cameras and sensors onto the ATV and headed out to install our surveillance equipment. That only took a couple of hours, and I was back at the house in time for dinner. I was happy to report that there weren't any new man made tracks and that there were numerous tracks left by deer, antelope, and other big game.

I turned the surveillance equipment on and was surprised to find all working very well. My guess was that since it was now dark, we were sheltered from some of the solar energy and that the CME was now much further away from the earth.

I watched the monitors until dinner was on the table and only saw a couple of deer grazing by the old cabin.

I was also pleased that the motion sensors worked, as they should. I heard several warning beeps while eating and each time saw an animal passing in front of the camera.

Mary was now able to sit at the table and eat with us. Her wound was slowly healing, and she was in good spirits. Patty had prepared a big pot of Chili with hot dogs and a side salad.

"Patty that was the best Chili I have ever tasted. I have gained a couple of pounds since you two have been cooking."

"I enjoy cooking for a man who appreciates the effort."

I smiled and thanked her.

Changing the subject, I said, "I think we should all stay in the house tonight and keep a close watch on the monitors. The cameras are hidden, and we have the sensors, but I don't want to be surprised by the attackers. We will rotate every 2 hours watching the monitors. If you get too drowsy to properly keep watch, wake me. I'll take the first watch at 10:00 tonight and that places me back on watch at 4:00 am. I want everyone up armed and ready just before daylight.

Patty, when I relieve you at 4:00 please stay up and start the coffee and some breakfast. I'll get Mary up around 5:00 and get her in position.

"I know this is going to be painful because of your wounds, but you just have to suck it up. I'm sorry, but that's just how it is, unless, of course, you want to be back in George's hands, and Mary turned over to his friends."

"We get it! So, knock off the pep talk. We pulled the trigger before, and we will pull it again. We are with you, and they are dead, they just don't know it, yet."

The girls went to sleep in the great room and I took my place in front of the monitors. The night passed very slowly and a large number of animals and predators that crossed in front of the cameras both surprised me and helped keep me awake. The rotation worked very well, and we all got some sleep.

We kept the lights off, so Patty only made sandwiches and coffee for breakfast.

The sun was just peeking above the horizon when the first sensor went off.

✪ ✪ ✪

★

Chapter 10

George Gale

Patty's home

4:30 a.m.

The men assembled and were ready to become the rulers of their domain by taking the Williamson place. Most had spent the night with George who cut the liquor off at 10:00 that night and told them to get some sleep.

There were six armed men in the back of the old pickup and another in the cab with George. Their plan was to arrive at the Williamson place before sun up to get in position and ambush Matt when he came out of the house.

They were cowards. They would never confront another armed person. Hell, they had to get half-drunk just to get the courage to make the drive to my place.

"George, I know you want to get Patty back, but I want Mary for myself. She's my age and a damn good looking woman."

"You can have her. I don't care as long as we kill Jones."

"Just you tell the guys not to shoot her by accident is all I'm saying."

"I will, but don't forget that she has been called for by every one of you. When this is over, you'll have to sort that out among yourselves."

"George, you'd best back me if you want my support for anything else you may have planned. You comprehende, amigo?"

George smiled and said, "She's all yours Jorge, and together you and I will rule everything within 200 miles."

Jorge smiled and said, "Now yer talkin' old buddy. It all belongs to us. Let's do it, I'm in the mood fer love."

"Roger that," said George, but he thought; you dumb redneck, threaten me, will you? You don't know it, but you are a dead man walking.

George drove down the side road that passed by the cabin on the backside of my property and dropped two men off with deer rifles. They were to sneak up on the backside of the house and get into position for the attack. The minute I walked outside, one of the bastards was supposed to ambush me.

They doubled back and headed to the front of the property. One of the men took a crowbar to the chain and broke it free from the gate. They rode in the truck a little closer to the house before hiding it in the bushes before it could be seen from the house.

George knew that once he captured Patty, he could convince her to come back to him and be his loving wife again. Perhaps they would have children and live happily ever after. He daydreamed about their life after he captured Patty. It never dawned on him that he would die that day.

**

Mary was watching the monitor when the alarm went off, "Matt, two guys with rifles are at the back by the cabin. They're walking towards us."

I came in from the back porch to watch the men skulk through the woods. I was trying to decide if I should go get rid of them when the alarm went off again.

"Make sure your guns are ready," I warned.

"Those idiots are breaking the chain on the gate.

I counted six men at the front gate and said, "Patty, I know it will hurt, but please sneak out to the barn when the two out back get closer and shoot them before they get to the house. Take the .308 with the suppressor. Shoot them at about 100 yards, and they will never even know they are under attack. I'll take on the ones in front."

"Okay, but are you sure you can get them all?"

"No, that's why I want you to come back and join us. I'll post Mary with the monitors by the middle window. She can warn us if any more show up and she might take a couple out."

"We'll do our best."

"Girls our best defense is to pick them off as far away from the house as possible. Shoot center mass and kill these vermin."

Mary had an M&P15 and two Glocks. She was itching to kill George. I raised her window about 6 inches before I crept out the front door.

I made my way west through the pine trees until I had a great view of the approach to the house. I saw their tracks in the snow before I actually saw these two would be Rambos. I moved my scope on the area below the tall grass.

A small dark object appeared to be an elbow, just below the moving grass. I placed the cross hairs in the middle and squeezed the trigger. A man jumped up, grabbed his arm, and screamed. I pulled the trigger again, and he stopped screaming.

I heard, "Someone shot my brother."

The person came out from behind a tree and ran to the dead man. I squeezed the trigger; he fell beside his brother never to rise again. Two down four to go.

I heard a rifle bark from the direction of the house, and a man staggered out from behind a tree with a big red stain on his chest. He gasped for air and fell to the ground. That must have been Mary making that shot. Three down.

These guys weren't the clowns that Patty had talked about to us. One or more had military training, and we still had three more to contend with today.

Patty watched the monitor until the men disappeared behind a hill about 200 yards from the house before she ran out to the barn. She grabbed a ladder from inside and used it to climb up on the roof. This proved to be more painful than she had anticipated. She told herself to buckle up buttercup because she knew their lives depended on killing every one of these men. She was also still torn up about the loss of Wilma, and she wanted blood, George's blood.

Her pain subsided significantly, as she forced herself to walk across the loft to the southeast corner of the barn. She crept to the air duct and peered over the yard to see two of the men about 150 yards out. She watched until both came into view and placed the cross hairs on the trailing man.

Even suppressed, the AR made a significant pop when she pulled the trigger.

Her real advantage with the suppressed AR was that the sound convinced the men she was to about to kill that the shot came from much farther away.

She had her sights on the second target before the first hit the ground. Both of the attackers took a bullet to the chest. She took a deep breath before shooting both in the head to assure the kills.

Patty ran across the loft, slowly climbed down the ladder. Her wound hurt, but she ignored the pain and forged ahead into the fight.

Mary had the rifle sticking out the window with the stock propped on a chair. She watched me work my way to the side as she split her surveillance between the scope and the monitors. She saw me take out two of the bastards and then found one trying to close in on me. She shot him and started looking for another target.

"There are two men hiding behind the large bush straight across and 75 yards from you. The one with the Blackbird."

"I see the bush, but don't see the men."

"I'll put a couple of rounds into the bush, and you shoot when they jump."

I heard her rifle bark several times, and dirt flew up on the left side of the bush. One man jumped out and hit the ground. I nailed him on the way down. I couldn't see him, but he kept screaming.

"The other one didn't move."

"He can't move. I got him with a lucky shot."

"I took care of the two on the back forty. Are there any left for me?"

"I replied, "Way to go, girl. Mary and I have killed all but one, and that bastard is hiding. We've taken out all six of George's army. Let's go find that chicken shit bastard."

She replied, "I'll bet he's hiding behind a tree just waiting to escape after starting this turkey shoot."

"Work your way up on the right side as I come up on the left. Mary, watch our backs."

We both arrived on either side of the pickup to see George frantically trying to start the truck. He didn't see us come up behind him.

"George, drop your gun."

He opened the door with his hands raised. He suddenly turned with a pistol in his hand, and I shot him before he could fire at Patty. He fell to the ground, raised the pistol, and got off one shot at me as I leaped around the front of the truck. Patty kicked the gun from his hand and placed hers on his forehead.

George said, "I love you and have to have you back. Forget Jones and come back to me."

Without apparent emotion, she looked upon George with the eyes of a King Cobra about to strike. "You murdered Wilma, and for that, I'm sending you straight to Hell." She shot him twice while I lay on the ground bleeding.

"Let me check your wound. Pull your pants down."

I pulled my pants and shorts down to expose a wound in my ass. The bullet had gone in from the lower side and came out beside the top inside of my right butt cheek. It hurt like hell; however, it was in all honesty just downright embarrassing.

My first thought was that we now had three wounded people who couldn't take care of themselves.

"Matt, don't you even think about whining. I've cut myself worse while shaving my legs. The bullet passed through just below the skin. It will hurt like the dickens, but you should be okay in a couple of weeks."

I think she really did try not to smile; she failed in that attempt.

She tore a large strip off her shirt, wadded it up, and said, "Keep the pressure on the exit wound while I get the ATV and a wagon to haul your pitiful butt back to the house."

I used my rifle to help me stand up, and keeping the pressure on the wound I started walking back to the house.

"Patty, I appreciate your help, but I don't want you to strain and open your wound. We can patch me up when we get to the house."

"Thanks for being a regular Quick Draw McGraw and keeping me from getting shot. George was like a mad dog and willing to kill me.

Matt, I want to correct something between us. I do care for you, and something might happen between us down the road, but I just got rid of one husband and don't want another for a while."

"That was supposed to make me feel better?"

"I just meant that I don't hate you and don't give up on me."

"I didn't propose. I just like you and wanted to see more of you."

I was struggling to walk the remaining 50 yards to the porch when I broke out laughing and replied, "Perhaps a dinner and a bird watching or skinny dipping and snuggling? Dating will definitely be different in the days after The Flare."

"Okay, I'm interested enough to go to dinner and a movie."

We both were in pain and moved slowly as we walked up the steps and into the house. Mary saw us come in the door and said, "Aren't we a bunch of crippled warriors. We need to find some purple hearts and pin them to our hospital gowns. Patty, will he live?"

My face turned red as I replied in my best southern drawl, "Ma'mm, it's nuthin but a small scratch high up on my right leg. I'll be a rubbin' some dirt on it and be as good as new, so I can protect my women folk from the Injuns."

"He got shot in the butt after shooting, but not killing George. Actually, it was rather chivalrous of him to leave that final pleasure to me.

George tried to shoot me, and old Quick Draw was faster. George can rot where he lies."

"I was wondering why he had his hand on his ass as he walked to the house. Does it hurt?"

"Damn Skippy. I mean, no ma'am, it's just a little old scratch."

Thankfully, the medical supplies needed to treat my wound were on the coffee table between Mary and Patty's chairs. Patty went to the kitchen and came back a few minutes later with a pan of boiled water.

"Move your hand, drop your pants and bend over the arm of the couch so I can clean and dress your wound."

I loosened my belt and pulled my pants down just enough to expose the top wound. Patty moved the coffee table to her then sat in a chair behind me. She pulled my shorts down to expose both wounds.

"The bleeding has mostly stopped, and it does appear that you will need a couple of stitches for each. Thank the Good Lord George didn't have hollow points in his pistol. You'll have two scars on your butt and won't sit down for a while on this cheek, but you'll be fine."

She cleaned around the wound, and then washed it with the sterile water. She popped two antibiotic pills in my mouth and went to work on my ass.

Patty said, "I cleaned the wounds, applied antibiotic ointment and sewed the edges together. We'll keep you on the antibiotic pills and save the IV antibiotic for serious wounds. You need to lie down and let the wound heal before you move around too much. We'll keep an eye on it to make sure it doesn't get infected."

"My ass is throbbing; don't I get some pain pills?"

"Sorry I forgot that big strong men have terrible pain when they get a boo boo."

"That was just plain old mean. Give me the pills."

"One a day for four days and then you're on your own. We have to ration them for real wounds. Matt, I know it hurts, and I'm sorry for teasing you."

Mary chimed in, and said, "Well, I'm not. Patty, what a wuss!"

They both nearly busted their own stitches howling in laughter.

Mary interrupted with, "I'll watch the monitors while you two rest up from your victorious battle.

"We can take turns checking his ass for infection."

Both women laughed until I threw a pillow at Mary and said, "We have to keep someone on the monitors 24 hours a day and someone on the front porch window at night, awake and on guard duty. Patty and I will pull that watch."

Since I was the most recently wounded, the girls allowed me to rest for the remainder of the day as they took turns watching the monitors. Only a few buzzards had started picking at the dead so far, but larger scavenger animals would soon follow behind them. I knew I had to get up the strength to go out and bury the bodies.

I thought about the job of burying the bodies, but the frozen ground was like concrete. I came to realize that the bodies were already frozen, and would remain that way for around 10,000 or so years.

We all giggled at what the archaeologists who would eventually find them would think.

In truth, I could think of no better end for any of those bastards.

I slept until Mary woke me with, "Get up sleepy head. You have to pull guard duty by the window."

"Whose stupid idea was that?"

"It's your stupid idea and keep your voice down," she said as she pointed to Patty who was asleep in the recliner.

"Sorry, I was still asleep," I whispered. "I'll get a bite; make a thermos of coffee and head on over."

"Patty made you a couple of sandwiches and a pot of coffee before zonking out for the night."

"Bless her little heart, as my dear sainted mother used to say. I'll hit the bathroom and headed to the window and monitor."

"That reminds me that at some point we'll have to check to make sure the septic tank is working properly. The truth is that the lateral lines can't handle too much waste water. You need to reroute the bathwater, and any gray water from the waste water or the septic tank will be overwhelmed."

"Is this digging ditches or turning valves.

"Turning valves."

"That's a bit of good luck 'cause diggin' ditches is not in the cards for a few thousand years."

164

"Frank planned for this day and has the system set up for most contingencies. We put a lot of thought into this bunker."

"Thank God for that."

I went to the kitchen to get my coffee and sandwiches.

"Matt, come over here, drop your drawers, and let me see your butt."

"Why Mary, I didn't know that you liked my butt so much."

"Well, yeah, I do, but more importantly it's the only male butt around, and even an old gal like me likes to look at a good butt every now and then. Now stop the bullshit and let me clean and bandage that wound."

I smiled and said, "Wound, you say? Well, that is an upgrade from scratch and boo boo."

I walked over to her, turned my back to her, and lowered my pants. She cleaned the wounds with Patty's help, placed antibiotic ointment on the wound, and applied a bandage. Before I could pull my pants up Mary slapped me on my good cheek when she was done.

"Everything looks good."

"Mary, you said old woman. How old are you? You don't look like you are much older than I am."

"I'm 42, and Frank was 65 when he died. I was one of his students and a child bride."

"You didn't have any children?"

"No, Frank had two by his first wife who died in a car wreck. His two girls disowned him when he married me. I wanted children, but Frank had a vasectomy and couldn't father anymore children."

"Frank must have been a great man. He has certainly helped save our lives."

"Frank was a great man, but not a great husband. His work with NASA was his passion, and it almost killed him when they parted. Then preparing for this catastrophe became his life's work leaving little time for me. I thought about leaving him when I had an affair with Gary last year, but I couldn't leave Frank. I guess I really did love him."

"Wait a minute. You had an affair with Gary Allen, the restaurant owner. Did Betty find out?"

"Yes, it was Gary, and for over a year we slipped around meeting for our low rent rendezvous in the old cabin at the back of the property."

"Did you love Gary?"

"I don't know. I did love being with him. He made me feel alive where Frank just made me feel old.

Whoa, that is enough about that, 'cause I can't get off the couch to go take a cold shower."

"I'm sorry. Would you like me to go into town and check on Gary when I get better?"

"We both will."

"Speaking of Frank did you ever find his notes on how cold it could get here in Wyoming due to the collision?"

"He never mentioned a temperature, but always referred to 'Colder than a well digger's ass.'"

"Oh shit!"

"A cold 'oh shit' is more accurate."

166

★

Chapter 11

Strangers

The Ranch

Pinedale, Wyoming

Mary's recovery was slow, but she was getting better every day.

Patty was much better and tried to hide her pain from us. She was a real trooper and wanted to pull her weight even though her arm was still in a sling.

My butt was sore, and I watched how I sat, but otherwise I was able to complete my normal duties by favoring that leg.

Mary and I thought that Patty would take George's death hard, but she was like a new woman. Laughing, giggling at my corny jokes and full of life. I liked seeing her be herself instead of the repressed woman I met at the airport. I figured maybe for the first time in her life, she felt free, especially from George.

I split some more wood and got the fireplace cranking to allow the battery bank to stay topped off and ready. Each passing day brought lower temperatures and more concern. Later we learned that the reason our luck held out on the snowfall was that it was just too danged cold to snow, coupled with the fact that there are fewer storms because of the new environment, or some such, whatever.

I knew that our luck wouldn't hold much longer, but for now, the snow remained on the ground, the skies were bright and clear. We should be getting on the road, for every day, that we stayed at the ranch increased the chances that we would end up exactly like George, and his army of drunks.

We looked forward to the President's weekly broadcast and were always by the radio ready to listen an hour before airtime.

***

The radio crackled, popped and had static, but was getting better. Soon, we thought the airwaves would be clear again. Now, we could hear most of what the Director of Homeland Security said.

"My fellow Americans, I am filling in for the President who is in high-level negotiations with China and Russia concerning their recent annexation of large swaths of equatorial lands.

Now moving on, I must say that we, your leaders are proud of each one of you. You have braved the recent turmoil's, the lack of electricity, and the recent polar vortex that has yielded cooler temperatures than expected. Keep your chins up, and this too will pass with time.

169

The good news is that power has been restored to our government offices, our major military installations and we are slowly bringing power to our major cities.

The bad news is that it will be months until we have power back on in the smaller cities and perhaps years before power is restored to the more remote areas of our country.

Stay inside as much as possible this winter, and please endeavor to conserve your fuel, food, and strength. You may soon see the DHS Humvees in your area. This will serve as the first signal that reconstruction is ongoing to bring this nation back to normalcy.

Thank you for your support and goodbye until next month."

Mary became excited and in a loud voice exclaimed, "He said next month instead of next week. These are supposed to be weekly presidential addresses. The damned President hasn't spoken to the country for weeks."

Patty replied, "The head of the DHS must think we are idiots, I mean, we know that the country is in much worse shape than this DHS lackey says in his address to the nation, but how do we find out what is really happening?"

I replied, "Is this any different than when the news media told us what the government told them to tell us. The public has been in the dark, and only spoon fed what the party in power wants us to hear.

I'll make a trip into town and see if any state officials have contacted the mayor. Perhaps he knows something."

"She."

"She what?"

"The mayor is a woman."

"Okay, I'll talk to her. You two know her. Is there anything you want me to say?"

Mary laughed, swirled her martini around and said, "Don't tell Betty that you know me."

"I'm almost afraid to ask. Oh shit."

Patty looked confused.

"Her husband and I teamed up to perform some after hours work on improving constituent relations."

"Oh shit."

"Yep, say hi to Gary for me."

"Why didn't I know that Betty Allen is the mayor?"

"Humph, easy you don't listen. My theory is that men's ears are prosthetic, you know, not real. They're like zeros, just placeholders."

"Ha Ha, very funny."

I drove into town the next morning to see how the town's people were doing and gain some info on what was going on in the outside world. I wanted to fit in so I left my AR at home, shouldered a lever action 30-30, and strapped on a Ruger P95 9mm pistol. I also took a small backpack with a Ruger MKIII, plenty of ammo and my survival gear, which held rations for three days.

Patty suggested that I park my truck in the woods before the first major side road in case there was a roadblock. I drove for about 10 minutes, saw the side road and sure enough, there was a roadblock. I pulled off into a stand of pines before being seen and walked up to the roadblock.

"Who are you and what do you want?"

"I'm Matt Jones and why are you blocking the road."

"I said what do you want?"

I didn't recognize two of the three men and replied, "I've come into town to talk to the mayor."

"Where are you from?"

"Here, I live a few miles northeast of town and wanted to see how everyone was doing."

"Well go back home. We'll tell the mayor you dropped by."

The third man grabbed the other two and had a private conference with them. The man Matt recognized moved a barrel from the roadblock and said, "This is Matt Jones. The mayor will want to see him."

The smart assed guy said, "Then you take responsibility for him. Don't let him out of your sight or the Sheriff will have our asses."

"Willy, what the hell was that about? Who are the new people?"

"A bunch of them came into town a few weeks ago, and the mayor made their leader the new sheriff. Bob quit and went home for good."

"And my guess is, the new bunch is taking over the town and surrounding community."

"That's right. How did you know?"

"I read a lot, and that happens in most post-apocalyptic books."

Before Willy could answer, one of the men flew by, heading into town on an ATV.

Willie continued and asked, "Are you saying it's the end of the world?"

"Pretty much. Get your family somewhere way down south as soon as possible. That's my advice. I'm going to talk to the mayor and get my ass back to the ranch."

"The strangers have taken control of all of the food and have started banning guns in town. The mayor rubber stamps whatever the leader asks her to do. Talking to the mayor won't do much good."

"Has anyone heard anything from the outside world?"

"Some of the Ham Radio Operators are spreading rumors that the USA is fighting a war with several South American countries. The funny thing is; they are saying that Russia has taken most of Equatorial Africa and China has invaded India and Southeast Asia. The whole world is at war."

He obviously didn't know that many of those countries were fried by the CME.

While we were walking and talking, we passed several well-armed men with bulletproof vests and M&P15s. It was dawning on me that I needed to get my ass back home quickly. Then I saw several pickups head out of town loaded with men I didn't recognize.

"Willy, I think I'll catch the mayor later. I just remembered something I have to do back home."

Willy raised his rifle, pointed it at me, and said, "Sorry, but I have to take you to the Sheriff, or they'll kill my wife and kids. Mr. Steele wants your place to be his home and headquarters. I won't hurt you if you do what I..."

I grabbed the barrel end of his AR, chopped him in the throat, and dragged him into the alley. I removed a roll of duct tape from my pack, taped his mouth, hands, and feet after removing his body armor. I put his body armor and hat on, and I took his weapons and ammo. I stashed my rifle under the back stairs of the Diner. He would have a sore throat for a long time, but he would live.

I tried to remain inconspicuous and eased my way through back alleys until I was again safely in the woods behind the Riverside Subdivision. I walked around the subdivision being careful to stay out of sight.

My plan was to walk to my truck and head home to help the girls fight off what I was sure was an upcoming attack. I just hoped they attackers would recon the place before attacking. I wanted to be there with the girls when the attack began.

My truck was gone was the first bad news I encountered on my way back home. I started walking as fast as I could but knew I'd get there too late.

I hoped they surrendered without a fight and were unharmed. Then, as I neared the ranch, I had my second bit of bad news when I heard the sound of gunfire coming from the direction of my home. Ten minutes later, there was a large explosion and then silence.

I slowed my pace while I resigned myself to bad news about Mary and Patty. As I walked, I swore to myself that I'd kill every one of these assholes who had turned my upside down world, more upside down.

It took another twenty minutes to circle around my home and come in from the backside. I surveyed the house and grounds with my binoculars and saw a burned out Humvee between the house and barn, along with several bodies.

Something caught my eye in the shadow of the barn towards the house. There were several men with prisoners kneeling behind them. There was gunfire, and the prisoners fell to the ground. The shadows kept me from seeing who the two were, but down deep, I knew it had to be Mary and Patty.

My rage took over as I drew a bead on these murderous bastards. I shot four times, and four men fell dead. Several others jumped into a pickup and headed my way. I calmly shot through the windshield until the truck veered left and rolled over crashing into a tree.

A short while later I heard several more explosions and knew they must be trying to gain entry to the bunker.

I came to my senses and headed to the back of my property. Not leaving tracks was impossible in foot deep snow. Still, I hoped that in the fog of battle those tracks could go unnoticed. I knew exactly where I was heading and arrived at my cave an hour later. I stopped several times to see if I was being followed. The first good news of the day was that the area behind me was clear. Working around the house had left many trails in the snow; my new ones would go unnoticed.

Even I had trouble finding the opening to the cave, and I knew exactly where it was. I stooped over as I walked the first few feet into the cave before being able to stand up. I turned my flashlight on to find the light switch.

In my spare time, I had placed a solar panel high above the cave and ran the wire back through one of the cracks to the living quarters of the cave. With the aid of a few batteries, this gave me well-lit rooms thanks to the LED light string that I ran around the ceiling.

I was abnormally calm as I surveyed my supplies and developed a plan to kill Steele and his men. I ate cold MREs, washed up, brushed my teeth, tongue, and the roof of my mouth to get the cold grease from the MRE out. A few minutes later, I fell quickly into an exhausted sleep.

I jerked awake, scared shitless as I heard something at the mouth of the cave. I readied my rifle; crouched behind a large bolder and lit up the cave opening with my flashlight. There was a sight for my tired eyes. Gus and Tina had found me. They came bounding over to me and licked my face as we rolled on the cave floor. They were wet, and the noise I heard was them shaking the snow off when they entered the cave. I was glad to have my pups with me, but they brought additional concerns to mind.

If my dogs could track me down, others could also. I had to make sure my dogs didn't lead these raiders to my doorstep. I began to plan a long campaign to regain my home. These bastards would pay for this transgression.

I would make sure the dog food stored in the cave contained a lot of jerky, assuring they had the proper food to eat and thrive. I was very heartbroken over the loss of my girls, but now I had two reasons to want to live, revenge, and the simple fact I didn't want to die because I loved my dogs.

This reinforced the need to kill all of these bastards before they killed me, or anyone else.

***

The Ranch

The sensor alarms went off at the front of the driveway and the north side of the property a few seconds apart.

Mary yelled at Patty, who was in the kitchen, "Patty, intruders. We have company."

They watched as one of the men tried to pry the lock off the chain to no avail. Then one of the Humvees backed up and rammed the gate, which broke the lock, however, the sudden stop threw the passenger into the windshield cutting his head. Two of the men were attending to their wounded comrade while the others waited.

Mary and Patty watched and listened to the monitor, they heard, "Kill Jones, but take the women as hostages. They'll make great comfort girls."

Mary saw them stop and said, "We only have a few minutes before they arrive. I'm setting a few booby traps and locking us in the bunker."

"I agree we can hide there for a year."

176

Mary and Patty went to the bunker, grabbed several wirelessly detonated anti-personnel mines, and placed them along the driveway and entrance to the house. They finished hiding the bombs before scurrying back down the stairs to the bunker. Mary pushed the buttons to slide the walls into place that hid the bunker and cut off all power, heat, and water to the upstairs. No one could possibly find them, but they could see and hear everything by using the surveillance equipment.

They patiently waited until the intruders slowly drove up to the house. Mary pointed out that half of the men had left the vehicles and were beginning to surround the house.

"Mary, look, there is another bunch coming up from the northeast corner."

"Yes, I see them. Let's wait until they congregate in the driveway between the house and barn, then we'll send them to hell. Watch the cameras inside the house. There should be a couple of men walking in the front door."

"You didn't lock the doors."

"No. Why force them to knock down our doors and windows when they would get in any way."

Mary calmly held the remote detonator device and selected the bomb in the flower pot a few feet in front of the porch.

She pushed the button and felt the shockwave, but didn't hear any sound due to the thick concrete and steel walls of the bunker. She saw the explosion on the screen and saw the men trapped inside the burning wreck. She also saw the man they thought to be the leader barely escape the explosion.

Mary cursed herself for not setting the bomb off earlier. She hoped shrapnel from the explosion had at least, wounded the asshole in charge.

Again, they watched the monitors and saw the leader taken behind the barn and tended to by his men. He was shaken, but not mortally wounded.

The attackers quickly swept the barn and house to find both unoccupied. Mary allowed them to get comfortable for an hour then set off another explosion beside two men who had stopped by the barn for a smoke.

The leader was now resting in a recliner ordering his men to search the grounds for more explosives. Since they split up into individual searchers, Mary didn't want to waste a bomb on one man unless he was about to find one. She had killed seven of the invaders and hoped to kill double that if they grouped together near one of her toys.

Patty had closed the secret door that covered the monitor in the living room, so the strangers still didn't know they were being watched, and this act probably saved my life. The attackers could have seen me escaping into the back part of the property and that, my friend, would have significantly narrowed their search.

"Hey, Mary, someone has flanked the attackers. Another just had his brains splattered. Look! There is Matt on screen #7. He's heading to the back of the property. I'll bet he's heading to the cave."

They watched me head away until I disappeared into the woods.

***

The Bugout Cave

Wyoming

I woke up as the sun chased the shadows away. It was still dark in my ravine, but the top of the mountain to the west was awash in bright sunlight. I was surprised to see a light dusting of snow outside and suddenly knew that I had to kill every one of these criminals before the next snow fell. Looking to the east, I could see the tail of the squall line that had passed while I slept. Clouds were beginning to build to the west.

Good, I thought, if a storm front moves in, these piss ants will be more interested in the weather than in watching for me, big mistake for them.

I decided to kill the men in town first, to draw their search away from my house, then come back and eliminate those left to guard the ranch.

I thought, *No, this campaign might not take as long as I at first thought, fuck 'em. They attacked me, now they die.*

I blocked the dogs in the cave with enough food and water for a week. I knew I'd have a mess to clean up, but didn't want them getting in the way while I was trying to draw a bead on a thug's head.

I took the .17 HMR Savage rifle with a suppressor with me along with my AR and backpack. I brought a suppressor for the AR also in case I needed more killing power. The .17 HMR was perfect for medium range sniping for headshots but wasn't quite powerful enough for body shot kills.

These men were wearing body armor so I would need well-placed shots to kill them. Then again, if there were a lot of these dickweeds, I could take leg shots. That would cause their friends to stop and tend to their buddy.

I was ready to be in the field for a week killing Steele's men. I had also decided to kill any town's people who were too chummy with Steele and his men.

I was crushed at the loss of the girls, yeah, crushed to the point of making a game out of hunting these animals down. Bloodlust, berserker, hell, call it what you want, but yeah, I wanted blood, blood knee deep in the streets.

***

179

Mary and Patty took turns watching and listening to the intruders in case they showed too much interest in the basement and started looking for the bunker.

The intruders found one mine and disarmed it before Mary could push the button. There were still three more, well hidden around the driveway close to the barn. Mary was holding back on them to try for large groups. She hoped they would get complacent after a while and she would send them on a one-way trip to hell.

They saw me from time to time during the next week, but I had no idea they were still alive.

✪

Chapter 12

Ambush

Pinedale, Wyoming

I was in position on the outskirts of Pinedale before most people had crawled out of bed for the day. People were now going to bed at dark and waking up with the sun now that there was no electricity, and fuel was in short supply.

My mission was to eliminate as many of Steele's men as possible and capture Steele if he raised his head in public. I was betting that I could kill most of his men in town, get back to my house, and shoot the ones there before Steele even knew he was under attack.

I was about 75 yards from a three-man roadblock on the northeast end of town. I watched the three for 15 minutes and noticed that the two that stayed close together had body armor while the loner did not. He also only had a hunting rifle while the other two had an AR and an AK47.

I took aim, held my breath, and squeezed the trigger two times resulting in two dead guards. As I drew near, the third man dropped his gun and raised his hands as I walked towards him.

"Those were Steele's men, weren't they?"

"Yes, they force us to pull guard duty with these bastards. They have taken over our town. Fifty people have just disappeared. I saw five get murdered by Steele's men."

"What's your name? I know I saw you around town, but I don't think we've met."

"Jim Rayburn, I was a math teacher at the high school."

"Why don't you fight them?"

"They have taken several families hostage and threatened to kill them if we don't comply.

They also have semi-automatic weapons and a shit load of ammo. We have hunting rifles."

"Has anyone heard any more about the rest of America?"

"Sam, a ham radio operator, reports that he is hearing that there were major riots in all of the big cities the first couple of weeks and now people are either freezing or starving. The northern states are in the middle of a three-week blizzard, one of those polar vortex things."

"What about Pinedale?"

"Most people in Pinedale died during the riots over food. More died as their medicine ran out. Steele's men killed a dozen more taking the town."

"Thanks, now what do I do with you?"

"I'll help you fight the rest of them. If I show up alive now with the two of the other guards dead, they won't ask questions, they'll just kill me, and my family."

"Okay, get that M&P15 and all of his ammo. Hide the other guns over behind those bushes. Then let's go and improve the odds by taking out the guards at the other roadblocks. Perhaps we can get some of the town's people to join us."

We took the body armor, and Rayburn put one on and moved to the next roadblock. There, we found only one man and a woman guarding the road.

Rayburn said, "Steele is running out of men. Several of them were killed taking your place. Steele was injured in an explosion, and seven of his men were killed."

"I took out four more just after they killed my friends."

"Are Mary and Patty okay?"

"No, Steele's men shot them just before I killed the shooters."

"Steele lost two of his men after the bomb wounded him. He thought the two townies might have had something to do with the explosion, so he had them killed."

I passed my suppressed AR over to Jim and said, "Kill the guards and let's take their weapons and body armor."

"No, no, the woman is a friend who was forced to stand guard. Wait, was that a test?"

"Yes, life is full of tests and trusts, now, take out the man."

Jim aimed, fired, and the man's head exploded. The woman fell down behind a stack of tires and then looked up to see who was attacking.

Jim called out to her, "Alice, it's Jim. We won't hurt you. Put down your gun."

We walked up to Alice, who gave Jim a hug, as she asked, "Aren't you that Jones guy who bought the Williamson place?"

"Yes, that's me. What do you know about me?"

"Not much, except that George Gale was spreading talk around town that you stole his wife and had plenty of food at your home."

"Neither is true. Now, will you choose to fight to be free and join us in our little revolution against Steele and his men, or do you choose slavery? One thing I know, Steele is not the only tyrant running loose these days.

How many roadblocks are there and how many of his men are in town today?"

"There are two more roadblocks and only three men in town besides the Sheriff and his two deputies."

"So we have to take out about 10 more men in town and roughly the same number at my home. Let's get moving."

We eliminated all of Steele's men manning the roadblocks, and two more townies joined us in our crusade. I now had four well-armed men and women to fight by my side, and for their future.

Now I needed a plan to ambush the Sheriff's office and Steele's headquarters. I asked the others for their input. Alice raised her hand and said, "What if I run into Steele's headquarters and tell them that there has been an attack on the roadblocks and Steele wants his men to meet him at the Sheriff's office. I duck out, and we ambush them as they leave the office."

"I like the plan, but let's make one minor change. We shoot Steele's men as they come out of their building, and then we shoot the Sheriff and his crew as they respond to the attack.

Now, where is Steele?"

Jim Rayburn said, "He came back to town to see our Doctor. I guess he's at his home by now."

184

"Good, now listen up. I want him alive if possible.

This is your chance to get just a bit of justice for their brutality to you and the whole town. I guarantee it will make the people of Pinedale stronger because it is a truism that if you take a stand once, you will be emboldened to always take that stand."

Everyone agreed to the plan, we carefully got into position and placed a guard to watch the Sheriff's office.

Alice hobbled into the headquarters acting as though she were wounded and told them the story. They took one look at the blood and brains splattered on her from Jim killing the guard and hauled ass out the door into a hail of bullets.

There were five of them, and three were killed instantly by well-placed headshots. The others were hurting, but they were saved by their body armor. One was out of action, but the second man put up a good fight for a few minutes until Alice stepped out of the building and shot him in the back of the head.

I yelled, "Get ready; the Sheriff's men will be here at any moment."

The Sheriff's men were seen jumping aboard a truck and heading south out of town. They were never seen again. The town was now free of Steele's men, and we just needed to kill him and then the rest of his men at the ranch.

We inspected the dead and discovered that Steele was not among them. We went to his house and demanded he come out, hands up.

There was no response, so I slipped around to the back door and found it to be unlocked, dumb. I eased the door open and cautiously went from room to room in search of the, so called, Ruler of Pinedale. Steele was gone.

I walked out the front door and asked if anyone had any idea of his whereabouts.

Jim said, "Matt, his truck is here, so he can't be far."

I directed a search of all the surrounding buildings while I circled the house, and what do you know; I found his tracks in the snow, yep, tracks in the snow.

I thought *I'm comin' for you, you slimy bastard.*

I set out in pursuit of Steele, and by using his tracks in the foot deep snow, I made much better time than he, trudging through the snow, which must have seemed to be trying to hold him back.

I caught sight of him about a half a mile from his house. When I closed to within 100 yards, he turned and fired his handgun. Yeah, fat chance of hitting me with that popgun at this range.

I stopped, calmed my breathing, took aim at his right leg and using the pad of my index finger squeezed the trigger. Steele went down in a heap, squealing like the stuck pig he was.

I guess my aim was a tad off because the 9mm piece of lead hit him squarely in the right buttocks. Karma.

"No, please don't shoot, I give up, please don't kill me," whined the great tyrant.

I ordered him to his feet and directed him to hobble back to town. Every time he tried to stop to rest, I gave him a little prod to his boo boo.

When we arrived back at his house, the Doctor was treating two of the townspeople who had received minor injuries in the fight. The rest were pumped up and ready to whip the world, but I knew that the only reason we weren't burying half a dozen of them was that we ambushed unsuspecting men. Those guys would have torn us up had they known we were coming.

Dr. Kanady asked if Steele needed help. "No, Doc, you take care of the folks here."

Steele squealed again, and begged, "No, wait, Doctor, I've been shot. Please help me!"

The Doc told him to shut the hell up and said, "If Mr. Jones says you're not hurt then suck it up to you rat bastard because I personally don't give a rat's ass how to hurt you are."

We went to the jail and released the hostages as the crowd outside grew larger. My new friends were busy telling everyone about the recent events, and soon there was a chant being heard in the streets.

The crowd was becoming a mob wanting blood.

I told them, "Nobody here is going to hang Steele. He gets a military tribunal."

The squealing pig cried, "Yes, thank you, Mr. Jones. Thank you. It wasn't me, I wasn't the one really in charge, I swear."

"Shut up, Steele."

The crowd did not like my position on the fate of this pig and made their opinions known. "Hang him! Hang him, now!"

I drew my sidearm and fired into the dirt just in front of the crowd. They quieted right down…

"Now you people listen to me. This man gets a fair trial in front of a military or a duly selected militia officer.

Since there is no regular military officer present, we need a duly selected militia officer. Is one present?"

The crowd became silent, as there was no militia in Pinedale.

I said, "All right since there is no duly selected militia officer available, do I hear nominations for commander of the Pinedale Militia?"

The crowd was too stunned to respond for a few seconds when someone shouted, "I nominate Matt Jones as the Commanding General of the Pinedale Militia."

The crowd cheered, and it was a unanimous vote. I was the commander of the local militia, consisting of one member, me.

I said, "All right, I accept, and since we now have a lawful military tribunal established we can try Mr. Steele for his alleged crimes.

Mr. Steele, this tribunal finds you guilty of murder, treason, and theft. The punishment is death. Do you have any last words?"

That asshole had lots to say, but I stopped him after about four words.

Walking up to the convicted murderer I said, "Mr. Steele you have been found guilty of numerous capital crimes, and a duly elected military tribunal has sentenced you to death. The sentence is to be carried out immediately."

I looked down at this miserable coward, drew my pistol and carried out the sentence, with prejudice.

"Matt for Sheriff. Matt for Mayor " shouted the crowd.

I watched as the mayor and several others who had betrayed the town were gathered up and placed in jail cells.

"Sorry, but I'm going home to get rid of the rest of his murderer's row."

There was a rumble in the crowd as most of the sheeple decided the coming fight at my ranch was not their problem and went back to their homes. I was deeply disappointed and thoroughly disgusted by the cowardice of those who chose not to get involved, but very proud of the group that stayed with me to finish the fight.

Jim led the others to me and said, "What can we do to help get rid of the rest of those murdering bastards?"

"The first thing is to get body armor on all of our people and upgrade weapons to the ARs and AKs. Check their weapons cache for suppressors so we can kill as many as possible without

188

making too much noise, remember, a suppressed weapon is still loud, but it makes the shot sound as if it came from farther away.

Jim, give me your AR. You take mine with the suppressor. We'll slip into position after midnight and start sniping at anyone that shows their heads.

The hard part will be getting them out of the cabin where we can engage them. That house is a fortress."

Jim replied, "Damn, we don't want to burn your house down to get rid of them."

"Don't worry; I have an idea that should smoke them out where you can shoot them. I'm going to sneak into the cabin while you get into position. Give me half an hour before you start sniping, and soon, the rest will gladly run out of the cabin. Jim will take charge of the attack. Do what he says."

Several said, "Yes sir."

I took one of Steele's pickups and drove back to my place. I hid the truck and worked my way towards the house through a corridor that I knew to have the least sensors and cameras.

I made it to the back of the house and nearly tripped over the sleeping guard. I couldn't believe it, his hand was on a nearly empty bottle, and his head was flopped back exposing his neck. Well, not one to miss a great opportunity I slid my blade across his neck. He bled out quickly and without a sound.

I had hoped to get the door open. I knew I could get into the hidden bunker, retrieve the tear gas canisters, and place them in the house to run the invaders out into the open.

I started trying to pick the lock without success, and then switched to prying on the door to break the door handle when the door opened.

"Matt, shut up and come on in," whispered a very familiar voice.

"Mary, you're alive," I whispered as I hugged her."

"Patty is alive too. We hid in the bunker."

Mary ushered me into the bunker and into Patty's arms. I was resigned to the fact that they were both dead and this was one hell of a shock, a wonderful shock.

"We have to take out the rest of these men now, but I want to know how you survived the executions."

"They killed some town's people, not us. We were already hidden in the bunker. What do we need to do?"

"Help me find the tear gas canisters and a mask. I'm going to set one off upstairs and flush these rats out into the open so our friends from town can pick them off."

"Matt, we still have three bombs on the barn side of the driveway. If you send them that way, I can blow the bastards straight to Hell, on a long black express train."

"I'll block the front door before I set the canister off. Let's roll."

I put a tactical vest on and clipped a tear gas canister to it before checking my Glock and getting a kiss from each of the girls. I closed the bunker doors and slowly crept back upstairs. There was a guard posted outside by both the front and back doors.

All of the others were sacked out in the bedrooms, and one was passed out in the living room. I waited until the thirty minutes were up. I immediately heard a pop, as though from a long way off. I watched the guard at the front door drop to the porch dead. A second later the guard, still in his chair, at the back door slumped to the ground.

Without making a sound, I eased a recliner in front of the front door and moved on to the back bedroom. I pulled the pin on the canister and quickly tossed it into the hallway before hiding behind the couch where the drunk was sleeping.

I could hear the men in the bedrooms screaming "FIRE!" Then quickly began coughing and wheezing as they scurried to find their pants and guns.

The ever-growing cloud of tear gas was choking them. They had no choice but to run for the outside air. The man on the couch woke up coughing, grabbed his gun, scanned the room, and saw me lurking in the shadows. He whirled around to shoot me, but I already had my gun on him and pulled the trigger twice. He was in Hell before his head hit the floor.

As the men fled the house, the confluence of both gunfire and mines readily dispatched the invaders to whatever Valhalla murderers go once their miserable existence in this life is over.

I saw one move and without hesitation hurried him along to join his buddies. Then, I went from one to the other taking headshots to assure they would never bother anyone again.

I thanked God that I was the only one wounded. Shrapnel from one of the mines hit me, and the fall on my ass reinjured my gunshot wound. Patty cleaned my wound, dressed it, and put a bandage on it, as usual, saying, "Idiot, now I'm going to really put your ass in a sling.

Just what the hell were you doing running around outside when you knew explosions were on the way?"

She was angry with me, and scared when she said, "I cannot believe that you did something so stupid."

She screamed, "Mary, heaven help us, we're in the hands of a maniac. He's a moron!

Damn you, Matt Jones!" Now crying she said, "Please Matt, don't get yourself killed. I, err, we need you."

She kissed me on the forehead, yeah again with the forehead crap, turned me over to Mary, and ran sobbing into the house.

191

"Well, Mr. Moron, she's right you know. I am telling you right now; there will be no more of that kind of Rambo shit. It's not that we like you, but we are used to you."

She also kissed me on the forehead, yeah I know, before helping me up on my feet.

"Oh, one last question Matt. Do you always get hit in the ass?" Smiling she asked if I needed some help."

Damn, I was on someone's shit list.

I thanked the men and women from a town that helped us get rid of Steele and his men. They were happy to have their town back and anxious to get back to their loved ones.

I went back into the house and helped the ladies open all the windows, and turning on the fans, before going down to the bunker, and a cot.

✪

Chapter 13

Global Cooling?

The Ranch

The next few weeks were boring compared to the earlier battles. The burned out Humvee and the craters in the driveway reminded us daily that it was not safe here anymore.

Daytime temperatures hovered around zero degrees Fahrenheit, and at night, the temperatures dropped to the thirty below zero neighborhood, danged cold neighborhood.

Fortunately, for us, Frank had installed valves and drains to keep pipes from bursting, and I methodically drained all of the upstairs pipes since we had moved to the easier to heat basement.

I kept the wood burning stoves full, and we closed down most of the house. Moving Mary down to the basement was a chore, but with Patty's assistance, we got her down there without dropping her on her head even once.

My wounds were still tender, and I moved slower than normal, but I could move around as long as I favored my right leg. Patty recovered also, and was pretty much back to normal, but still favored her left side and couldn't lift much yet.

Mary had me worried because we needed to load up and get the hell out of Dodge, and she needed two to three more weeks before she would be well enough to help with the loading and be well enough to travel.

Her wounds were progressing better than expected, but she could only get around with the aid of a crutch for now. The upside was that none of us were in much pain unless we over did it and tried to do too much, which was, unfortunately, exactly what we needed to be doing.

Guard duty at night was next to impossible due to the cold and high winds, so we had to rely on the monitors. I personally thought that if anyone was stupid enough to attempt an attack on us when the temperature was thirty below zero he deserved to be added to the rock hard frozen bodies already placed.

Oh, I almost forgot to tell you. The week after the big brouhaha, I was feeling really bored. Mary reminded me about the archaeologists who would find those preserved bodies in a hundred thousand years, or so, and I got to thinking that I might have some fun, so I went out to the bodies, that were then like concrete.

I dragged them into a circle after building a 2-foot high pyramid in the center. I then placed a rock just behind each head. Now it looked like a crude ceremonial altar. I just wish I could see the archaeologists faces while they tried to figure out what it all meant.

We had a couple of days with snow and woke up one morning to another seven inches of the white powder. The bad news was that half of the monitors were blocked with snow. It's true, you just cannot fix stupid. I had forgotten to put the "snow shrouds over the lenses. I retrieved the lenses, warmed up the ATV, and made the circuit around the property placing the hooded shrouds on every camera and listening device. It was so freakin cold, and I hate being cold. We gotta' get out of this place. Okay, back to my story.

I didn't see anyone on the patrol around the property but did see smoke rising a few miles west of my position. I saw many signs of animals during my tour, the hide, and bones of a deer and even saw a Cougar eating a freshly killed dog. This reminded me not to let Tina and Gus out without me to protect them. The wind howled constantly, and I had to keep every inch of skin covered to avoid frostbite.

Frank had prepared well for subzero weather. There were several jumpsuits styled as zero weather suits with hoods, face masks and built in goggles.

I wore mittens over shooting gloves to be prepared to fight if necessary. The jumpsuits were white with varying shades of gray camo to blend in with the surroundings. If I stood still no one would notice me unless they saw the cloud my breath made. Really, it is true, at night our exhaled air would not dissipate. This actually happens in Siberia. The Russians call it a habitation fog. I'm serious, they really do.

I knew we had to prepare to leave my fortress home and all of its supplies, but just could not make myself think about the immensity of the task.

***

Then, one afternoon a helicopter landed on our front lawn and scared the crap out of us. We didn't hear it approach until it was landing because the wind was so loud. It was a military Lakota UH-72I, which is a small utility helicopter. It didn't have any armaments, but just being there scared us. We grabbed our weapons and headed upstairs to defend our home.

Two people covered head to toe with snow suits got out of the helicopter, raised their hands, and approached the front door. They stopped before walking up the steps and yelled something we could not hear. I opened the door, showed them my M&P15, and waived them to approach.

One of the men pulled his facemask off and said, "Is Frank Williamson here. We need to see him."

Mary responded, "Bill, is that you?"

"Mary, yes it's me. Can we come in and talk?"

"Yes, and please tell the others to join us."

Bill waved back at the chopper; the pilot cut the engine, and the occupants came running to the house. Six people ran up and into my house. We helped them remove their snowsuits and herded them down into the basement.

Mary asked, "Bill where did you get the helicopter and where did you come from?"

"We stole it, and we came here from Seattle. Where is Frank and what happened to you?"

"Frank died several months back, I sold this place to Matt, and I got shot by looters after The Flare is the short story."

"Damn, I'm sorry to hear about Frank, and you, of course. He would have wanted to see the fireworks. Why are you still here? Frank knew about the likely probability of an extreme weather change to colder temperatures.

We are rapidly moving into a new Ice Age and only the area roughly 10 degrees north and south of the Equator will have suitable temperatures for mankind's survival.

In five years, a one-mile-high glacier will cover everything as far south as Charlotte, North Carolina, and run in generally a line straight across the U.S. Everything from Charlotte south to Sarasota, Florida will be in a constant Alaskan winter. Sarasota south will be similar to Ontario, Canada.

The coastal shoreline will expand outward to the continental shelves.

Hell, England will be a part of the landmass of Europe, not that it will be habitable. The bottom line is we are screwed, and it could get even worse. The entire planet could become one big snowball."

"Yes, Frank did mention the possibility, but he hoped he was wrong and we decided to take our chances here. You know how he loved Wyoming."

"Mary, Frank told me that if his worst fears came about, he was planning to head south with us. We came here to pick him up and refuel the helicopter. Frank was supposed to have fuel for us. That was his payment for his passage south. We didn't know that you were still with him."

"What? Why would he lead you to believe that?"

Bill looked down at his feet and said, "Mary, I'm sorry to be so blunt, but Frank did not intend for you to come with him. He confided in me that you had betrayed him and that you would not be around when we arrived.

We thought it was strange when we couldn't contact him, but hell we were busy tracking the planets that have so abruptly ended our civilization."

Mary thought for a minute and replied, "Can we go with you?"

"Sorry, but the trip was planned for seven including Frank. We just do not have room for all three of you. Having said all that, I cannot begin to tell you how imperative it is that you move south immediately, all of you!

The snow is already two feet deep in Seattle and a minimum of four feet deep over most of Montana all the way down to South Dakota.

In another four or five days, you won't be able to get out. The temperatures are dropping so fast that your fuel will likely freeze.

This place will be covered in snow all summer long.

Do you have the fuel?"

I stepped into the conversation and said, "Mary, please go with them. Patty and I will quickly gear up and head south to join you later. Bill if we leave in the next three days, will we be able to get south of the snow and make it to where you are going?"

"Yes, if you leave before the snow gets too deep to be able to drive south. The question is will the Mexicans allow you to cross their border? The change in weather has been a major topic at the UN and nations are guarding against millions of Northern and Southern people from immigrating to their warmer countries.

I probably should not tell you this, but I know that the U.S. plans to annex Mexico, by force, if necessary and it will be necessary.

Northern Mexico will become similar in climate to the Mid-Atlantic States. Panama will be much like Ohio at best.

Only a band about 1,000 miles wide will be as warm as Kentucky in late spring. A high of 70 will be a heat wave. Crop production will suffer, and the estimation is that about half of the remaining world's population will die off."

"Could you squeeze both women in if I pay you in gold or silver?"

"Sorry, but no, the helicopter won't take the extra weight."

198

"What if we don't give you the fuel? After all, it now belongs to me."

One of Bill's companions began to become aggressive as he started to reach inside his coat and said, "I told you this shit was going to happen." He pulled a pistol and wheeled around towards me.

I also knew this conversation would go south, and drew my own concealed handgun saying, "Drop it or die," as I pointed my pistol at him.

He continued upward with the pistol, and I shot a split second before he pulled his trigger. My first bullet struck him in the chest, the second nearly in the same hole. His bullet missed me and shattered a display case on the other side of the room.

I pointed my gun at the remaining five and said, "Drop your guns on the floor, or you will be lying right beside him, do it, right now!"

Bill yelled, "Drop your guns. Damn, I told that asshole to stay calm. This is madness. Matt, the guy in the green snowsuit, is a soldier who forced his way onto the copter. You just killed his friend. They killed two of our friends, and my guess is that to expand the helo's range, they had no plans to take anyone with us. They just wanted the fuel and the pilot."

As Bill spoke, the man tried to get his pistol from under his parka. I stepped forward and hit him on the head with the butt of my pistol as Patty raised a shotgun and pointed it at his stomach. He fell to the floor, and his pistol skittered across the floor. He was dazed, but not out.

Bill asked, "What are you going to do with him?"

I replied, "We're taking him outside and telling him to walk to South America."

"That would be the same as murder."

"Normally, I would say that you are right, but as you stated, this man murdered two of your companions and intended to maroon, or kill all of you right here. So, as the duly selected militia commander of the Pinedale area I sentence him to banishment. Besides, we don't have a jail."

I kicked the man in the side and said, "Get your sorry ass up before I shoot you where you lie."

He rose from the floor and raised his hands as we walked outside. Patty followed with the shotgun as I pushed him around the corner of the house.

I asked him, "Do you believe in God?"

"Don't be ridiculous, look around you. Would a God allow this to happen? I have no time for fairy tales."

"Well, I have a different opinion, now here's the thing. If you are right, and I am wrong, then, what the hell, no harm, no foul, just blackout, but if I'm right and you are wrong, well, that's just going to be a bad deal for you.

Last chance, do you want to get right with God?"

"Yeah, right, go fuck yourself."

I turned him around and said, "Boots, start walkin"

I started feeling guilty about having him die by freezing in this frozen tundra, so I took pity on him and shot him in the back of the head, turned to Patty and said, "Sorry, but he would have killed all of us if he could."

"Yes, I know. Still, I hate that you had to kill him, couldn't we had left him here when we left on the helicopter?"

"Damn, *you* are right. On the other hand, there is no functioning 9-1-1 number, and now there are three open slots. We can all go with Bill and his friends. Sorry bud, but you would have killed me. I just got you first."

Patty stormed off mad as hell because I had executed the murdering scumbag.

Whoa! Just hold it right there, I know what you are thinking, and the answer is no, I did not murder him, nor did take any pleasure from it.

As the only available military commander, I held an abbreviated court-martial, found him guilty, and lawfully executed him. Yeah, it seems flaky to me too as I reread this, still, damn, I don't know.

I would, however, hope that you would consider this little factoid: If he set out on foot, how far would he go before he doubled back, and tried, or perhaps succeeded in killing one, or all of us. Still, think I'm a monster?

I followed her back into the house and found the remaining four glaring at me as I entered.

"You executed him. Didn't you?"

"Yes. He murdered your friends and had every intention of doing the same fucking thing to us. I am glad he is no longer a threat."

"So you get to be judge and jury?"

"Yes, as the duly elected Militia Commander in this Area of Operations, I am, by law, the judge, and jury, that is, until we leave this area, and no, I am neither sorry, nor ashamed of what I did. The bottom line is that there are no other judges, or juries available, and good men will have to take a hard stand to do what it takes to survive.

Toughen up, people. The world we grew up in is gone, dead, and is about to be buried under a mile of ice."

One of the women said, "I think you killed him just so you three can all come with us. Well, I don't want you near us."

I replied, "That's fine. Get the hell off my property, NOW!"

Bill jumped in with, "The helicopter was running on fumes when we landed. We can't leave without fuel. Barbara shut the fuck up. She doesn't speak for the rest of us. Of course, you three may travel with us. Matt, please understand, we are scientists, and we tend to be timid in these situations. Personally, I am thrilled to have teamed up with someone with your skill sets.

Now, please, may we fuel up the helicopter and leave in the morning."

I replied, "Let the three of us discuss the matter and we'll get back to you in an hour. By the way, what is our destination?"

Bill took a bit too long to answer and said, "Costa Rica. While you three talk, we'll get some personal items out of the copter."

"All right, but understand this; this home is a no gun zone for visitors. If you come back with a weapon, I promise that it will not end well for you. We okay on this little fact?"

Bill said, "Matt, we have no other weapons, and even if we did, none of us would be so foolish as to violate your, uh, local ordinance.

We agree on no weapons."

"Thank you, Bill, I believe in trust through verification, so you will be searched when you come back in. You good with that?"

"Of course, we are good with that."

The four of them went out to the copter as we headed into the kitchen to discuss our fate.

I opened the discussion with, "We just survived an attack by a group of strangers, and now these fine folks just drop in. Look, I don't trust these people any further than the rats that attacked you, or Georgie's little army. Their story stinks, even though Frank's notes back up the need to get the hell out of here. I vote we use them to get to safety and a warmer climate."

Patty added, "I understand why that woman is mad at us. You shot that man in cold blood without a trial. I know you think you did the right thing but I don't like it one bit. Having said that, I don't want to sit here up to my ass in snow and become a human icicle either. I vote to go, but Matt you can't be judge and jury again, or we part company."

I ignored Patty's comment because she would not have liked my answer.

Mary held back and then said, "I don't trust these people either, let's be prepared for trouble tonight. Frank was Bill's friend, but I barely knew the man.

My guess is that Frank found out about my affair with Gary and planned to let me die alone here in the snow. I vote to go, but we must be on guard at all times."

Let's pack tonight and be ready to fly out in the morning."

Even having calmed down, I decided to let Patty have the answer I bit back earlier, and said, "I'm sorry you feel that way about me, but I would do it again in the same situation. Sorry you don't agree, but don't get yourself killed worrying about a two bit asshole like that guy, so I suggest you get off your high horse.

Patty, there is a chance that we won't be welcome when we get to where ever we are going. If they say, "Go away," are you willing to just roll yourself up in a big ball, and die. I'm going to be right up front here; I'm not.

The old civilized world is gone. Now, it's a world of only the fittest survive, so get that through your pretty head."

Patty was mad, but she was smart enough to look at the floor and not continue this discussion, now. Knowing her, I knew this was not over.

To change the direction of this confrontation, Mary said, "Bill plans on Costa Rica."

"He lied, and not well. His first story places Costa Rica in the ice, but I don't believe that for a moment. Costa Rica is south of the Tropic of Cancer. It won't be tropical, but maybe like West Virginia, considering the mountains.

Personally, I think we should go all the way to Brazil. That will put us right on the equator. I think they plan to ditch us as quickly as possible and move on south."

Patty replied, "You might be right, the equator sounds like our best bet."

We all agreed and headed back to the great room when Mary grabbed my hand and pulled me back to the kitchen to say, "Matt, you did the right thing killing that prick. He would have killed us as soon as the helicopter was refueled. Please, don't give up on Patty. She is having trouble coming to grips with this new world."

"Thanks for the support, but it's too late for Patty and me. She made it clear that she isn't interested in me."

"Okay, but take good care of Matt."

She kissed me on the cheek and headed into the great room.

The others were waiting on us, and I told them, "Ok, shuck the cold weather gear, and we will then frisk you. I hope you understand but understand or not, this is gonna' happen."

Bill smiled, and said to his crew, "Do as he says, and no hard feelings. No one can be too careful these days."

"Thank you, Bill. I am pleased that you understand, now let's get to it."

Following the successful search, and finding no concealed weapons, I said, "Bill, here's the deal, we will give you the fuel in return for a safe trip down south. If you agree, we will fuel the helicopter and take off first thing in the morning."

Bill answered, "We agree, and will be happy to have you with us on our trip."

We've talked it over and have decided that our chances of survival are distinctly improved with you along."

"Well, all right, the first thing is to get the helicopter moved to the back yard as close to the west corner as possible, or we'll have to put the fuel in cans and fill it one five gallon can at a time."

The pilot quickly replied, "Not a problem, I'll move it now. Oh, we'll have to run the engine from time to time during the night to keep it warm, so it will start in the morning. We can top the tank off before we leave."

"Okay, let's roll."

I remembered the comment they made about flying in on fumes and wondered if these people ever told the truth. We fueled the copter and came back into the house.

Funny how the helo only took about ¾ of the fuel that was expected…hmmm.

Everyone was now downstairs in the heated part of the bunker. Patty was watching the monitors while Mary helped one of the women prepare supper.

I heard Patty say to Bill, "Yes, the cameras and sensors make guard duty bearable. We were very vulnerable for a while after The Flare pulling guard duty until Matt re-installed the cameras and sensors. It was weeks before we were able to obtain a good signal from most of the cameras due to the CME interference."

"Frank really set this place up for survival. Too bad we have to move on south."

Mary chimed in, "Yes, I love this place, but I don't like starving any more than freezing. We are lucky you came along. I hope you like deer soup and fried potatoes."

Mary caught my eye and winked.

Bill asked, "Do you have any food or weapons and ammo that we can take with us?"

I interrupted with, "What, sorry, but if you could only take the three of us, how can you take more supplies?"

Bill stammered for a second and replied, "We have some scientific equipment we can pitch. Our South American counterparts will have the same equipment."

Hmmm?

"Yeah, well sure, we have some MREs and some frozen deer and raccoon meat. We will, of course, bring our rifles, pistols and what little ammo we have left. Let's make it an early night, so we'll be rested in the morning for our trip."

Mary placed all of them in a separate room so we could have some privacy.

"Something doesn't add up. Now they want more food and weapons on a helicopter that could barely get there if Frank joined them," said a visibly upset Mary.

"That's why I downplayed our resources. We'll load extra food for them and ourselves but no weapons for them. We need to use them to get down south and then part ways with these clowns without a fight.

I'm not giving them their guns back until we get to our destination. Now let's keep two of us up at all times. Patty and I will take first watch."

As we packed, I noticed that Mary was doing very well considering her recovery, and a little giddy in some respects.

"All right, Mary, what gives? There is no way you can do all this work, yet. What did you take?"

She smiled, and said, "Dang, I had hoped you wouldn't notice. Yes, I took two hydrocodone tablets to mask the pain to allow me to pitch in. I'll be fine, but let's get this done before it works off."

Trying to look stern, but knowing that she was right, I just hoped she didn't reinjure herself.

"Okay, I get it, but once we are out of here, we need to talk about taking such heavy pain killers without talking to me first."

We packed light on personal gear and clothes. We figured we would just have to find what we needed down south. Our duffle bags had two extra weapons, plenty of ammo and MREs.

We packed three extra duffle bags with MREs and about two thousand rounds of a mixture of .22, 12 gauge, .223, and 9mm rounds. I placed their side arms in a bag that I would keep away from them until we parted company, or I learned to trust them. I found it interesting that an extra 200 pounds of gear now magically could be taken along on the flight.

"Damn, the pilot went outside and started the engine again."

I replied, "I heard him, and it makes me nervous. You don't think it's a ruse to take off without us, do you?"

"No, because everyone else is sound asleep."

At the end of my watch, I heard a whine coming from the fuel pump room at the far end of the bunker. It took a minute to realize that fuel was being pumped into the helicopter and it was only 3:00 am. I turned a light on in the hallway and was certain I heard someone sneaking around in their quarters. I alerted Mary and checked on our guests with a flashlight. They appeared to be asleep.

I turned the lights out and crept up the stairs and out towards the copter. The pilot was closing the fuel door with his back to me.

I coughed to get his attention; he turned and whispered, "Bill is everyone ready."

I pretended I didn't hear him and replied, "It's a bit early to be topping off the tanks isn't it?"

"Oh, sorry, um, I didn't mean to wake you. I'm just nervous and want to be prepared for anything that happens. Almost running out of fuel scared the crap out of me the other day."

"I wasn't asleep. I was on guard duty watching for threats. Not much gets by us since The Flare."

I followed him back to the house and went into the monitor room with the others.

"Mary, no question, they were going to leave without us."

"That's what I'm thinking. Keep your guns handy. Go wake Patty and get a bit of rest. I'll babysit our visitors."

"You need some sleep too."

"I can't sleep, and I don't trust these people."

"Well, I don't trust them either. I'll keep you company."

We talked for the next two hours and took turns watching the monitors and checking on the pilot as he started the engine twice more. Finally, the sky was getting lighter above the mountains as the sun came up

Mary went into the kitchen and placed sandwiches on the table along with bottles of water. I woke everyone up, told them to grab their sandwich, water, and gear, and said, "Let's hit the road."

After they had started loading up, I went through the shutdown list for my home heating system and drained the water lines.

I ran across the back yard with my gear as the helicopter engine fired up and began its high-pitched whine. I shoved my gear into the cargo department, and then took my 9mm from a shoulder harness to be ready to go. Just as I stepped up to get in the helicopter, the pilot took off as I hung on for dear life. I heard the girls yelling and then saw the end of a pistol pointed at me.

"You missed one, Matt, no hard feelins'." Bill pulled the trigger on a .25 caliber pistol and shot me in the chest. I fell backward five feet to the ground and saw a figure being shoved out of the door. Mary landed a few feet from me as the helicopter roared off and away.

Mary got up, hobbled over to me, and placed my head on her lap as she ripped my parka open to find my wound, "Matt, are you okay? Where did he hit you?"

I was wheezing, huffing, and puffing, but finally looked up at her and replied, "The asshole shot me in the chest. I'll be sore for several days, but I'm not hurt at all."

Son of a bitch but that hurt.

Mary looked at me as if I was crazy and had a dumb look on her face.

I reached around, lifted my sweater to reveal my body armor as I said, "I never trusted those bastards and took out an insurance policy. Where's Patty?"

"Oh, shit, she's still on the helicopter! They took her with them. We have to rescue her."

"We'll try, but they will be over a hundred miles away in an hour and 400 miles away looking for more fuel in about three hours. It will take several days to get a truck ready to travel south."

She took me in her arms, hugged me, and said, "Then get off your lazy ass big boy and let's get moving."

"You know I just got shot and it hurts like hell, right?"

"Yep, two Tylenol then rub some dirt on it, and you'll be good as new."

"Oh, I see how this works. You get the good stuff, and I get Tylenol. Thanks for the sympathy."

"Matt, seriously, one, you are not hurt badly enough for the good stuff, and two, I don't know what I'd do without you."

She helped me up, and we went back in the house. I restarted the heat and turned the water back on before Mary corralled me to make me take a pain pill. Then she made me take off my shirt and rubbed some pain relief cream on my chest. It felt good, and I was having thoughts that I hadn't had in months.

Mary said, "Now don't get too excited, that was for pain. You're still Patty's man. I just need to keep you alive long enough to get you two back together again."

"Yeah, like that will ever happen. Let's get to work," I said as I buttoned up my shirt.

I put my cold weather gear on and started out the door when she said, "Do we have a plan?"

"Why, funny thing you should ask, yes we do have a plan, a very good plan. I'm getting your 4X4 ready to pull a trailer all the way to Brazil. I'll load it with as much fuel as possible, add weapons, ammo, MREs, a cold weather tent, subzero sleeping bags and whatever else we think of while we're packing. You pack several meals from our perishable food stock to eat right away, get clothes for both of us, and start thinking about anything I missed."

"Like the First Aid kit, survival gear, a snow shovel, a snowmobile, etc., etc."

"Yep, that about sums it up. Let's get the gear out in the barn by the truck, and we'll see what we can stuff in, and onto the truck and trailer without flipping them over."

"Why don't we take theF350 as far as possible and then acquire a smaller 4X4 for the rest of the trip. It's a 4X4, and yeah, I know, loaded down like this it'll only get around 10 mpg, but it will haul a bunch more than the small truck. We'll be traveling very slowly until we get out of the snow and the dual back wheels and front winch could come in handy."

"You're right, I like the idea. How large are the fuel tanks?"

"It has two 50 gallon tanks, and there's a 50-gallon reserve tank installed behind the cab. At 1o mpg, that gives us a 1,500-mile range and even if we only get 5 mpg, that's a 750-mile range. I'd really like to add some of the 55-gallon drums on the trailer and fill them, but I'm afraid it would just add too much weight. If we get lucky and don't get killed on the way, we might only have to find diesel once during the entire trip. The truck is older, but Frank had it totally rebuilt, and it's in perfect condition."

"I like the idea even better. Let's not put the camper on to save weight. Maybe our luck will be about to change, and we'll be able to get at least one drum of diesel on board.

We will take turns driving and sleeping until we get close to the border. We can sleep in the cab. The back seat is small, but we'll just have to make it work. Mary, are you up to all this? I'm worried about you."

"Well, let's see, am I up to freezing to death, no, definitely not. Am I up to getting this done, so we get somewhere where it's warm? Uh, yeah, with a little help from my friends, I'll get through it."

"All right, then, I'll check the fluids, grab an extra battery and an extra spare tire."

Mary looked over at me and said, "We have to warn the town."

"Yes, we do. They helped destroy Steele's army. I'll make a quick trip into town in the morning."

Mary insisted on going with me the next morning. We drove my old Ford and stopped at the Sheriff's office. I was

211

knocking on the door when Jim came up behind me and greeted us. The new mayor was with him.

"Jim, we only have a few minutes here and need to get the word out to everyone that they must pack up and head much further south. The heavy snow and arctic temperatures are not going to go away. In fact, they are going to get worse, much worse!"

Mary told him her husband's story and what we heard from the helicopter people.

The mayor replied, "If that were true the President would tell us. I don't believe you."

Mary replied, "Then freeze to death. Come on Matt; we told them. Our job is done."

I added, "Jim, we're heading south later this week. You will die if you stay here. Goodbye."

We got in my truck and drove back to my home. I never found out if any of them survived.

I stayed busy loading and unloading gear to get the most on the truck bed and trailer while the pile of items Mary brought from the house grew larger and larger.

"What's in that bag?"

"My jewelry collection, feminine hygiene supplies, and a small amount of makeup. I have to have all of it."

"What's in that box?"

"Whiskey, vodka, tequila and rum."

"Moving along, is there anything in your pile that we don't need?"

"Well, a lot of it is clothes. A naked lady would be safe around you so we could cut back on clothes."

"Funny. We only need two changes of clothes, five pairs of underwear and 10 pairs of socks."

"So we'll stink up the cab of the truck, and the banditos will puke when they smell us and let us go across the border unchallenged rather than smell our funk."

"Yeah, that sums it up rather well!"

"You didn't mention bras. I have a need for them. Can I take five?"

Mary's face was getting red, and I'd never seen her mad before now so I thought quickly and replied, "Sorry, I didn't think you wore them."

"I don't know if that is a compliment or you are just bullshitting me. I'm taking five and you can go...."

I interrupted with, "Mind my own business, and throw something out so you can make sure we both have adequate clothes."

"Works for me, thanks, handsome."

Later that day I saw Mary inspecting the pile of things I needed for the trip, she called me over and pointed at a book in her hand and two 50 pound bags of dog food.

Mary said, "I'm not eating dog food. We have plenty of those Meals Rejected by Ethiopians and won't need this stuff. And why the hell are you bringing several books on how to fly an airplane?"

I pointed over at Tina and Gus and said, "Surely you don't want them to become pupsicles, and I brought the books to keep me busy while you drive."

"No, but there went sleeping on the back seat with the dogs along."

"You can still sleep on the back seat. They will come up front with me or lay on the floorboard."

"I was just messing with you, but don't think I'm flying with a self-taught pilot either. I wonder how many house pets are dying because of this nightmare."

"Tens of millions. Let's save these two if we can."

Mary produced two ice-cold bottles of Blue Moon beer and said, "Let's toast to our upcoming trip that will lock us in the cab of this truck for about a month."

I raised my bottle, clinked it against hers and laughed before I said, "Here's to fair weather, good luck on the road of life and great friendship."

Mary laughed and added, "Here's to fresh air, cold meals, and great friendship!"

"Are you hinting at something by that comment about fresh air?"

"I was just thinking about being cooped up in the cab of that truck with two dogs and a man that fart constantly."

I couldn't help but laugh when I replied, "It's the dogs."

✪

Chapter 14

Heading South to Warmer Weather

The Ranch

Wyoming

I thought of Patty being held by those thievin' maggots every minute of the day. I also realized that the odds of finding her, freeing her, and making her fall in love with me were probably similar to winning the Power Ball Lottery twice, so I kept busy loading the truck and tried to keep my mind off her plight, and on my own. Still, my mind kept wandering back to what might be happening to her.

With only two people to pull guard duty, we split the night into three-hour shifts and took turns with the hand held alarm box during the daylight hours. I was on duty the next morning and watched the mountains around us take on their beautifully bright, glittering shapes from the rising sun. I wondered how long if ever, other human eyes would again behold such a wondrous Wyoming sunrise.

The morning promised to be, yet another sunny day with no additional snow. I knew that our luck could not continue to hold, and promised myself that today was the day to leave our beloved stronghold.

I went to the great room to wake Mary and found her up and in the kitchen preparing sandwiches for our trip, along with several thermoses of coffee. We ate a quick meal, fed the dogs, and let them out to take their morning toilette before heading for the barn.

The sight before us was a big Ford truck and trailer that looked like something out of a Mad Max movie, or maybe The Beverly Hillbillies. It had stuff sticking out everywhere, and both truck and trailer were piled disconcertingly high.

"Do you think the engine can pull all of this weight?"

Mary replied, "Oh, sure, three times that much. What worries me is whether the trailer can handle the load without busting a spring, or breaking an axle, shoot, and the floor may collapse. Other than that, the biggest concern is the gas mileage. We only have to get to the border without issues, and then we bulldoze our way through Mexico."

"Uh, Mary, did I just hear you say the biggest concern is the gas mileage?"

"No, Matt, you did not hear me say that poor gas mileage was my biggest concern. What you did hear me say was that after a busted spring, a broken axle, or a floorboard collapse, the gas situation would be the next biggest thing to concern me."

"Oh, yeah, well, that makes all the difference."

Mary smiled her Mary smile, and said, "Yes, well, what else can we do other than try, and hope for the best. If it breaks, it breaks, and we dump it, nuff said.

Now, Matt, this is serious, let's get something straight, so we understand each other, no riders, and no involvement in other people's problems. Stay focused because we have our own fair damsel to rescue."

"Roger dodger, we are completely agreed on riders and strangers. Come on Mary, you know I never insert myself into the problems of others."

"Matt, you really are a shit, you know that?"

"Yep, it's just a part of my undeniable charm."

"Oh, dear God in Heaven."

Changing the subject, she said, "I can't imagine why they kept Patty. The men and women were paired up, and it's not like they need to import a woman into a region that will soon be flooded with people from the U.S. and Canada."

"Yeah, I agree, it makes no sense. I can't keep my mind from thinking about several different scenarios on why they kept her. None of them seems to offer a good outcome. I know she doesn't care for me, but I still count her as a close friend and want to help her."

"Come on Matt, it's time, let's stop talking and get on the road, Brazil or bust!"

We offered up a sad farewell to our home. We drank several toasts and got ready to leave.

At 7:00 am, I pulled out of the driveway, and onto the road in 19 inches of dry blowing snow, and as we thought, the truck drove like there was no trailer behind it. I started out in two-wheel drive thinking I would save gas, but Mary told me there was very little savings of gas and the extra traction might save our lives. I quickly shifted into four-wheel drive and kept it there as long as we were on snow for the rest of our trip.

Our plan was to take Hwy 191 southwest, turn east on 80 and head to Denver where we'd drive south on Highway 25.

This was not exactly the shortest, and definitely not the safest route, but thought it would be quickest.

At first, we felt it would be best to get through Colorado as quickly as possible, and hoped to make it into New Mexico before the passes were clogged with 20' snowdrifts. Still, I was worried about going down those steep Colorado mountains. I was scared shitless thinking about the possibilities.

Did I share my concern with Mary? Nope.

Once into New Mexico we hoped to make it unscathed into Texas, and cross over into Mexico at Nuevo Laredo. That would put us in Mexico for the fewest miles.

Since the solar flares had started out on the weak side before culminating in the monster CME when Alpha Omega hit the sun, there weren't quite as many cars abandoned on the highways as expected, but there were still way too many. There were enough to keep us on our toes, and the bad news was they were covered in snow, so they were hard to see in the daytime and much harder to see at night, right up to the point of being dangerously close to crashing into one.

The upside was there were many dead semis providing us with a good source of diesel fuel that fortunately had not, as yet gelled. We brought five gallons of the anti-gelling additive and hoped it would be enough.

The point of this was that we had to drive slow in the daytime and crawl at night. Hitting a stalled car could kill us, or at a minimum end our trip south and leave us freezing. The cold seemed to be getting worse by the hour, and we were crawling along. I do not think I have ever felt so vulnerable in my entire life.

Traffic was nearly nonexistent. The few vehicles we did see were filled with people on a mission. Their eyes were straight ahead focused on the task at hand.

We only hoped to get to Rock Springs by the end of the first day, but even at 25 miles an hour, we found ourselves north of the town in less than four hours.

I stopped about a mile north of town, stood on top of the truck, and scanned the town with my binoculars. I did not see any movement, but there were numerous columns of smoke coming from chimneys scattered around the town, tragically there were just too many to count. By the time the fireplaces had no more fuel, it would be too late to escape.

"Mary, I plan to go around the larger cities, but we have to go through Rock Springs. If we want to arrive safely in South America, we cannot stop for anything but fuel, and whizzes. There will probably be former cops who will try to confiscate our truck, criminals will try to rob us, and there might even be women and children needing food. We have to ignore them all and be prepared to fight it out to get our butts south."

"How do we handle the police?"

"Respectfully at first, Failing that I will shoot them if they try to take our truck. Keep your carbine and pistol handy at all times. I'll do the talking and decide when to fight, or run roadblocks."

"I hate not helping people, but have no problem with taking out anyone trying to take our ride."

Yes, I did remind her of that other people's problems thing. Yep, she shushed me.

Our map showed that we would hit the Highway 80 interchange about a mile before the town, but in fact, the area was built upon both sides, well before the interchange.

We drove towards Rock Springs, and as feared, there was a roadblock on the south side of the interchange blocking entrance to the town, but also blocking us from taking the down ramp. As we approached the roadblock, several men with guns yelled for us to stop. I saw a man in a police uniform get out of a parked car and start running towards us.

"Mary, duck down, I'm going down the exit ramp, and we'll worry about which side of 80 we need to be on later. Duck!"

I twisted the steering wheel, floored the gas pedal, and careened down the snow packed ramp dodging and sliding around stalled cars.

I heard several shots, and a bullet hit the trailer's bed. We didn't shoot back, and soon we were out of range; slip sliding away.

Well, at least I thought we were until Mary yelled, "Someone's coming up behind us on a snowmobile. They're a mile or so back."

I knew I could not outrun a snowmobile so I stopped the truck, pulled out my AR10, laid the bipod legs on a box in the trailer, aimed and squeezed the trigger. The man was still a half mile away, and the bullet struck the road ahead of him. I aimed three feet high, held my breath, squeezed the trigger, and saw the snowmobile explode in a ball of fire. I knew it was a lucky shot and wondered if the man's wife thought to steal a truck was worth his life.

Just then, several bullets struck the cab and bed. There was another roadblock on the east side of the town on our side of the road.

I stopped and quickly aimed the AR10 at the men at the roadblock and fired 20 quick rounds just short of their position. I heard Mary's carbine firing, and a man fell. One fired back, and I emptied another magazine of 30 rounds at them. Three dropped, and the other two went running back towards town.

I quickly checked the truck, found it to have no serious damage and we hauled ass thru the roadblock. Only two of the men were moving. I thought of ending their suffering but decided not to as they may have access to medical help.

The others had died because they wanted our truck and our supplies. I used the bumper to push several drums out of the way, and we again headed south.

"Do you think those men wanted our truck?"

I looked her in the eyes and said, "Yes, some of them died for a damned truck, but it's our truck, and much more will try to take it from us before we make our destination."

She looked at me, raised her carbine, and said, "Try is the right word. You are right, Matt, we will do what we must do or die trying."

"Yeah, our motto is the same as the one used by the Ranger School: Can't quit, won't quit, die first."

"All right, I'm fully onboard, crap we've only covered a hundred miles and three maybe four people are dead because they wanted to rob us. We have to get better at this."

We headed on down the road at 30 mph and only had to dodge an occasional car or truck. The drive was monotonous. I drove another three hours before switching places with Mary.

I reminded her that there were only a few small towns off the interstate so she shouldn't have any worries until we get to Laramie. That was 230 miles, so I told her to wake me in six hours or about 50 miles from Laramie.

Once we made Laramie, I planned to get off the main road and cut down below Laramie and Cheyenne to Highway 25. I'd figure out how to handle Ft. Collins when I woke up.

I felt a hand patting my shoulder and woke up needing to pee.

"Is everything okay?"

"Yes, I hate to wake you, but I have to go."

"Oh yeah, me too, you get the bathroom by the trailer, and I get the one in front of the truck. Don't get your butt frostbit."

I looked around and noticed that we weren't on Highway 80 and the snow was still over a foot deep. I actually didn't see that we were even on the road. I could see that there was a raised line corresponding to a road leading away from us.

I finished and asked, "Mary where are we, this doesn't look like Highway 80? You made good time."

"Oh, we're just southeast of Laramie at the junction of Highways 12 and 130, just northeast of the Laramie Airport. I fly out of here...er...flew out of here many times and I know the area quite well.

Look here on the map. I know a short cut over to Highway 25 that will avoid several built up areas."

We looked at the map, and I felt compelled to point out the absence of any roads where she pointed.

"Yeah, well, it's true, there are no paved roads, but there are dirt roads, and I've been through there many times."

"Really, dirt roads, and pulling 9 million pounds of gear? Wait a minute."

"The roads are frozen, and yeah, I'll wait."

I went back to the trailer, returned with two 12-gauge pump shotguns, and placed them on the console.

"You're driving. I'll ride shotgun."

"Can we go now, or do you have some other little thing to take care of?"

"Nope, I'm ready, thanks for asking." I know my natural charm just seems to overcome all obstacles."

I looked over at the Laramie skyline and saw large columns of black smoke rising over the city. I knew the rioting had started; people were freezing, being murdered, and dying of hunger. The road would be tough from here on. I also wondered why we had heard nothing from the federal government of late.

Mary really did know the way as she had me wind around the countryside. The truck went off the side of the road a couple of times but kept on chugging until we were skirting subdivision after subdivision as we traveled around Laramie. We crossed several railroad tracks before getting back on a real road heading south.

"I fell asleep thinking about Patty and how to find her. My mind finally connected several facts as I began to fall asleep. The reporter's questions about major powers invading countries located around the equator and my friend Sam and Frank's warning finally matched up. The major countries kept the collision and resulting disaster a secret so they could prepare to take over other warmer countries and start their new homes at the previous owner's expense.

Sadly, that is just a repeat of human history. It's kind of like, boy meets girl, boy loses the girl, new boy gets the girl, only now it's invaders like land, invaders take land, and then invaders lose land to new invaders. Traveled

I'll bet the "New USA" is now somewhere near or on the Equator in South America. That's where we are going."

"Do you think Patty's captors know about this?"

"The world heard the same broadcast we did. I think the race is on to get to warmer climates and the countries between us and the equator will try to stop the invasion of immigrants."

"I can't fault them for protecting their countries. The USA installed the wall across the border back in 2018 to stop terrorists from attacking our country. Millions of people will die from this disaster because the southern countries will try to protect their resources.

It reminds me of a story I once read about a one-armed Confederate Major, whose troops kept fighting after the war was over. When a Union Major asked him, under a flag of truce, why did these rebs keep fighting when they knew the war was over? He replied, 'Because this is our land and you are on it.'

I think that is what we are going to find. I don't think we will be welcomed as rich tourists."

"Crap. Mary, we have to cross the wall ourselves. If the USA doesn't stop us the Mexican government will surely try."

"So we need a plane or a boat."

"I guess we'll cross that bridge or border when we get there, but yeah, I think you are spot on."

I caught myself and said, "Damn, if we decide on a boat, it would be nice to be by one of the oceans."

"I was going to say that myself, but what if Patty escapes and is waiting along Highway 25 for us to come along and rescue her."

"We can't have a plan for every possible scenario for rescuing Patty. I know it sounds cruel, but we have to rescue ourselves and do our best for Patty as things develop."

"Matt, I know you are right; however, I can't get Patty out of my mind."

"Me neither."

"Now changing the subject to our trip; this is Highway 287. It takes us south to Ft. Collins, Denver, and Colorado Springs. We need to stay as far away from them as possible.

I plan to go about 15 miles east above Ft. Collins then head south until we get near Colorado Springs. That route avoids the most people and puts us in ranching country where we have less chance of running into criminals or having the police try to steal our truck."

Mary replied, "I like the plan; what do I need to do?"

"Take over driving while I navigate when the time comes."

"Just let me know when."

I added, "Okay. We can make our way to El Paso and then decide one if by land or two if by sea. If we decide by sea, we can work our way over to Corpus Christi or South Padre Island and then go by water down to Brazil."

"The Corpus area may have way too many other people planning the same thing, besides the fact that there will still be crooks trying to take our shit.

There is also no chance of making it to Padre Island. The Naval Air Station is there, and I do not think they will be too friendly, either."

"Do you know much about Open Ocean sailing or boating?"

I replied, "Damn near nothing, I know fresh water boating and can sail and navigate a sailboat, but navigating without a GPS on the open ocean will be dangerous."

"Matt, we need to stop at a few libraries along the way and pick up the books holding the necessary knowledge."

"We'll also need to pick up food, water, and ocean type stuff to make a long voyage."

"Your ocean stuff comment did not instill confidence in me at all."

"Me neither, but I'll read some books and figure it out. I kind'a like the idea of driving all the way there better all the time, but I don't think it will be possible, but we'll see."

"Yes, driving safely through 15 Latin American countries that weren't safe before The Flare makes me feel so much better."

The realization that we had little chance to make it to South America had begun set in, but I knew that freezing was not a good choice either. The second thing that had set in was that the almost million dollars I had spent on a safe home to live through a disaster were up in smoke. I just hoped that a chest full of gold, silver, platinum, and jewels would help us bribe enough officials to get to our destination.

Yeah, bribes always work, I mean, surely they wouldn't kill us and take it all.

★

Chapter 15

Patty

The Ranch

Wyoming

Patty slid over to the far side of the helicopter to make room for Mary and Matt to join her in the back seats. She was shocked to see that there were only two seats and one of them would have to sit on the floor with the baggage. Mary climbed in behind her, followed by Matt.

Just as Mary was dealing with where to sit, Bill yelled, "Now, take off."

Patty yelled, "No, they're not in," as she saw Bill shoot Matt and then push Mary into Matt and knock him out of the helicopter. Bill then hit Mary's hand, which caused her to fall out and to the ground. Patty tried to jump out to join her friends, but Bill grabbed her, and they were soon too high off the ground for her to jump.

Patty yelled, "What the fuck is going on? Why did you kick them out and keep me?"

"Because we don't need them and we can trade you for fuel."

"I thought you were Frank and Mary's friends."

Bill laughed and replied, "We met Frank's friends a week ago, and the idiots told us of their plan to head south. We killed them and stole their helicopter. If you want to live, do what I say when I say, and I won't pitch you right out of this bird."

The UH-72A Lakota helicopter had a cruising speed of 150 mph and a range of 426 miles. The helicopter had a fuel cell added that added another 100 miles to their range, but this still meant they had to make a series of 400-mile hops to cover the 2,500 miles to the edge of South America. It was an additional 2,300 miles to the equator. They had to assure that they never ran out of fuel so many of the legs would be short due to the low range of the helicopter.

It only took a little over three hours to reach Four Corners Regional Airport in Farmington, New Mexico. The airport was covered by six inches of snow. It was below freezing, and the wind was blowing at 10 mph. The pilot tried to make radio contact with the airport tower to no avail.

"There's no response. We'll have to go in blind. We have plenty of fuel, so I'll circle the airport and find the refueling station. The worst case is we siphon fuel from another aircraft."

"I agree. Team... be ready for hostiles. Some government do gooders might try to confiscate our copter. Worse yet, some criminals might try to steal it from us. Have your guns ready. Barbara, shoot our captive if she causes any trouble or tries to talk to anyone."

As planned, they circled the field, found where the fuel tanks were located and landed close to them. The pilot and one of the men found the tank with the proper fuel and ran a hose to the helicopter. They only had a hand pump and slowly filled the fuel tanks.

Barbara, and one of the men took Patty into the nearest building to look for anything useable, but only found some candy and chips in a vending machine. Patty was hungry, so she took a bite from a chocolate bar.

"Bitch, who told you to eat," said Barbara as she slapped Patty across the mouth drawing blood.

Patty covered her face with her arm and said, "I'm sorry just tell me your rules, and I'll obey."

The leader replied, "My rule is, don't do anything until I tell you to."

"Please tell me to use the bathroom."

"Don't be a smartass. Barbara, take her behind the fuel tank."

Patty searched for something to use as a club or knife and came up short. She did her business and walked back to the helicopter with Barbara pointing a pistol at her the entire walk. Patty knew she had to escape soon or she would never be able to get back to her friends. She was mad as hell and focused her anger on finding a way to escape. She knew that most of the time they would be in the air and thought it was about 450 miles to Farmington so she would be approximately 900 miles away unless she could make them land without getting herself killed.

She felt strongly that Matt and Mary would head south earlier than they planned and would look for her. She had to figure out how to get away and then increase her chances of being found.

She racked her brain to remember the roads and cities of New Mexico. She convinced herself that Matt would end up coming down Highway 25 on his way south. Assuming they left the next day, she would have 2-3 days to reach Highway 25 and still be there before they arrived.

Barbara was looking at a map, and Patty saw she was looking at New Mexico. She confirmed that she would fly over or near Highway 25 about two-thirds of the way from Farmington to El Paso, before heading into Mexico. Barbara caught her looking and told her to mind her own damned business.

Patty surveyed the area around her and saw Matt's bag was against the back of her seat. She knew Matt had his survival gear, ammo and some guns in the bag.

"Barbara, can I get a blanket from my bag? I'm cold, and I want to take a nap."

The woman was annoyed, but reached behind her seat and threw a blanket at her. Patty covered herself and slouched down in the seat to hide her attempt to get into Matt's bag.

She reached down from under the blanket and felt his bag. She slowly pulled it closer. Then she waited until the pilot started the engine and pulled the zipper to open one end. During the takeoff, she pushed her hand into the bag and felt around, but only felt MREs, a compass, and some pistol magazines.

She slowly pulled the bag around the bottom of the seat to reach the other end. She reached back into the bag and found the barrel end of a pistol. She slowly moved the pistol closer to her as the others looked out the window. She placed the pistol in her coat pocket and then pretended to be asleep. She knew she had to force the helicopter down as close to Highway 25 as possible but wasn't sure how to tell when 25 was close.

"Where are we crossing the border? I heard the Mexicans had blocked all traffic into Mexico?"

"Dip shit this is a helicopter, we can fly over roadblocks. Shut up."

"Don't you think the Mexican Military will be ready to shoot down intruding aircraft? Matt told me that we could take a plane down there if..."

230

Barbara slapped Patty and told her to shut up.

Bill knocked her hand away and said, "Let her talk."

"We planned to fly south until we found all of the plane's electronics fried. Anyway, Matt said our best chance was to fly into Mexico very low from El Paso into Mexico."

"Why El Paso? We planned to fuel up there and then cross the border fifty miles east of El Paso."

"There will be a lot of air traffic around the city, and it will be easy to get lost mixed in with the other planes. If we are noticed, I speak Spanish, and he wanted me to convince the Mexican authorities that our aircraft was one of theirs that had communication problems. By the time, they got suspicious; we'd be much further south and would just have to deal with the locals to get fuel. I assume several of you speak Spanish."

Patty knew this was flimsy as hell, but it was the best she could quickly make up.

"The two men your friend killed were our interpreters. You have that job now. Have you been to Mexico lately?"

Patty had been to Cancun a couple of years back and replied, "I go all the time to the resorts, why?"

"With all of the drug gang violence, I want to only land in safe areas."

"Damn, make it hard why don't you? Let me see the maps and give me the range of this copter, and I'll make some suggestions. Until then I'd make for Highway 25 and come in from the north."

"Okay. Jack, you heard her. Do it."

She was shocked when the pilot steered due east towards 25. She knew she had a chance now. It was a tiny chance, but much larger than an hour ago. She studied the maps and started penciling in names of drug gangs that she'd heard on the news. She was now convinced if she talked fast, she might be able to blow some smoke up their asses and she might just pull this off.

She thought, *Now, I believe I truly understand Matt's thinking. These assholes want to sell me into slavery for some fuel, fuck 'em, either they will be dead, or I will. Matt, I hope to live long enough to tell him how sorry I am, and for what a fool I've been.*

Patty knew that they would be landing in El Paso in just under two hours and felt she had to act as soon as they were close to Highway 25. She watched the sun and knew they were flying southeast and guessed they would intersect Highway 25 about halfway to El Paso in about an hour.

She quietly rummaged around in Matt's bag to find something, anything that would help her escape. She felt around until she found a military bayonet. She took it and slid it under her right leg.

"That's Highway 25 on our left. It looks like a big runway. Okay, let's follow it south."

Patty looked ahead and saw nothing but highway and dirt for 10 minutes. It hit her that there was no snow then a patch of green showed up ahead, and she saw buildings a couple of miles farther down the road.

She aimed at one of the captor's duffle bags and fired a shot into it to get their attention while sticking the knife against Barbara's side.

"Don't move; stick your hands in the air. I'll kill Barbara and start shooting. I have 16 bullets, and I'll kill all of you if you don't let me go."

The man in front of Patty turned to shoot her. She had steeled herself for this moment and proved to be quicker on the trigger. She shot him twice. The first round entered Bills forehead, propelling him into the windshield and splattering blood and brain matter across the now bullet pierced glass. The second round passed through his neck and also exited the windshield. Cracks began to form, and it was only a matter of a

232

few moments before the windshield would be blown into the cabin.

There were screams, and Barbara tried to reach for Patty's gun. Patty rammed the knife deep into Barbara's side puncturing her lung and spearing her heart. Death overtook her as she slumped down into the seat. The only sound now heard in the cockpit was the whistling sound made by the air screaming through the holed windscreen.

"Anyone else want to die? If so, I can certainly oblige, 'cause I am thoroughly pissed. No takers? Fine, now land this piece of shit right now!"

The pilot landed in the middle of the road, and Patty kept the pistol trained on them while she tossed her bags out. She took Matt's AR10 from one bag, slid a magazine in, and jacked a round in the chamber. She stuck two more magazines in her pocket.

"Okay, I have my stuff, and I have a 30 round mag in my .308 AR. Get out of here and don't fuck with me or I'll put all thirty in your fuel tanks."

The pilot began to plead with Patty, "But, if we take off now, the windshield may shatter, and cause us to crash. Please let me stay long enough to put a hundred miles an hour tape over the cracks. It will only take 3 minutes."

"If this piece of shit is still on the ground in 3 seconds you will be dead. Now fly, or die."

She slammed the door, ran to the side of the road, and ducked into a shallow ravine where two dry creek beds came together and puked.

The pilot lifted off inside of 2 seconds. He was not much more than a mile down Highway 25 when the bird nosedived into the ground and became a massive ball of flame.

She said aloud, "Dang, I guess that windshield didn't hold after all, pity."

She had excellent cover and could defend herself from all directions by moving only a few feet.

She hauled all of the bags over to the rocks and hid them.

***

Patty took a pair of field glasses from one of the bags and surveyed the surrounding area.

Looking south, she saw a small village on both sides of the highway about two miles ahead. She could only see the tops of the houses.

The built up exit overpass was the tallest structure for miles. The overpass was a mile and a half away. It took her three trips to move all of the bags to the exit and tuck them into a high ledge under the overpass.

She kept an eye out for people while eating an MRE and drinking some water from her canteen. There were three backpacks and four duffle bags to sort through since she knew she couldn't carry everything. She laid everything out on the concrete and started placing the items she had to have on the right, items she wanted in the middle and items she could live without on the left.

The *have to have* pile had:

- her 9mm carbine
- Glock 17 and all of the 9mm ammo and magazines
- M&P15 and ammo and mags for it
- Ruger MKIII .22 caliber pistol plus three mags and 500 bullets
- Weapons vest

- MREs

- Three canteens filled with water.

- One change of clothes, two more sets of underwear, a jacket

- Rain poncho

- First aid kit.

- Bayonet

- Backpack

Her wild assed guess was that she had nearly 100 pounds of gear selected and didn't have some of the survival gear such as water purification tablets, fire starter, ax and 20 other important items. She moved the M&P15 and its mags and ammo to the middle pile along with 400 rounds of the .22 ammo.

She then added several of the survival items to the backpack, loaded everything into or onto the backpack, strapped the 9mm holster on, and tucked the Ruger into her belt. She strained to get the backpack in place. Her life's work had made her strong and determined, but Sylvester Stallone she was not, several somethings still had to give.

She reassessed her situation while guzzling most of the contents of a canteen and eating another 2,000-calorie MRE. She ditched the jacket and rain poncho since her parka was waterproof and reviewed the remaining gear. She moved a canteen and only kept three magazines for the Glock and Carbine leaving 250 9mm rounds. The pack was heavy, still weighing around 60 pounds, but manageable now.

For the first time in her life, she was glad she had thrown all those hay bales, feed bags, and stock boxes. Yeah, she knew she could manage, but dang, she hated to leave all those treasures, and thought, *I sure hope the good guys find this stuff.*

She made up a second backpack with only some MREs, water and a FA kit along with spare survival gear to take with her as she scouted the area to prevent losing her primary backpack to "the good people" of this tiny hamlet.

She tucked everything else tightly under the overpass and hid them with brush and rocks. She didn't want to take everything with her and lose it all to robbers. She kept her carbine with its 31 round magazines and her Glock.

She decided to curl up under the overpass and spend the night there. She would scout the area before everyone was awake in the morning.

Patty was startled when she felt something snuggle up to her in the dark. It was whimpering as it tried to bury itself under her parka. She slowly turned her small flashlight on and lifted her parka to reveal a medium size gray dog with dark eyes and a long wet tongue. It began licking her face and wagging its tail. It was shaggy, and she couldn't tell what kind of dog it was, but she couldn't bear pushing it out from under her parka. Things were definitely looking up because now she had a much-needed friend.

They soon fell sound asleep and woke up just before sunrise when the dog made a low growling sound.

Patty looked around and saw three Coyotes sneaking up on them.

She threw a rock while yelling, "Go! Get out of here!"

The nasty beasts ran away, and the dog sat in front of Patty wagging its tail and staring at her. Patty opened an MRE and ate it along with some water. She offered the dog a small bite of the MRE, but the dog turned up its nose and ran off.

She saw the dog leaving and said, "That's the shortest time I ever had a dog, so much for making a new friend."

She busied herself getting ready to scout the area and didn't notice the dog had returned until it dropped a small rabbit at her feet. Patty saw the freshly killed rabbit and placed it in a plastic bag for supper.

She petted the dog and said, "Thanks for supper. Hey, what's your name?"

She held her hand out, and the dog licked her hand. She rubbed its ears and peeked at its collar. The dog's name was Max.

Max smelled like wet dog. Yep, he desperately needed a bath and some flea treatment if he was going to sleep with her in her parka. She already had several bites and was itching by morning.

She took off towards the village on the west side of the highway. Max followed and stayed out of the way. She found a position behind an abandoned tractor to watch several of the houses. There were about 30 people living on this side of the highway, and she quickly noticed that one small group was in charge and packed guns. The others did all of the work

She watched for several hours with Max by her side. She knew this village was not for her and was obviously dangerous. Max followed along as she headed back to her hiding spot.

It was well past noon when she offered Max a piece of dried meat from her MRE, and again he ran off. She finished eating, and about 20 minutes later Max dropped another rabbit at her feet. This rabbit was almost as large as Max.

"Good boy Max, good boy. I like rabbit."

She noticed he had some blood on his muzzle and knew this dog could feed himself, and her, in a pinch. She covered up Max in her Parka and took a nap for a couple of hours while waiting for late afternoon.

Max's growl woke her again to see a man driving an ATV on the road below. He didn't see her hiding under the overpass.

237

"Good boy Max for warning me about the man. You are a good watch dog for a pint-sized furball."

They went scouting again that afternoon to the east side of the road. The villages of Ramamillo and St. Lucia consisted of about twenty houses each. There was a gas station with a small general store with a pool table.

Patty surveyed the houses until she saw two young kids playing outside as a woman stacked firewood. She tied a white handkerchief to the barrel of her carbine and took her parka off. It was midday, and the temperature was around freezing, but she wanted the woman to note that she was a woman walking up in a peaceful way.

She walked slowly with Max towards the house when one of the children alerted their mom. The woman turned towards the house, a few seconds later a man came out with a shotgun and watched Patty walk towards them.

"Ola Senorita. Since you ain't from around here, what do you want?"

"You are right, I'm not from here. I'm heading to warmer places. My name is Patty, and I am not here begging."

Keeping the shotgun aimed at the ground, but ready, he said, "My name is Antonio, and this is my sister in law Carla, mucho gusto. What can we do to help you? Did that helicopter drop you out in the desert, before it crashed?"

"Yes, the helicopter dropped me off. Those were bad people. They kidnapped me. I had to force them to let me go."

"Why they kidnap you?"

"I don't know. They offered three of us a ride down to Mexico, but shot one of my friends and threw him and another friend out the door while taking off. My friends will be coming down Highway 25 in a couple of days looking for me."

"You and your dog need to move on. We have some bad peoples here also. You don't want them to find you."

"Are they a part of a drug gang?"

"No, but they don't like strangers. It's our mayor and his familia. They took over the area when the lights go out.

Anyone who disagreed with how they run things disappears. We have doubled in peoples in the last two weeks since the snow started up north.

Peoples, they do their best to go south. We have seen them pass through on foot, horseback, old trucks, and even ATVs.

We don't have extra food, so we give them some water and send them on their way. The mayor recruited one group to stay, and they have become his enforcers."

"Aren't you afraid of the mayor? Openly bad mouthing him could cause you trouble."

"Mayor es puta. We go my cousin's casa in Guatemala this weekend. We have an old truck and almost enough food for two weeks travel. We find the rest on the way."

Patty quickly thought that this family was leaving in 5 days and that her friends should be coming through in 2-3 days at the latest."

"How many of you are going?"

"Just my sister-in-law, my ninos, eh…kids and me."

"Is your wife going?"

"She die two years ago."

"If my friends don't get here before you leave, can I go with you?"

The woman spoke first, "We don't know you. Why we trust you aroun' the children?"

"I can help drive, pull guard duty and I have my own food. It's going to be a long, dangerous trip, and we could help protect each other. I also have better weapons stashed a short trip from here, Glocks and M&P15s plus ammo."

"I don't know, me and Carla, we go in me casa and discuss it."

"Fair enough."

Patty didn't want to let them know that she also had enough extra food for two more people for two weeks. She was thinking about how dangerous the trip south would be when she heard Max growl his low alert growl. She turned to see Antonio at the door.

"Come on in. It must be 30 degrees out there. Please share our fire."

"Thanks. Can Max come in also."

"Yes, bring him. Will he bite my kids?"

"No, he's very gentle. What have you decided?"

"You can come with us, but you'll have to help and share the guns and ammo with us."

"That sounds like a deal. How do you plan to get to Guatemala?"

"We go to Corpus Christi, find a boat, and cruise down to Guatemala."

"I like what I'm hearing, but what about food?"

"We scrounge along the way and find enough food to take on the boat."

"How many people do you think will be on the boat?"

"If we find Carla's familia there will be 12 counting the five of us here."

"We will have to find a lot of food."

240

"Si, we search warehouses, abandoned trucks, and stores."

"I'm in if my friends don't show up in time. Max and I will be ready."

"Perhaps your friends could join us, but I don't know about the dog unless he is maybe on the menu."

"I'd like it if they joined us. I won't go without Max, and hell no he is not food. He is a good guard dog, and he catches his own food."

Antonio smiled and said, "If he catches his own food, he's better than most people. Si, he can go, but none of our food will be wasted on a dog. You and the dog can sleep in the living room."

"Thanks, I'll go fetch the rest of my gear and will be back shortly."

Patty really didn't like that they had more people joining the party without a certain food supply, or the thought that Max would be in a stew. She also knew who would be kicked out if food ran short.

She was careful to assure that no one was tracking her as she traveled back to the overpass. She sorted through her supplies and decided to keep most of it hidden until needed. It's not that she didn't trust the family; she didn't trust anyone, well, except, of course, Matt and Mary.

Patty returned an hour later with enough food to last three days. She also brought an extra two days' worth of MREs for the family.

Antonio saw her meager possessions and said, "You going to need more food if you go with us."

"Hold on. I just brought enough to get by until either my friends show up or I know they won't be coming. I brought your family a two-day supply of MREs for the trip even if I don't join you."

He seemed satisfied with the gesture and helped her carry her gear into the living room.

"Muchas Gracias, Senorita Patty, I did not mean to offend you."

He asked, "How your friends to stop and look for you here?"

"I made a big sign on the overpass that says *Patty is here!*"

***

The time passed, and Patty realized that Mary and I were not coming, or worse, had missed seeing the sign and gone on south.

Antonio asked, "They didn't come today. We are leaving in the morning. Are you coming with us?"

"Yes. I don't know what happened, but I'm thankful that you will let me travel with you. I'll go get the rest of my gear.

"I drive you over after the sun go down. Can we find it in the dark?"

"Yes, I stuffed my things up under the overpass."

They drove to the underpass and with Antonio's help; they quickly loaded her things and arrived back at his house safely.

Antonio was curious how she had come by such high-quality guns and survival gear. Patty gave him the AR10, a Glock and the ammunition she had discarded as too heavy to carry.

"Thanks for the guns; they make me feel better about protecting my family. How did you get the guns and survival gear? Most people were caught by surprise by the solar flare."

"I was one of those Doomsday Preppers, and I owned a grocery and hardware store in Wyoming. We carried a large selection of guns, camping and survival gear. My two friends had been warned that the solar flare was going to happen and they helped me prepare.

NASA also predicted the recent cold weather. Antonio, this place will be buried in snow in a year."

"How did they know and the government didn't know?"

"Her husband was on a team that discovered Alpha Omega III, the planet that hit the sun causing the solar flare. He quit NASA because the government planned not to tell its own people."

"I don't believe you."

"You don't have to, but why would I lie to you?"

"I don't know."

Antonio brushed against her several times while they were fetching her gear and it made her feel very uncomfortable. She had assumed that Antonio and Carla were living as man and wife, but his actions said otherwise. She would stay on guard the rest of the trip.

They loaded everything into the back of the pickup and a cargo trailer and then got a good night's sleep before heading out the next morning. Twice during the night, she saw Antonio staring at her while he thought she was asleep.

The next morning we drove away and didn't look back. The temperature was below zero that night, and Antonio knew

243

his propane tank was very low. He knew his family could not survive if they stayed there. Moving south was the only possible choice.

They drove down to the small town of San Antonio on Highway 25 and took a road east that would take them to Highway 54, where they would head south to El Paso. They drove through the city without stopping even though several people tried to flag them down. Patty rode in the cab of the truck with the small girl in her lap. Three adults and two kids made for a crowded cab in an old 1959 Chevy truck.

They were about halfway to Highway 54 when the girl asked, "Why did that truck park behind the hill?"

Patty looked back and saw a semi with its trailer parked by its self.

"Antonio, stop and go back. That truck might have something we need. It's a Wal-Mart truck and might have food or something we need."

"No, I don't like stopping. Very bad to stop."

"Trust me."

"Si, but be quick."

He stopped, turned around, and carefully pulled off the road and behind the truck. Patty grabbed her rifle and cautiously walked up to the cab and found the driver slumped over the wheel. He'd been dead for weeks. She went to the back of the truck and found it locked with a plastic seal. She cut it with her knife and opened the doors to reveal pallets of food.

The trailer was filled with can goods, dry foods, sanitary products, bottled water, and drinks.

Antonio looked at the vast amount of supplies and said, "There is so much. How do we know what to take?"

"We need to take as much canned food that has high caloric content as possible. We can find water along the way. I'd also add some of the sports drink, so we make sure we have the right electrolytes."

Patty climbed to the top of the back pallet and crawled all of the way to the front. She cherry-picked several boxes of can goods and sanitary supplies while Antonio unloaded the trailer. They stacked three layers of canned goods on the floor of the trailer and then stacked their possessions on top of them. This helped them fill the trailer and hide the can goods from prying eyes.

They finished loading the trailer and pickup with all they could safely hold, and Patty made a stack of can goods beside the road.

"I'd hate for someone to go by here starving and miss this pile of food. I hope someone finds this and it saves their lives."

Patty and Antonio marked the location of excess food and supplies on numerous occasions during their travel south.

★

Chapter 16

Angel with an M&P15

The drive around the Denver metropolitan area was slow at best and filled with danger lurking around every corner.

Our first major challenge came between Loveland and Greely while driving down a back road when a group of farmers blocked the road with a tractor and tried to take our truck.

It was one of those heat of the moment things, where the guy on the tractor lurched out across the road and blocked it.

The others backed him up with raised shotguns and one pistol. We were about a hundred feet from them when we came to a stop.

The guy on the tractor yelled, "Now you folks need to come in a little closer and talk with us."

I replied as I grabbed my AR, "Y'all need to get out of the way and let us go through."

"No, we don't. What we do need is to borrow your truck to help us move south. I don't care what the government is saying this winter is bad and getting worse. If you play nice, we'll take you with us."

I signaled Mary and said under my breath, "I'm going to shoot the headlight on the tractor. If that doesn't scare them off, I'll start shooting the gas tanks on the ATVs."

I aimed, squeezed the trigger, and the headlight exploded. The men dropped behind the tractor and three ATVs for cover. I carefully aimed again, took a deep breath, held it, and shot the closest ATV's gas tank. It erupted in a fireball catching several of the men's clothing on fire. They scrambled away from the vehicles trying to get their coats and overalls off.

Everyone, but the man on the tractor took off for the hills. He fired the tractor up, turned towards us, and drove straight at us while firing his shotgun. The shotgun peppered us with spent birdshot. Again, I took aim and put two bullets into his chest. The tractor veered off the road and sped on until it turned over when it encountered a small dry creek bed.

"Matt, what makes people think they need our truck more than we do?"

"They are terrified for their families and now are beyond caring. They see the world closing in on them and go into survival mode. Kill or be killed. I hated killing that dumbass, but he was shooting at us. He should have run with the others."

We continued our trip south around Denver and didn't stop until we saw the signs for the Airforce Academy. We almost ran into a Humvee where four Airmen were guarding the Main Gate.

"What's your business in this area?"

"We're heading south. What have you been told about the strange cold weather?"

"Make sure you stay on this road. We've been turning people away since the lights went out. We were told to prepare for a long cold winter and will be leaving in a few months."

"How is the rest of the country doing? For that matter what's happening in the rest of the world."

"Most of the population has died off due to starvation, disease or killed during the riots.

The truth is, we only hear what they want us to hear, but scuttlebutt says most of the United States will be arctic tundra by next Christmas.

The entire world is suffering the same cold weather, except for the tropics, of course.

At least we have a warm room and food. That's more than most of the world."

"What about South America?"

Another soldier spoke up, "I heard it's much better down there. Did you know we declared war on Mexico and Brazil after they closed their borders? We were told yesterday that all the countries between Mexico and Brazil have been invited to join the U.S. as new states.

We're pretty sure that if they refuse, well, we'll just take 'em anyway. I know, it doesn't sound like the U.S.A, but really, what else can we do?

There is also open warfare between the equatorial countries with Russia and China, again, what else can they do? I hate to think about what is happening to the native populations."

"Airman, shut up."

"Sir, John is just spreading these stupid rumors. In truth, we don't really know nothing. All we hear is bits and pieces."

I nodded my understanding, and said, "Yeah, we understand, anyway thanks. We'll move on south until it gets warm if there is such a place."

"Sounds like a good solid American plan, be careful and stay safe. Keep a close eye out for bad guys, there's lot of 'em out there. A truck like this is an awfully tempting target for desperate folks, be tough."

"Thanks and you stay safe also."

"Mary, do you think the military will abandon those boys?"

"I don't think so. They'll be needed to win the war."

"Probably in South America."

"That's my bet."

We drove on south without any real issues, trading seats every 4-6 hours. It took a while, but we both got used to sleeping sitting up with our pistols and rifles ready for action. Gus and Tina were getting tired of the ride, and I tried to stop a couple of times to let them run for 15 minutes.

We were leaving Santa Fe when Mary yelled, "Look up ahead on the left. There's a school bus off on the side of the road."

"What the hell?" I said as I brought the truck to a stop in the middle of Highway 25."

"It's a bunch of kids and two Nuns."

I replied, "Oh, crap, be alert for an ambush."

"The kids won't shoot us."

"Someone could be using them as bait."

We slowly approached the kids while watching for anything strange. The nuns and the kids waved frantically at us, as we got closer.

"Thanks for stopping. I'm Sister Angela, and this is Sister Nan. You are the answer to our prayers. We have been stranded for several hours and everyone else just honked as they drove past us. I don't want to have the kids out here after dark. They will freeze."

"Hello Sister Angela, I'm Matt, and this is my friend Mary. What happened and where are you going?"

"The engine died, and we were stranded. We are heading to El Paso to live in a warmer climate. We couldn't heat our orphanage in Denver and decided to head south."

"What makes you think that El Paso will be warm enough?"

"Our people there always are complaining about the heat in the summer."

"Ma'am, you need to be thinking about going much farther south, about 2,000 miles farther south."

"Oh my, that would be South America. No, we'll move in with our convent in El Paso, but thanks for the advice."

"Well, I guess I can look at your bus. Mary, please park the truck and trailer between the bus and the side of the road."

The bus was from the early 1970s and had a large Ford V8 under the hood. I retrieved my tool bag and went to the front of the old bus, raised the hood and started diagnosing the problem.

I performed a quick visual inspection and found all of the wiring in place. Then I checked for fuel delivery to the carb and found the fuel pump working well. The accelerator pump was squirting gas, so I moved on to the electrical system.

I found my spark plug wrench, removed a spark plug, and had Sister Angela crank the engine over while I grounded the spark plug threads against a bolt. There wasn't any spark, and the spark plug gap looked good, so I removed the distributor cap and checked the points. There was the problem. The points had come loose and destroyed the condenser; both were mangled.

"Sister, I'm afraid you need a new condenser and points for the distributor. Your bus isn't getting any spark to explode the gas."

"Where can we find these parts?"

"Normally at an auto parts store."

"I'm sure Santa Fe has several of those."

I found Mary talking with several of the children and told her that I would have to go to Santa Fe to find the parts to fix the bus.

"I'm going with you."

"Why don't you stay here and keep the nuns company?"

"You don't want me with you, or are you protecting me?"

"You are a dear friend, of course, I want you with me, but I also want you to stay safe."

"I can watch your back while you search for the parts."

"All right, let's roll."

I told the nuns we were going into town to find the parts and leaving the dogs to play with the kids.

We turned around and headed to one of the main streets thinking we would find an auto parts store. We saw three in the same block a mile into town. I chose the NAPA store.

We parked off the street and went to the back door. It had been pried open and was ajar. We drew our side arms and cautiously entered the building to find what looked like millions of parts.

I told Mary what to look for, and we searched for two hours without success. Then I totally appreciated computerized parts management systems.

I heard a crashing sound from the back of the store and heard, "Matt, come quickly."

Mary was in the employee breakroom eating a candy bar. She had smashed the glass and had a large pile of candy bars, chips, and candy at her feet. She held a chocolate bar in front of my nose, and I took it. Damn, I missed chocolate.

"I'm taking these back to the kids. I doubt if they've had much candy since the flare."

"Save a couple for us."

"Well, yeah."

"Mary, we need parts for a Ford 390 distributer. I think any old '70s Ford V8 distributor probably had the same points and condenser. Let's look for a complete distributor."

I found an auto repair manual and showed her the exact parts. We then looked for a complete distributor and found a few, but no Fords of that era. We searched for hours.

"Oh, man, what's wrong with me? Mary, let's go to that auto salvage yard we passed on the way here.

When we get inside the yard, keep an eye out for any old Ford trucks from the late 60's to the early 70's."

I grabbed a phone book from behind the counter and ripped out the auto parts and salvage section.

As we walked out to the truck, a voice from behind us said, "Hey, puta, why are you stealing from my store?"

I slowly turned toward the voice moving so that my sidearm was away from the man. As I turned, I eased my pistol out of its holster. Looking over my shoulder as I moved I saw three Latino gangbangers leaning against the building.

Their posture was relaxed, as they felt they had complete control of the situation. Before they could react, I raised my pistol and shot each of them. As I walked up to the one who was still alive, although barely as he was already spitting up blood.

I said, "Thug, this is now my store."

I didn't give him a chance to respond as I slit his throat. I had already made too much noise and didn't want to attract any more attention.

Mary looked stunned, and said, "Matt, that was incredible. I'm glad I'm with you because anyone else might have tried to talk his way out of a no-win situation. Damn, I'm proud of you."

"Thanks, Mary; I'm glad you realize it was the right move."

Her laugh had a hint of hysteria as she said, "Right move? Are you crazy? That was the only move that could get us out of that alive."

As we drove to the salvage yard, we saw a few people scavenging around town and more going through abandoned homes as we passed, but no one tried to bother us. Instead, they immediately tried to hide. Things were not good here, gang rule.

It was only a twenty-minute drive to the salvage yard, and the gate was open. We stopped in front of the office, and I went in and saw a large whiteboard with the locations of the various cars and trucks handwritten on little magnets.

The board, organized into several sections, was titled Chevy, Ford, Dodge, and "Damn Foreign Shit." The owner was obviously a fan of American iron. I looked outside, then back at the board to get my bearings.

I ran outside and said, "Mary move down this aisle, turn left at the second Isle and go until we see Fords."

She followed my directions, and we soon found ourselves surrounded by Fords from the 1990s through late model cars. I told her to keep going to the back of the lot. The cars and trucks got older as we progressed.

I saw several old trucks on the left side of the aisle and immediately went to the first one. It was an old pickup with the correct engine, but someone had taken the distributor and carb. The next was a dump truck, and there we got lucky. The complete distributor was there. I removed the distributor and backed myself out from under the hood to see Mary standing there with her hands in the air and her rifle on the ground.

There were two young boys, and a girl standing nearby and the tallest had a revolver aimed at Mary. He saw me clear the hood and pointed the gun at my face.

I calmly replied, "Get that fucking gun out of my face."

"Shut up mister, or I'll blow your head off."

"What do you want? We haven't hurt you and don't want to. Now just relax, put the gun back in your pocket, and no one will get hurt."

I saw the other boy bending to pick up Mary's rifle. The kid with the gun was distracted for just the second I needed to grab his pistol. While making my move, I held the barrel and pushed it back toward his side, twisted his hand to the right forcing his arm back and up. He screamed and dropped the revolver. Bending him over I used my knee to kick him in the ass, knocking him to the ground.

I pulled my own pistol and told all of them to freeze.

"Do what I say, when I say, and no one dies."

"Mary, pick up your rifle and keep it on them. Now what are your names and why did you pull an unloaded pistol on us?"

"Mister, how did you know the pistol wasn't loaded?"

I showed her the cylinder from the barrel end and pointed at the empty chambers.

"Oh, I guess we're not very good at this kind of thing. I'm Jane, this is Billy, and that's Bobby. We needed one of your guns to protect us from the drug gangs."

"How old are you?"

"I'm 11, and they're both 12."

"Where are your parents?"

"Dead, the gangs killed our dads and took our moms to their clubhouse."

"So you aren't dangerous criminals?"

"No, and we're sorry. We wouldn't really hurt anyone. We're just scared, and we thought you were part of the gang."

"How would you like to get out of here and go to a warmer place?"

"That would be great. We've been living in that van over there and freezing at night."

Mary looked at me with surprise in her eyes, and I quickly put her fear to rest by saying, "We have friends that are taking a bunch of kids like you farther south to a warmer and safer location."

"Oh, yes, can we really go with them? Will you be going with us?"

"Yes, well, until we get to their location and then we're moving on south."

Bobby said, "But what about our moms?"

I looked at him and said, "I'm sorry son, but I'm afraid it's too late to help them. They are in God's hands now."

Angrily Bobby shouted, "God's hands! If there were a God, he would never have let this happen to us. I'll never believe in any god, again."

Now, in tears, Jane asked, "Do you really think our folks are really and truly with God, right now?"

"Yes, Jane, I also know that you are being given a chance at a new and better life than you have now.

I guess what I'm really trying to say is just give God a chance. Times are hard, but if you open up to Him, life will get better.

Now, all three of you get over here and let's all have a group hug."

Mary joined in the hug, and I saw her eyes were wet with tears.

I just think these kids needed to hear that all was not lost, that hope actually does spring eternal.

We told the nuns about the kids, and they were happy to help three more homeless kids. They took them into their arms and made them feel at home.

I replaced the distributor, cleaned, and adjusted the points, and the bus fired up and ran like new. I gave the Nuns one of our walkie-talkies so we could stay in contact on the road, then we drove south and led the way for the bus all the way to El Paso.

"Matt, I gotta' tell you that I believe that saving these three kids more than makes up for killing that guy on the tractor."

"I'm sorry? What do you mean by that?"

"Look, Matt, I've known you for a while, and I can see you've been beating yourself up for ending that miserable asshole's life. He would have killed us for a freakin' truck.

Whether you believe it or not, you are a hero, and besides saving my life, you have added 11 kids to your list of lives saved. Put a smile on that face."

She reached over, kissed me on the cheek, and gave me a pat on my shoulder.

"I know you are right, but even when killing has to be done; it still doesn't go down easy."

"Matt, if it ever becomes an uncaring thing, well, you just become one of the bad guys, but even though there is much more life taking ahead of us. You will never become one of the bad guys, so get over yourself."

My thoughts turned to Patty as I drove south. We lost two full days because we kept getting involved in other people's problems and now I knew that I would never see Patty again. Mary and I didn't talk about not seeing her again. It was always when we find Patty.

"Damn, I just realized, we are out of the snow, it's gone. The road is dry, and we can speed up."

Mary barely woke up and mumbled, "Yeah, okay, that's nice."

I shifted into two wheel drive and slowly sped up to 50 mph, and the bus kept pace. I had not asked Sister Angela if they had enough gas to make it to El Paso. Fortunately they did.

It was midnight, and we were cruising at 55 mph, passing many small villages on the left and right of the road. I wondered, *how are we going to find Patty?*

***

The kids were bored and were playing on top of the overpass when one pulled a can of black paint out of his backpack and started painting over someone else's tag.

257

"Now it says Greg was here. Write your names on it."

The kids were being kids and had no idea of the chain of events that a little paint could set in motion.

***

I pulled over to allow Mary to drive and the Nuns to switch drivers. We all took a bio break and then hit the road again. I had stopped under an overpass and saw the painted over message on the side of the overpass.

We drove for another four hours at 50-55 mph until we were northwest of El Paso, where several of the communities we passed through looked like WWII cities that had been bombed. We were high on an overpass and saw a section of El Paso that looked the same.

We stopped at a roadblock at the entrance to the Woodrow Bean Highway. This was a US military roadblock. We pulled closer, got out and a guard told to get back in our vehicles until the guards could check us out.

"Sir, what is your business, and where are you from?"

"We are from Pinedale, Wyoming and the school bus full of kids is from the Denver area. We are trying to get the kids to the Mother of God Orphanage on the southeast side of El Paso."

"Sir, are you planning to travel south through Mexico?"

I got the drift and replied, "No, we plan to stay in El Paso and work at the orphanage. Why does that matter?"

"Just trying to save your lives. Thousands of Americans and Canadians are streaming towards the border to escape the polar vortex and lack of food.

The U.S. and Canada are now at war with Mexico. Remnants of the Mexican Army and Federales are killing any gringos they find.

They have killed thousands trying to run roadblocks and have even shot planes down for invading their airspace.

Basically, they are real, really pissed."

"Thanks for the advice. May we proceed to the Orphanage?"

"Sure, but don't get off the road. There are hundreds of desperate people, and the whole town is running out of food. We've only had one battalion guarding the whole area. Ft. Bliss has been closed, and all equipment was shipped out a month ago."

"Where did they go? Where is our government?"

"The Army attacked across the border when Mexico refused our offer to make them a part of the USA. As for the Government, I can't answer that, but there was a large shipment of cold weather gear, snow cats and snowmobiles brought in this week for our use. Put two and two together."

"What happened in the city? There are sections that looked like they were bombed and are still smoldering."

"The riots were horrible. We bombed those bastards. They were looting and killing for days. We sent jets in to stop them from hitting the suburbs. Now, go on and get those kids to the orphanage. I bet they are worn out."

I filled Mary in on what she'd missed as we drove around the north side of El Paso. It took another hour to get to the orphanage, and we had to wind through several small communities to get to it. There were no people on the streets, and most windows were boarded up.

We arrived at the orphanage and found the windows also boarded up and the front door was broken in. Mary and I

259

carefully went in and cleared the place. It really pissed me off that the looters didn't spare an orphanage.

There was a message spray painted on the wall inside the entrance. It read, "Sister Angela, we are starving, cold and under attack by gangs. We have headed to South America. Come to Quito, Ecuador. Watch out for the Diablo's. They are everywhere." It was signed Sister Grace.

Sister Angela fell to her knees and broke into tears frightening the children. Sister Nan and Mary tried to console them while I tried to get Sister Angela back on track.

"Sister Angela, do you believe in God?"

She looked up at me still sniffling and replied, "Of course I do!"

Then why do you doubt his decision to have you and the children move farther south? He told us to move south with several messages until we got his point. The weather here will be near zero for seven months of the year."

"Did he also provide us with two angels to guide us to our promised land?"

I knew my play at using her religion to get her calmed down had backfired, but neither could I leave these kids stranded.

"I don't know about angels, but we are going to get you to a safe place and God willing, find your friends. You can believe that!"

Crying herself, Sister Angela managed to say, "Thank you for reminding me to place my faith in God. I won't question his choice of Angels, but most aren't armed with assault rifles."

"This Daniel needs all the firepower he can get with modern day lions. Oh, we also shouldn't forget the Archangel Michael. He didn't need an AR, but I'm no Michael, so I do need an AR."

I told Mary about promising to help the children travel south, and her reply was, "I already knew we would help them until they were safe. You just took a while to process it in that small man brain of yours.

Seriously, this is just something we have to do, and we will do it, or die trying."

Mary and I were sitting in the truck eating when I noticed two of the children were staring at us. I called them over and asked them if they wanted a chocolate bar.

"Yes, please, we haven't eaten in two days."

"What? Mary, please dig out the chow while I check with the nuns to see what's going on with their food."

I walked over to the bus and signaled Sister Angela to come outside to talk.

"Ma'am, are you short on food?"

"Yes, that's why we were anxious to get here to feed the children. We ran out yesterday."

"Why didn't you say something?"

"I trusted that God would provide, has He?"

"He did, but all you needed to do was tell me. Ask two of the older kids to come with me, and we'll take food back to the bus."

I took the kids to the trailer, found three cases of MREs, and helped take them to the children.

The kids were very hungry and ate the rations as though they were a Thanksgiving feast, which I guess it was.

I would never make jokes about the MREs to the kids, but they must have been starved to eat this stuff with smiles on their faces."

All of the children thanked and hugged us several times for the food. I knew we could only feed 15 people for a few more days with our supplies, so we had a new mission to find food.

Later I watched as the light show ramped up as the sun went down. I wondered if the Northern Lights stretched down to the equator. I was getting used to the magical display of lights and colors.

I walked over to the bus and gathered the nuns and Mary to help discuss our next move, and eventual destination.

Sister Angela said, "We plan to go to Quito to join the rest of our friends."

"That may not work out well because we are heading to the east coast of South America. We can travel together until we get you somewhere safe."

"Are we going to drive there?"

"Sister, I don't think it will be possible to carry enough food, water, and fuel to drive to Quito. I think we have to hire, buy, or borrow a boat."

"So we travel across Mexico to the Pacific and cruise down to Ecuador?"

"No, we will either travel to Corpus Christi, on the Gulf, or San Diego on the Pacific. We have a much greater chance of finding a boat or buying passage on one in a port city.

The problem with that is that it will just be far too dangerous. One of the smaller fishing villages will probably be our best bet to acquire a boat."

"But, Matt, we have no money to purchase a boat. Please tell me that you do not plan to steal one."

"Sister, no, we do not plan to steal a boat, but if there is no other way, that is exactly what I will do.

Mary and I have sufficient funds to purchase a boat if one is available."

Again, Sister Angela began to tear up. She said, "Matt, we will pray very hard for you, and for a boat to be available to purchase.

I hope you understand that we have no way of repaying you for all of your kindnesses."

I looked at her, then hugged her and said, "Sister, your prayers and getting you and the children to safety is all the repayment we could ever ask for.

Now, stop worrying about that repayment nonsense. We love you and will do all we can to never let you down. Okay?"

"Okay, but we will forever in your debt. Have you decided which direction we should go?"

"The drive to the Gulf would be the safest for finding food and water, but there is no way to get through the Panama Canal.

The drive to the Pacific is across the desert and mountains; still, crossing the desert seems like certain death, so I guess we'll head to one of the fishing villages just south of Corpus.

Sister, I meant what I said about getting you to a safe place, but Ecuador is probably going to prove to be impossible. I hope you realize that we cannot cross the desert, nor can we traverse the Panama Canal."

"I understand, God's will be done, so Corpus Christi it is Mr. Jones."

"Okay, now we need to search the area for fuel, food, and water before we head out. We have enough diesel fuel to make it, but your bus needs gasoline, and we need about 70-100 gallons to make the trip.

We can load the bus with water and food, but I don't want a bunch of gas cans inside the bus, so we'll have to secure them to the back of the bus and in our trailer."

Mary responded, "Matt come with me to the auto parts store and the hardware stores we passed a few blocks back to get some gas cans. We'll take the bus so we can fill it and the cans."

"Sounds good, as a last resort, we can siphon gas out of the abandoned cars. I will search for a hand pump at the auto parts and hardware stores."

Mary and I took the bus to find gas and kept an eye out for food during our trip. The auto parts store had 21 one-gallon fuel cans, but only six of the five-gallon cans. We took them all since they were clean and we could store water in the one-gallon cans.

The hardware store proved to be more fruitful. We found a dozen five-gallon cans along with two hand pumps and several thirty-gallon trashcans that we would use to hold water or food.

The hardware store also held 16 cases of bottled water, three bags of dog food and 9 cases of Gatorade, which we loaded into the bus.

I also found a full toolbox and several bundles of rope I added to our collection.

All of the ammo, had, of course, been stolen from the hunting section, but I found several hunting knives, axes and thermal underwear. The knives and axes I found in a drawer under the showcase. How they were missed, I had no idea, but I was sure glad they did. The thermals were in an unopened FedEx box in the stock room.

I was worried about the kids and gathered the entire display of long johns. I also found two 50-foot garden hoses to cut into siphon hoses.

"Matt for grins and giggles let's try that gas station for gas."

"It's worth a try."

I was glad the garden hose had to be hooked to a clear plastic smaller hose to adapt it to the pump when I saw the muddy foul concoction heading to the pump.

"Oh shit. Bad gas. "

"Sorry."

"Don't be sorry. It was worth a try."

We drove over to the car lot and began pumping clean gas out of the first car. The problem was that car lots don't fill cars up that are going to be sold until they *are* sold.

We decided to check the abandoned cars that lined the street. We were doing fairly well when we came upon an F150 with a full 36-gallon tank.

It took two hours to pump the bus full and to fill the 18 five-gallon gas cans.

Mary pointed out that there was a new and used truck sales lot across the street and that we should find plenty of diesel fuel there. We returned that afternoon and filled the tank on the Ford.

I was changing the hose to another truck's tanks when Mary said, "Matt, we've got company. There are two men walking towards us over by the sales office. They are doing their best to not be seen."

I took her binoculars and saw the men. One had a shotgun, and the other had a pistol.

"Mary, let's try to scare them off. They only have a shotgun and a pistol, not much of a match for our ARs.

I'll yell over to them when they get to this end of the building. If they shoot, place a bullet close to one of their heads, and I'll bet they run for their lives. I don't want to kill unless they get stupid."

"Matt, get a grip. If they shoot, I intend to drill them."

"Yeah, I guess you're right. Damn."

I stayed low and out of sight as I moved closer to the men.

I was only about 50 feet from them when I popped up and yelled, "Why are you sneaking up on us and what do you…?"

"Die pendecho," was all I had heard before they began shooting at me.

I ducked and scrambled for a better position to repel their attack when I heard two shots, then silence before Mary yelled, "All clear."

I peeked over the back of a truck bed and saw both men lying in front of the sales office. Mary and I kept behind cover as we worked our way to the men. One was clearly dead since half of his skull was missing. The other was writhing in agony on the pavement.

"You fucked up shooting a Diablo. We will hunt you down and kill your mothers and your dogs."

"Where does this so called gang hang out, turd?"

"You are in the middle of our turf, Gringo."

"You are dying and still talking tough?"

"My brothers heard the shots, and they will be here in a few minutes. You are walking dead."

I cut his throat and urged Mary to help me load up our stuff and hit the road.

Mary called the Nuns on the radio and told them to get ready to bugout.

We were a couple of blocks away when we heard the roar of motorcycles coming from the direction of the truck lot. They were searching for us, but luck was on our side today, as they didn't find us.

"Mary, we need to load up the children and get the hell out of here now. I don't want to get into a war with a bunch of drugged out gangbangers while trying to protect the children."

"I agree, you load up our stuff, and I'll help the nuns get the kids ready."

"Sisters, there is no time to talk. We must leave now. That gang, the Diablo's, is in the area and looking for us. We have to leave now."

It only took 10 minutes to get our stuff loaded, then I pitched in and helped load up the kids and their equipment.

Herding kids are similar to herding cats, or like trying to load jackrabbits on a flatbed trailer.

I started wondering about being trapped on a boat for several weeks with 11 kids and 2 nuns.

In another 15 minutes, we were on our way out of town.

***

Patty didn't know it then, but while Mary and I were tending to the kids in El Paso, her group passed us by on their way to Corpus Christi.

✪

Chapter 17

Patty's Journey

Patty experienced a very harrowing journey, and I wrote her story just as it was told to me. Her journey hardened her and gave her the resolve to survive; no matter what it took.

***

Hwy 13

New Mexico, USA

Antonio stopped for the night at an abandoned hotel in Artesia, NM just off Highway 13. The trip had been uneventful except for a small scare in Roswell when several men jumped in front of the truck when they slowed to get around two stalled cars.

Antonio was driving when it happened and floored the gas pedal knocking one man down and running over another. The truck bucked and Antonio took them on out of town as if it never happened. Patty looked back in time to duck as the injured man shot several times at them as they fled the area.

They drove around a motel to check for any threats and found none. They split up and began kicking in doors until they found two rooms that were clean and hadn't been used.

He parked the truck in front of the rooms so they could keep watch for thieves.

Patty brought her backpack and Bug Out bag in from the truck and settled in for the night with her dog Max. The first thing she did was to wedge the chair under the doorknob so no one could get in the room.

The second was to place a hammer by the window so she could escape if needed. Max and she ate alone by moonlight in our room before turning in for the night.

Patty came instantly awake hearing a low growl from Max. The doorknob again jiggled, and she heard a bump on the door. She drew her pistol and heard a whispered curse from the other side, as the intruder retreated.

She had felt that Antonio might be trouble and this convinced her to stay on her guard around him.

Their sleep was interrupted several times by sounds in the night. It would be a long time before she was able to get a restful night's sleep.

The next morning Carla fried eggs covered in cheese and hot sauce, thanks to Antonio's early morning scavenging trip. The tasty meal was a great change from the MRE's.

She was a bit surprised that Antonio was his normal self as he joked and played with the kids. He acted as though nothing at all had happened in the night.

Carla got the kids dressed, and they loaded everything back onto the truck and drove towards Highway 10 passing through Carlsbad, Loving and Pecos before getting on Highway 10 east at Fort Stockton.

They stopped for lunch on the outskirts of Fort Stockton and hid behind a large delivery truck near a Walmart parking lot.

Antonio wanted to park in the lot, but Patty felt sure that with all the treasures inside, that there would be some well-armed squatters, that would not want company.

They siphoned gas into the truck's tank while Carla prepared lunch. Patty tried to help Carla, but she told her that she didn't need any help.

The children still thought they were on a road trip to visit relatives and were oblivious to the danger and tension, except for the bandit thing, but Antonia said it was the Frito Bandito, and that it was just a game. Some kids will believe anything.

Patty joined them in a game of checkers while Antonio tracked down more gas.

Things changed dramatically when they started east on Highway 10. They were passed by a string of Humvees heading east at a high rate of speed and saw several other cars and trucks ahead and behind them.

Patty told Antonio, "I think we are beginning to see other people heading south. We need to concentrate on staying on guard."

"I think you are right. They are all heading towards San Antonio. I hope they stay there and don't go on to Corpus

Christi. I don't want to find a million people looking for a boat to take them south."

"I'm hoping they're just driving south and trying to stay in the USA as long as possible."

"Maybe, we'll see," said Carla.

Either they passed a car, or a car passed them every half hour on Highway 10 west of San Antonio. Most were families with their possessions stacked on the car's roofs or in trailers. They saw several military convoys heading east, but only one heading west. Most of the people waved; a few focused straight ahead.

Antonio waved his hand and pointed ahead. There was a truck on the side of the road with its hood up, and several people were trying to flag down passing cars. No one stopped. Patty felt horrible as they passed the truck. There was a young woman with three kids standing by a man who lay on the ground. Still, they didn't slow down so Patty couldn't tell what had happened to the man.

Matt's voice began ringing in her ear. It could be an ambush. Yes, even though Patty felt bad, she didn't really feel that bad.

Patty said a quick prayer hoping the man was okay. They kept driving, and Patty knew stopping could place them all in danger.

They finally saw the first signs for San Antonio, and a short while later Antonio pulled the truck off the road into the garage at a new Chevrolet Dealer in Kerrville. He had to jimmy the lock on one of the overhead shop doors, but he quickly had the door up.

"Carla, fix dinner while Patty and I go get some gas. We'll spend the night here."

He poured all of the gas from the five-gallon containers into the truck's gas tank and gave two to Patty. He retrieved a short piece of garden hose and two more five-gallon cans and followed Patty. They walked out to the lot, stopped at a Chevy Z71 4X4 pickup and he was able to fill all four cans.

Antonio looked over at Patty and said, "You haven't said much about yourself. Are you married or is one of your friends a boyfriend?"

"My husband died a few weeks ago, and the two people I'm trying to find are my best friends. I don't have a boyfriend. What about you and Carla, I know she is your sister-in-law, but is she your girlfriend?"

Antonio laughed, "The puta would like that, but oh Hell no! She's too much like her sister. I had a nice young girlfriend back home after my wife died, but Carla ran her off. I was about to throw Carla out when everything went dark."

"Sorry, I didn't mean to pry."

"It's okay, don't worry. I just need someone to talk to every now and then that isn't muy loco.

Where will you go when you leave us? You know that you are welcome to stay with us."

"Thanks for the offer, but I need to find my friends. I'll keep searching for them."

"I like you and want to be your friend."

"You are my friend."

Antonio confused Patty, he was so sweet, caring, and tender in person, but skulked around at night trying to get into her room. She liked him but intended to keep this friend at arm's length. She noticed Antonio was different to her in front of Carla, and she wondered if they were much closer than he told her.

Carla was polite enough, but she wouldn't speak to Patty unless she spoke first. Patty knew she had to get away from this family as soon as possible because she just wasn't sure what the danger really was.

They carried the gas cans back to the truck and filled it before having dinner with Carla and the children.

Dinner was quiet when Carla spoke up, "Antonio, please hurry up. It's cold, and the kids need the heat in the truck. They are freezing."

He looked over at his children playing and replied, "They look okay to me. Oh, what the hell, come on Patty let's go get some more gas."

Antonio and Patty went back outside with the empty gas cans to go fetch more gas before dark. They had no trouble finding cars with half-full tanks.

Antonio talked a lot about his life and his children. He disliked his dead wife, but he really loved his kids. He spoke several times about his dislike for Carla and her being too much like his wife.

"Antonio, why do you keep her around if she is mean to you and the kids?"

"She's not mean to the kids. She's just stern. If she were mean, I'd get rid of her in a single heartbeat. She cooks, cleans, and takes care of the kids, so it's like having a free maid."

"Is that fair to her? I think she loves you and is jealous of any woman around you."

"You got that right. She hates you and asks me every day to leave you on the side of the road."

"Will you do that?"

"No, you are my friend, and you are a big help with protecting my family. Carla couldn't handle a rifle or help get petrol, but watch out for that dagger she keeps under her apron."

273

That scared Patty to the bone and probably explained who was trying to get into her room at night.

The sun was ducking below the horizon as they walked back to the truck. Patty could see Antonio's breath dance in the waning sunlight as he spoke. Patty guessed she was growing a bit fond of this man, but still feared him, she definitely didn't trust Carla.

Antonio found a motel and they performed their regular routine of checking for other people before settling into suitable rooms. This time they had to search three hotels before finding one with no one present. He drove to the far end before choosing rooms for the night.

Patty secured the door with a chair, cleaned up the best she could and went to sleep. She awoke in the middle of the night again, to hear Max's low warning growl because her door was yet again being rattled as someone tried to force their way into the room. The door wouldn't budge, and the noise soon stopped. This happened once more during the night, and again the person couldn't budge the door and gave up. It had to be that bitch Carla or was it Antonio who tried to get her to fear Carla.

Patty lay there unable to sleep thinking that Antonio must have a dual personality. He never made a pass at her to her face, but he kept trying to break into her room to…well, she didn't want to think about that.

Antonio smiled at Patty and said, "Good morning sunshine. I hope you slept well last night."

She didn't want to call him out, so she just replied, "I slept very well thank you. How are you doing this morning?"

"Mui Bien, gracias."

They had a cold breakfast of leftover sandwiches before getting on the road again.

274

Antonio pulled away from the hotel and drove down Highway 10 towards San Antonio. The kids were asleep in the back all bundled up against the cold air. They decided to take Highway 37 south around the city and drive straight to Corpus Christi. Patty remembered Matt saying something about Corpus maybe not being the best place to go but just couldn't remember why, but she was a bit worried. The traffic was very low for normal traffic in a city this size and they only saw a few cars heading either way on Highway 37, so they took that as a good sign.

Antonio spoke up after a few minutes, "What do you see that's odd about the traffic besides there are only a few dozen cars and trucks on the road?"

Patty looked around for a few seconds and replied, "They are all older cars without electronic ignition."

"Damn, you are right. I wonder why new cars aren't running."

Patty replied, "The solar flare destroyed the electronics in all new cars, phones, TVs and the electric grid."

"How do you know this?"

"Scientists have known this could happen for many years. Nuclear bombs will also destroy electronics by producing an electromagnetic blast. Preppers like me study and prepare for this possibility."

"I feel dumb."

"Don't feel bad. Most people have never heard of the possibility that a solar flare could wipe out our electronics and power distribution."

Carla said something in Spanish that she understood to be, "That bitch thinks she is so smart. I'll show her how dumb her ass is."

Antonio replied in Spanish and Patty caught most of the meaning, "Shut the fuck up you old puta. She is a nice lady."

Patty coughed and said, "It's not nice to talk in another language in front of people."

He replied, "Sorry we were rude."

They drove around San Antonio before noon and were only 10 miles from Corpus Christi by mid-afternoon. Stalled cars on and beside the highway slowed their pace considerably. They had to weave between stalled cars and personal objects left in the middle of the road from people trying to carry too much luggage after abandoning their cars.

He drove much closer to the town than they planned because there were so few people. The place was practically a ghost town. Then they noticed graves everywhere beside the road and rotting bodies in alleys and front yards. Buzzards were everywhere. The stench was sickening, but they kept moving towards the Gulf of Mexico.

Antonio wanted to find a safe place to hideout while he went to the docks to find a boat suitable for the journey to Guatemala. They chose an abandoned house beside a park about half a mile from the Gulf. He parked the truck and trailer in the garage, and then they prepared to stay there until he found a boat. He would get up before dawn and walk down to the harbor to search for a large deep draft powerboat or perhaps a deep sea fishing boat.

Antonio headed out an hour before dawn since he wanted to get to the harbor before anyone was awake for the day. The city was almost too quiet. The only noise was the occasional bark of a dog. About half way to the docks, a pack of six large dogs started following him. They kept getting closer until he found a garbage can lid and banged it against the side of a building. He was very glad they took off, but he would keep an eye out for them and other dangers. After all, he didn't want to be eaten before he got his children safely to their new home.

He struck out that morning. There were only wrecks, burned out hulks and a few boats in dry dock of the size needed to go out on a deep water cruise.

He had expected to see many more boats at the Corpus Christi Yacht Club, but there were only a few dinghies and four sunken boats. He sat on the dock at the Yacht Club thinking about his next move when he heard a voice from the shore.

"Mister, there ain't no boats left here in the city. The people got scared of the snow coming and hauled ass south. Hell, they fought for the boats. Hundreds were killed, and a shit pot full of boats were burned."

"Where can I find a boat?"

"Not in Corpus Christi. You might have to go up or down the coast and find a small village where they haven't heard about the permanent winter."

"How did you hear about it?"

"My son is in the Coast Guard and was stationed here. He wanted me to go with him, but I'm 71 years old and I ain't moving to South America. I might freeze my brass balls off here, but I won't go to no dang "ferrin" country."

"Thanks for the help. Have you seen any gangs?"

"There were at first after the shit hit the fan, but they either killed each other off or moved south. Now, don't you be fool enough to try to cross the border, even if you are a Mex. Hell, you'll end up drafted in the Mexican Army. We're now at war with them damned Mexicans. Them that didn't git pushed south, or kilt, are killing Americans on sight if they catch 'em trying to cross into Mexico.

Our Army wiped their military out before loading up and moving south. Still, the soldier boys from Fort Hood left an Infantry Battalion, and one of them Tank Companies. Biggest danged things I ever did see. Yep, them tanks scared all them gangbangers back across the border, though they is some still around, so you best grow eyes in the back a your head, ya' hear?

Now down in Mexico the drug gangs run things wherever our army ain't. It might take a while to settle 'em down, but Mexico will become a part of the Union. You just wait, things will be better for them Mex's, too."

"Thanks for the advice."

Antonio didn't know what to make of the old man, but he believed what he'd heard. He traveled back to them quickly.

***

"Ladies, there weren't any boats in the harbor that I would trust to make it off the wharf. I'm going to drive north to several small towns, and maybe I can find one there. If not I will come back and then travel south until I find a boat.

There's one out there waiting for us, there's got to be."

Carla was disappointed and replied sarcastically, "Are you sure you checked every marina?"

"Si, I know what I'm doing, so shut the hell up, you old bat. People took every good boat and headed to South America just like we are wanting to do."

"Thanks for braving the city and searching for us," Patty said and gave Antonio a peck on the cheek.

Yes, she purposefully kissed him to goad Carla, who had been a bitch to her while Antonio was gone. Patty does have a bitchy side when you get her riled.

Oh yeah, she could see Carla was furious all right, but she did keep her mouth shut for a change. Patty knew that Carla would have to disappear before she would get on the boat.

Antonio didn't like her, and she always treated Patty as a threat, and from the way she related this story to me, she was a threat to Carla. I mean, hell, she didn't want Antonio, but she most definitely didn't want Carla around, especially with that damned knife she always carried.

She fell asleep that night thinking of ways to get rid of Carla without killing her.

***

When Patty came to, she was dizzy and felt like crap. She thought her head might explode as she tried to wake up. She heard strange sounds and instinctively knew the smart move was to play dead.

She overheard to two men talking about this 'new hot piece of ass that they had traded for. She felt sorry for the poor woman after peeking through her eyelids across the room at the rough men seated at a bar. They were drunk and slugging free whiskey down one after another.

The men talked about a wide range of topics from women to the cold weather. One mentioned the recent rumor about the permanent winter and the flight of people to Mexico and South America. They thought they should head south, but the local bars were full of alcohol, and it was above freezing most days.

Besides, they had their choice of homes to live in, and most houses outside the city limits had full propane tanks that could heat a house all winter. They decided to wait until spring to move south.

She moved her head slightly to look around the room to find herself in what was once a nice bar with a nautical theme. She saw most of her possessions on the floor by the jukebox, and then the room swayed a bit when she moved her eyes too fast, so she closed them.

She tried to rub her eyes, but couldn't move her arms. That's when the realization set in that she was the new woman

279

and she was lying on her side on a pool table with her feet and hands tied together.

Her mind raced to what could have happened, but the last day was missing from her memory. The last thing she remembered was Antonio saying he had to travel north to find a boat and kissing him on the cheek.

Then it hit her, that bitch Carla had drugged her and sold her to these men. She had no idea how long she had been unconscious and then she wondered how Carla had moved her from the house.

She slowly felt around her right ankle and was relieved to find her Keltek .380 still in her ankle holster. She also found her knife strapped to the inside of her other leg.

As her wits began return, she was amazed and relieved to realize these guys were so drunk they didn't find either of her weapons when they tied her up. She vowed they would pay for that oversight.

She had adopted this precaution after being kidnapped in the helicopter. She'd vowed that she would never go anywhere unarmed again.

She was startled when a third man appeared and started groping her from behind.

"I get her first. Let's wake her up and get our money's worth."

"No, I called dibs first, and I'm the one who found that crazy bitch that sold her to us. I go first."

Patty knew this was just going to be too easy from the way they had tied her, wrist to ankle. She retrieved the knife and the pistol; cut her hands free from their bindings while the two men were arguing over which one went first.

When dibs guy came over and ran both his hands down her inner thigh, she clamped down on them with both legs, drove the knife into his stomach, and shot the other two.

As the man fell to his knees, the knife caught on the table's edge dragging it across his naked stomach. He used his hands trying to stuff his intestines back into his abdominal cavity with no luck.

His screams of pain became feral as he fell onto his back, blood pooling along his sides. The other two drunks fell off their barstools and lay writhing in their own blood.

Neither was mortally wounded but would bleed out in a half hour or so without treatment.

"So you three assholes think I'm a hot piece of ass, do you? This is the only piece you're going to get today," Patty said as she shot both in the stomach.

Through his screams, one pleadingly said, "But, I traded a good boat for you."

She looked both men in the eye and replied, "Damn, I'm worth more than some leaky old boat, oh well.

Tell me, bucko's, was it good enough to die for? I just gotta' tell ya' that it was great for me, you big hunk of man, you.

Now just die with your friend by the pool table."

Remember how Patty was when I first met her, a regular Nancy Nice. Well, I'm tellin' you this those days were gone. Why our little girl was all grown up.

She told me that she hoped they would die a slow, painful death, but she became worried that someone might find them in time and save their lives.

So, instead of leaving them with their wounds, she went back over to them and put one bullet into each kneecap.

She said, "Boys, help might come in time, and you might live, but watching you try to walk, would be worth the price of admission. I'll see ya' around boys."

She also told me that in thinking back on that situation she hoped they did get help and lived." She said, "Damn, but I'd love to see them walk."

***

Patty went over to the bar, poured three fingers of Bourbon, and drank it down in one gulp.

She checked her supplies, found all of her guns except for one Glock. She hid what she couldn't carry in her backpack and headed out to kill Carla. As she left the bar, she wondered if she would ever find Matt again or if she would have to live out the rest of her life alone.

As she left her paramours in the bar, she looked both ways before stepping into the street and saw poor Max lying by the building dead from two gunshot wounds. That made her feel better about making those perverts in the bar suffer; after all, a little suffering is good for the soul, right?"

Patty had been unconscious for some time and had missed Antonio and his children's departure. She found his truck by a dock north of the city and realized that she had lost Matt and Antonio. Suddenly she felt very alone and very afraid.

Yeah, alone and afraid she may have been, but helpless she was not.

The truck had plenty of gas, but the bed and trailer were empty. She ditched the trailer, drove the truck, and started scavenging for food.

She knew the stores, warehouses and trucks were a waste of time, but searched for food processing plants, hoping that she could find nonperishable foods that were in the packaging process.

Patty knew that she would be seen walking or driving around town and decided to get away from the northern part of town and drove south until she was just south of Oso Bay and below the water treatment plant. She found an abandoned house on the waterfront and made it her base of operations. Patty made sure she came and went by different routes so following her would be more difficult. She was always on the lookout for people following her.

Several followed her, but they only did it once.

She drove to the manufacturing side of town and found large warehouses, light manufacturing, and several food processing plants. She found the holy grail of breakfast cereal boxes on the packaging lines and loaded her truck to the brim. She made several trips back to her hideout before moving on to other buildings.

Her most significant find was a canning plant that had potted ham, chicken and Spam. She also found a plant that made packages of jerky and sausage sticks. These would last for months to years without spoiling. Again, she filled her truck several times. Her food supplies were now more than sufficient for the near future. She now needed ammunition and medical supplies for her trip south. She also needed a boat.

✪

Chapter 18

Corpus Christie

We made it to the outskirts of Corpus Christi two days later, a little afternoon and because there were so few people, we decided to stay while I searched for a boat.

We spent the time hiding at the Emerald Beach Hotel, on South Shoreline Blvd, with our vehicles in the parking garage. The rooms were pretty classy, but with billions, worldwide dead, or dying, the room service sucked. Still, the price was right.

We unpacked only the necessary items and settled in for a while. Mary and I took turns guarding the vehicles both day and night.

With the wind howling off the Gulf, it was really cold, but with our cold weather gear the time on guard duty was tolerable.

Still I so wanted to climb into my arctic sleeping bag, but I knew I would fall comfortably to sleep, and might even wake up dead.

The Nuns took the kids out to the beach and Gulf; they were excited to play on the beach. Playtime lasted about thirty minutes. The temperature was in the low thirties.

So, dear reader, if you don't know anything about Corpus Christi, let me enlighten you; the wind blows hard. The "feels like" temperature sat around ten degrees Fahrenheit, with blowing sand. Actually, it could often feel like standing in front of a sand blasting machine.

There were the remains of a recent dusting of snow against the northern side of the buildings, which only re-enforced my desire to head farther south. It was late March, and the temperatures overnight should be in the fifties, not the teens, and now they were always in the teens.

Mary and I planned to leave the Nuns and kids safely at the hotel while we searched the docks for a boat, or purchase passage south.

We left before dawn and worked our way down to the waterfront where our map said the Yacht Club should be located. The only person we saw was the proverbial little old lady, all bundled up and sitting in a chair, fishing from a pier just south of the Club.

We braved the wind, and cold sea spray, approaching her with open hands, "Hello how's the fishing?"

"Much better without all of the boats and people stirring up the water," she replied as she held up a stringer with a half dozen small fish.

"Where did all of the people go?"

"Most are dead and rotting in their houses or buried in the parks. The rest either drove off or took a boat south."

"Why did you stay?"

"I was born right here in Corpus 66 years ago, and by God, I'll die here in my home when the Good Lord decides it's time to call me home. Hell I like snow, a'course livin' here on the Mexican border I don't ever see any, but I don't mind this weather.

I went to New Hampshire once and played ice hockey when I was a bit younger. I plan to do that again, right here, once it gets a mite colder a'course.

Folks here 'abouts' call me Meg. You got a name?"

"Yes, ma'am, we do, I'm Matt, and this is Mary. We came down from Wyoming. I guess it's turned into a frozen tundra right about now."

She smiled with a disconcertingly pleasant grin and said, "Yes, I reckon it is, or soon will be. Glad ta' meet'cha.

Now, since I doubt y'all be out here for your health, is they sumthin' y'all want or is they some way I can be of help ta' y'all?"

"You surely can, if you know where we can find a boat. We have a bunch of orphans, and we need to get them safely down to Central America."

She began with a chuckle that slowly became a cackle, "Damned if I know, boy. The Yacht Club is up there, but they ain't nothing that'll float or move.

Y'all might go north, or south where there are several marinas, and a couple of fishing communities down close to the Mexican border, and if you go there, you best be packin' and extra careful. Still, I don't spect you'll be findin' much. Maybe a sailboat. Them damn Yankees that come down here a'lookin' for a boat didn't seem to know spit about sailing."

"Thank you, Meg. We'll remember your advice. Good luck with your fishing."

We gave some thought to what Meg had said. Mary thought she was like deciding to eat at a shaky looking roadside diner because the parking lot was full of trucks. The drivers know where the good eateries are.

Yeah, Meg was a trip, and I wondered if she would ever get to play ice hockey. I'd be willing to bet that even at 66, she could check like a pro. What a gal!

We proceeded a short distance north to the Yacht Club, and old Meg was right, nothing there except burned out sunken hulks. It was late morning when we saw a man fishing off the dock.

"How's the fishing this morning?"

"It stinks. Only got me one lousy Flounder. A man could starve to death at this rate."

"Where can we find a boat?"

The old boy's face turned stormy, and he said, "Damn, boy, cain'tcha even say hello to an old man?

My names Brett Starnes, you?"

I grinned and said, "I'm sorry, sir, I guess I was a bit rude, and I sincerely apologize. My name is Matt, and this here is Mary. We are shepherding a couple of Nuns and their orphan charges.

Sir, do you have any idea where we might engage a boat to take us all the way to Brazil?"

"Now, see, that warn't so tough was it?" and Brett burst out laughing. Nope, they ain't none here. You might could try goin' south until you find a marina, or that little Mexican village just this side of the border. They might could be able to help you out, seein' as y'all are on such a mission of mercy.

Yep, herdin' Nuns and Orphans might just help, cause, you know, all them Mex's is Catholic. Whole area was founded by Catholics.

287

Why even the name Corpus Christi is Spanish for Body of Christ. Now I ain't no Catholic, but I plum like the name Corpus Christi, Body of Christ.

Fact is, most folks my age like the name, 'course we ain't a'goin' nowhere. That old sayin' about home is where the heart is, is true. Well as you get older, if'n you do," he laughed like a loon over his little pun, then added, "Wait, what was it you wanted, agin?

Oh yeah, a boat, well, just go south. You just might find one, but be careful what you wish for, cause ya' just mite git it."

He kept right on talking, and we weren't sure if he was still with us, or just lost in his own thoughts.

"Yeah, they used to be plenty of them, but a lot of people done come through here over the past few weeks and ever danged one of 'em wanted passage to South America. They stole boats, killed boat owners, and shot up boats when they couldn't get on board them. Yeah, I'd try them other marinas.

Say, did I tell you 'bout the time."

Whew, half an hour later we were finally able to say, "Thank you Mr. Starnes for all your help. I hope you don't mind my asking, but are you by yourself?"

"No, my best friend, my ex-wife," again with the laughter, "is fishing off the pier down south of here."

"Aren't y'all afraid someone might try to harm you?"

The man pulled an Uzi from under his jacket and said, "Not if they want to live, 'sides, why would anyone want to hurt me. Son, I've been a life taker and a heart breaker on four continents when I was a Navy Seal, and I may take a few more lives afore I die in this new fangled shitty-assed world we find ourselves in. Don't rightly reckon I'll be a breakin' many more hearts, though ya' never can tell. Shoot, ya' never can tell.

I can't get the old lady to go south with me. She doesn't think old people should be out on the water alone."

"Can you navigate on the ocean?"

"I've sailed a 30 footer from the west coast to Hawaii and then on to Fiji and back. So, yeah, I reckon I can."

"Well, we have to find a big boat that can handle 15 people. You see, we have 11 orphans and two Nuns that we picked up along the way here and have to get them safely to their sister orphanage in Central America before heading on to South America. If we find one, would you two go with us?"

"Well, let me see if we can get the old woman to go along. I warn ya' that I'll not be a'leaven the old bag again. We've kinda' grown used to each other's company, but I gotta' meet the kids before I commit to this crazy plan. Still, I might know where you can find a boat that I could still skipper."

I was a bit concerned about Brett's age and mental capacity, so I asked, "Sir, I promise you that I do not wish to be rude, or insult you, but I must ask are you sure you can do the job, I mean, at your age."

He laughed again, but this time it seemed somehow different. He said, "Matt, please, call me Brett, and I assure you that I am completely competent and up to the task.

All that crazy old man shit was to put you at ease in case you wanted to rob me. People at ease are not ready, and that's where my Uzi comes in handy.

I'm mentally sound and probably could give you a run for your money; still, before I agree I want to meet the Nuns and kids first. Deal?"

"Oh, hell, yes! We are staying at the Emerald Beach Hotel, on South Shoreline Blvd a few blocks from here.

Whoa, wait a minute, Brett; is your wife like you? I mean mentally?"

Brett lowered his head and said, "No, son, I'm afraid she isn't. She's much smarter than I am, and could probably whip your ass."

"Oh, sure, we know the Emerald Beach Hotel, on South Shoreline Blvd well. Let me call the old bitch and get her to meet us there."

He pulled a walkie-talkie out of his pocket and said, "Meg, I want you to meet me at the front of the Emerald Beach Hotel, on South Shoreline Blvd. We have friends there. Bring protection."

"Okay, what the hell have you got us into now?"

"Trust me and shut up. Love you."

"Love you, too, ya' old coot."

He reached under his lawn chair, and pulled an M-14 rifle, scoped and prepped as a snipers weapon. Then he shouldered his Uzi and came along with us.

Well, damn…

The man who came with us was definitely not the old "step and fetch it" he portrayed. He was, indeed, sound of mind and body.

He talked about his career in the military, but still asked several questions probing our backgrounds. He stopped a couple of times to rest, but always got back up and walked, as if nothing was wrong. I heard two clicks on his walkie-talkie, and he reached into his pocket for a second before pulling his hand out.

He stopped at the front of the parking garage and said, "Not that I don't trust you, Matt but, I will feel much more comfortable if you bring the kids and Nuns out here so I can meet who we are going to be stuck with on a boat for weeks on end."

Mary pulled out her walkie-talkie and said, "Sister Angela, please come down to the front entrance to the parking garage and bring the kids. We may have found passage south."

"Okay, it will take a few minutes to herd them down."

We passed the time telling Brett about the events in Wyoming and our journey to Corpus Christi until the Nuns and kids arrived. He picked a little girl up and immediately became the grandfatherly type, and immediately fell in love with all of them.

I noticed he reached into his pocket again and that was followed by two clicks on his walkie-talkie. A few minutes later a woman dressed in fatigues also carrying an M-14 sniper rifle came walking up to us with her hands raised. Her face looked familiar, but she was not the same lady we saw on the beach fishing.

I said, "Ma'am, you look different."

"I hope so. My wig and pillow for my belly do tend to put most would be bad boys at ease."

"Who were you trying to fool?"

"Well, you at first, but mostly there have been some scumbags preying on some of our friends. I was the bait this morning, and Brett was the sniper."

"So I guess you were the sniper making sure we weren't the bad guys."

"That about sums it up. Now, who are you?"

The Nuns introduced themselves and the children, and then Mary and I told them about us."

"Wow, moving 11 kids to Central America. That is quite a chore. Brett, are we up to this. That's only four fighters protecting 13 innocents, bad odds."

"We can teach some of the older children how to shoot. Looks like some are 12-13."

The Nuns objected at first, but Brett calmed them down by saying, "Ma'am, there are now a lot of bad people in this world that would enslave the kids, kill the rest of us, then take our boat and supplies.

We'll need all of the firepower we can get if you want to make the trip. We won't have them do anything unless it's for the survival of the others."

I caught the part about "our boat" and said, "So you have a boat?"

"Yeah, well, we actually have two boats. One is too small to take this size group. We could have sailed out by ourselves, but we decided to wait until the rush of people was over.

The large one is an older Oster 56. It will be a bit uncomfortable, but the boat will make it anywhere in the world. We have been stocking it for a cruise to South America for a month. It looks like we'll need to rip out some furniture to make room for mattresses and supplies."

I replied, "We have enough MREs for three people for a month, several ARs and Glock 9mms and several thousand rounds of ammo. We also have 200 gallons of diesel and 100 gallons of gas. We can help scrounge for food in this area."

Brett added, "Sisters, I am sorry that you have to face this with us, but there it is. It is and will be, kill or be killed for a long time coming. Can you deal with this new world?"

"You do understand that we do not believe that violence is the only way, but just let some pirate try to take one of my charges. We are willing to learn how to shoot, so you'd better be ready to teach us," said Sister Angela.

Just a bit stunned I added, Sister, I wonder if God would forgive you if you did not take that stand. They are his children, too, and I'm pretty sure that is why he has chosen you to protect them."

Brett let out a deep breath, and stammered, "Whew, okay, good. I still have some friends over at the Naval Air Station CCAD. I happen to know that we can have a shit pot full of slightly toasted MREs. Some idiot grabbed what he wanted and set fire to the building so no one could use the rest. It rained that day and put the fire out.

Sister, I am going to look at that rain as a sign that the remaining food was meant for us, especially the children, wow."

We helped sort through the mess and found perfectly good supplies of those delicious MRE's under the burned stuff.

Brett said, "We have enough together to feed the entire bunch for about a month. We can extend that by several weeks if we stop and fish along the way."

Brett even managed to hustle a few thousand more rounds of ammo, and four squad automatic machine guns (SAWs) equipped with pintle mounts, and an old ambulance to carry out booty. Things were definitely looking up.

I asked, "Is there any hope of finding any warehouses or trucks with food that haven't been found?"

"No, I think we have pretty much searched every square inch of the immediate area, and can only find drinking water, alcohol, and fuel. Alcohol, yeah, who'd have thought it, but every corner bar in town had lots of that stuff."

"Are there any distilleries or beer brewing facilities in Corpus Christi?"

"I like your thinking. They use grain. Hell, what about granaries?"

"Let's split up into two teams. One loads what we have on the boats and the other searches for food."

"Works for me. Take Meg with you since she knows the town and I'll put the kids to work on the boat. We'll need to get rid of anything not needed to safely get there so ladies, be ready to wear one set of clothes while the others are drying in the breeze."

Brett stopped on the road, got out of his truck and walked a few feet into the woods. A few minutes later, he waved for us to go around his truck and wait for him.

He rejoined us and said, "Follow me, stay close and do what I do."

Brett drove about a hundred feet further then pulled off the road and drove in the grass for a while before getting back on the road. A minute later, we saw his home up ahead.

Brett and Meg's place was a few miles south of the city and had access to Corpus Christi's very shallow Oso Bay.

Their home was a nice ranch style house, with a large barn and a dock extending out into the water. As Brett had promised, there were two sailboats tied to the dock. The large one appeared to be in much better shape than its smaller sister was.

"Brett, how were you able to keep two boats when every boat around Corpus Christi has been stolen?"

"Well first, we're off the beaten path, and the roads in have traps, trip wires and land mines guarding the place. Several have tried to come here, and several have died. It's a shame that some may have simply innocent people just trying to get by in a cruel world. These days, bad things happen to anyone who goes where they should not go.

Let's not waste any more time. Meg, please show the women the supplies while I show Matt the boat."

"How soon do you want to leave?"

"Matt, there is a group that's been trying to find us and our boat for several weeks. Our mission in town was to flush them out and take them out before they kill us and take our boat. Therefore, the bottom line is that we need to leave in two days.

We'll finish loading, and I'll give you and the others a crash course in sailing. I'll use the small sailboat tied to the back of my large boat."

We had a quick lunch while we stripped the boat of any unnecessary furniture and dead weight. The couches, beds, and tables were torn out. We would sleep on the floors in sleeping bags.

We shuttled supplies from our vehicles, their house, and barn to the boat. Everyone pitched in to carry supplies to the boat. It soon became clear that the boat wouldn't handle all of the supplies. Brett and Meg had also been preppers and had several years' worth of food, medical and sanitation supplies. He had as much buried in drums around his property as he had in the house and barn.

By late evening, the work was completed, and Brett proclaimed, "We all must be aboard before sailing the day after tomorrow. Boarding will be before daylight and set sail with the tide.

Time is critical because Oso Bay is so shallow, we must depart at high tide. If we miss it, we will be stuck here for another 12 hours.

Everybody, eat a good meal and get plenty of sleep. Be prepared for sailing lessons in the morning. We'll need to split up and share guard duty until we leave."

I took Brett off to the side and asked, "Why did we discuss the need for finding food when you have enough for all of us for many months?"

"Easy question, easy answer, we were feeling you out to see if you and your little Scout Troop would have a chance to survive on your own. You passed."

"Brett, are we towing the small Venture behind your boat when we leave?"

"Yes, why?"

"I'd like to store some survival gear in it, and also I thought it would be a good idea to use it to scout out islands and go ashore without exposing the larger boat to gunfire."

Brett shared a huge smile and said, "Nope that is not another stupid question. Do it. You know, Matt, I like you."

We spent the next morning sailing around the harbor during high tide learning the finer points of sailing and tacking the small boat. Lessons in navigation would come once we were on our way.

We tacked back to the dock as the tide began to wane. I loaded the little craft with my survival gear, which included half of my silver, gold, and jewels. Another watertight bag had guns and ammo plus a weeks' worth of MREs.

I tied the craft to Bret's other boat, and I planned to tie the small boat to Brett's larger craft just before we left. I didn't want him or his wife snooping around my cache.

***

The men were following Patty from a distance when they lost her. She made three turns and waited each time to see if she was being followed. They drove past after her first turn. She waited for five minutes, drove to her next turn, and waited. She never saw the car again and went on to her house.

One of the men shouted, "Look up ahead. Slow down, there are several vehicles heading south. It's not the girl, but they could be easy targets."

"Yeah, there's a bus and a truck towing a trailer. Let's hit them."

"Hold your horses, dumbass, let's follow them to where they're holed up, and take everything."

***

The men had seen my truck, the Nuns bus, and Brett's truck as we headed to his home. We didn't know they were preparing for an attack on us, or that Patty was just a few miles north.

I was sound asleep in a back room snuggled deep in my sleeping bag. I felt something bump up against me and fell back asleep thinking it was one of my dogs.

Later I woke up with a head on my chest and arms around me. It was Mary, and her body felt good against mine. I fell back asleep trying to decide if I should give up on finding Patty. Mary snuggled tightly against me the rest of the night. I stroked her hair as I fell asleep.

Mary woke me up at 5:00 am to pull guard duty. I went to the kitchen and found coffee and a sandwich waiting for me. Mary was suiting up to check our vehicles and grab a bite herself. It was about an hour and a half until we would awaken our motley crew for debarkation.

I walked up to her from behind, gave her a hug, and said, "We will be okay. Thanks for staying with me last night. I needed the company."

"Me too. We don't have anyone but us anymore."

I walked up the road and stood in the shadows to guard the entrance as Brett and Meg finished getting the boat ready.

I remembered that I had to tie the Venture to the main sailboat and kicked myself for not doing so before I came on guard duty.

I watched from a distance as the kids were herded onto the boat with Mary and the Nuns behind them.

I took one last glance over my shoulder to check the road to Brett's house and caught sight of several men running at me just as a blast knocked me off my feet. I heard gunfire and more explosions, and that's all I had remembered before unconsciousness took me into total darkness.

The men were trying to capture the boat and my friends but ran afoul of the trip wires and anti-personnel mines. The mines had killed half of their crew before they got within a hundred yards of the boat. The mine that knocked me on my ass killed three of their men and wounded four more. Thinking I was dead, they ran around me and charged onto the boat dock.

Mary and Meg opened fire. They shot several more as the marauders ran across the driveway. This pinned the remaining assailants down as Brett used the inboard diesel to motor away from the dock. The gun battle was fierce with bullets hitting the cabin and stacks of supplies on the boat. One child and Sister Angela received minor wounds though the rest remained unharmed.

"Brett, wait for Matt, "Mary yelled."

Meg replied, "Dear, I'm afraid he is dead. He was thrown down by the blast, and several of the attackers ran right over him. If the blast didn't kill him, they most certainly did."

Mary cried as the boat moved out of range and they headed out to sea. Upon clearing the bay, Brett dropped the keel and hoisted the sails. With Meg's help, they were soon skipping along the waves headed south.

I woke up in time to see the three surviving attackers jump into their truck and try to chase the boat down. They apparently hoped to use their automatic weapons to stop the boat before it headed out of the channel and into the open sea.

I forced myself to get up and run to my truck in an attempt to stop them.

They drove like lunatics at breakneck speeds to no avail along with the channel heading north. The boat had already made the turn out of the channel, and I could see the sails being unfurled.

I came to an abrupt stop aimed and fired several bursts at the men who were firing at my friends. Two of the scumbags dropped dead with my first burst, and the other ran to the other side of their truck. I hid behind the motor and front wheel while we exchanged shots. Then I dropped to the ground and shot the bastard in the knee that was poking out from behind the back wheel of the truck. He fell, and I ended his suffering by placing one more round into the back of his head.

I ran over to the truck, yelled at my friends, and then fired several bursts into the air before again lapsing into the soothing darkness of unconsciousness from exhaustion and my wounds.

My last thought before dropping back into darkness was that I'd lost Patty and now Mary was gone. I was alone, and I already missed them very much.

Chapter 19

The Ocean is a Vast Desert

The Gulf of Mexico

I don't know how long I was unconscious, but I had bad dreams, good dreams and some dreams I won't mention because they are too personal. I remember sweating, freezing and sweating again. A dragon chased me through a city and had me in his jaws when an angel smote him with her sword.

I remember waking up in my dreams; the same angel was wiping my face with a cold, wet rag one minute and placing blankets on me the next. My head hurt as though it was in a tightening vise. I remember waking up with my angel in bed beside me. She kissed me, and I fell asleep in her arms. Mostly I remember being tossed about in my bed between periods of blackness.

I was dreaming about my angel when I realized that there was a bright light in the room above my head. Damn, I must be dying because don't you always see a bright light as you slip into death. Then I felt pain in my butt, right shoulder, and side. I tried to roll over and felt something damp and cold being placed on my forehead, easing the pain in my head allowing me to return to dreams of my angel.

I heard my angel's voice, "Matt Jones, I think you might just live."

I opened my eyes and saw the most beautiful angel I had ever seen, and she looked just like Patty. I blinked my eyes, and this beautiful angel hugged and kissed me for a long time. I was in love with my angel. This dream was very real to me.

"Matt, you are going to be okay. Open your eyes."

"Patty?"

"Yes it's me, Oh, Matt, I have been so lonely, and I have missed you more than I can ever say. I promise that if you'll have me, I'll never leave you again."

She hugged me tight and kissed me again for a long time. I kissed her back and hugged her as tight as my injuries would allow.

"Patty, you must know that I have loved you since the moment we met at the airport. Please, don't leave me again."

I fell back asleep and didn't wake up for several hours, well into the evening.

I looked around in the twilight and saw a goddess at the wheel steering what I believed to be a sailboat. I looked around and saw I was below deck looking up at this angel who had saved me from certain death.

Slowly, I began to realize that we really were on a small sailboat and moving along at a fair pace. The cabin was filled with boxes of cereal, Spam, and cans of vegetables.

Gathering my strength, I forced myself from the bed and started up the steps to join my angel.

When Patty saw me, she tied the wheel in position, came to the cabin door, and helped me up the steps. She helped me walk until we were able to sit. We simply held each other for several minutes without uttering a sound.

Easing away, she said, "Matt I was so afraid I might lose you, again. I just could not allow that to happen, and I vow to die fighting before ever losing you again.

I have grown and learned so much since being kidnapped on that damned helicopter.

I killed them all, Matt. Now, I understand how wrong I was to push you away. I love you.

Please, can we go forward together? I do understand, Matt, and I will fight at your side against anyone who tries to harm us. Please, I have been so lonely, and wanting only to be in your arms."

I gazed into her tear-filled eyes and realized my eyes mirrored hers, as I said, "Patty, please hold me again, for a long time."

And she did.

I touched my finger to her lips and said, "I love you, and I am yours, now, and until death part.

I know we need to catch each other up on events since we last saw each other, but right now I just want to hold you for a very long time."

Kids might read this book, so I won't give any detail about that night, but I will say we had a very enjoyable day and wonderful night. That is all I have to say about that.

I woke up in Patty's arms with the sun streaming through the cabin windows. She felt good against my skin, and I kissed her closed eyes. Her eyes opened, and she had a big dopey smile on her angels face.

"Darling, what happened to Mary?" she asked as if afraid of the answer.

I looked away for a second, before recovering my composure and said, "She was on a sailboat, and we were getting ready to leave when we were attacked. I was on land when the attack started. The kids, Nuns, Mary, my dogs, Brett and Meg, everyone, got away and are now half way to South America."

"Kids and Nuns?"

We took the time to fill each other in on the events since the helicopter took off up in Wyoming. We were both amazed at what the other had been through to survive. I was so proud of this woman.

We got dressed and had breakfast above deck in the sunshine. The temperature was in the upper-forties, so I guessed we had sailed a long way south.

I looked behind and saw the small sailboat that I had forgotten to tie to Brett's boat. My supplies!

"Patty, you brought the Venture!"

"I guess it must be pretty important to you because you kept talking about it while you were unconscious.

I saw guns and MREs, so I tied it to our boat and brought it along. I was never so relieved when I saw that there was another small sailboat capable of sailing on the open ocean. Your friends left enough weapons, food, and water for a small village."

"How long has it been since the attack?"

"Darling you have been in and out of consciousness for over a week. It took me three days to get the boat ready and packed.

We have been sailing since then. I figure we've sailed nearly 600 miles southeast. That probably amounts to about 400 miles straight south. We have to go between Cuba and Mexico, at Cancun, before continuing southeast to Brazil. We're sailing into early spring so we shouldn't have to contend with storms, but we'll keep relatively close to shore in case we have to find a sheltered cove."

"I'll be able to help steer, so we can sail 24 hours a day to cover the 3,000 miles to our new home. At 6 miles an hour, if my math is correct, we should be there in about 21 days without stopping. A thirty-foot boat like this one tops out at about 8 MPH."

"Oh, I'm guessing the warmer weather is probably caused by the warm water coming north in the Gulf Stream."

"Yeah, that makes sense. How about slipping over here and warming me up."

"You only get five minutes of warming up before I have to get back to the helm."

Patty sat down on my lap, we enjoyed the ocean breeze for a few minutes, and then she began teaching me how to sail. I didn't tell her that I already knew how to sail, well, a little.

I enjoyed the training and the one on one contact. I was in pain while she sat in my lap from the shrapnel wound in my butt: however, I loved every minute of it.

In thinking about the attack, and the explosion, I didn't even know I had been hit. I don't remember much about trailing the thieving rat bastards or killing them. After that, I don't remember squat until waking to my Patty's voice.

Yes, this was the second butt cheek wound in two months, and my ass hurt like hell, but I was so happy, and she felt so good I didn't let my knickers get in a knot and sucked up the pain.

She also did a wonderful job of sewing up my ass, again.

"I think you've got the hang of keeping the sail with the wind. Keep an eye on the compass, and you won't go wrong. I'll teach you about tacking tomorrow. Now how long do you think we ought to sail before switching?"

"I vote for changing every four hours. That gives a decent sleep and won't be too boring."

"Yes, that sounds about right, we can always lash the helm down long enough for pee breaks and a stretch every now and then. The boat pretty much holds course unless the wind changes."

"Okay, but we need to stop for an hour every day when the wind is the slowest to err..."

Patty replied, "And go skinny dipping. The air temperature is in the high 30's, but the water is in the high 60's."

"Sounds great."

Patty winked at me and added, "We need some personal time also."

"Yeah, I need some personal time. Hey, what about protection?"

I brought enough birth control pills to last about two years, assuming they don't go bad."

"But what about until they begin to take effect?"

"Okay, I guess it's time, I don't really know how to say this, so I'll just blurt it out. I have been on the pill since I was 16. George and I didn't get along, but even so, we did have sex, and I realized early on that I was never going to have a kid by him.

Besides, I knew two months ago that we'd end up in bed together. "

"I knew you loved me back then. Why did you push me away?"

"I don't know. I've kicked my ass a whole bunch of times over that one. Matt, I'm not the same person I was then. I hate to keep saying it, but I just didn't get it, and since change is the only constant in the Universe, now I do."

We quickly found that at the end of our personal hour was a good time to take a dip in the water and bathe. The water was much warmer than the air, and it was the highlight of our day. We kept an eye out for sharks but never saw any nearby.

This must be what heaven was supposed to be.

★

✪

Chapter 20

Betrayal

The Gulf of Mexico
10 nautical miles from the East Coast of Mexico

One low spot was that there wasn't much in the way of fish in the open water away from the continental shelf. There must have been whatever those tiny things that whales eat because we saw several. We also saw many flying fish near the continental shelf. In the Gulf of Mexico, the shelf runs out to about twenty miles. That's why the water is so much calmer than in the open ocean, where the shelf usually doesn't run out more than about five miles.

The ocean waves hit the shelf and build up making for higher surf on the ocean side. On the Gulf side with the much longer shelf, the waves settle down before cresting on the beach.

That wasn't a problem once we figured it out. We just sailed in closer to the islands as we made our way southeast from Cuba, the Caymans, and Jamaica. We fished and stopped to fill our water drums every chance we had. We changed our route to follow the chain of islands all the way to South America.

Of course, sailing closer to the islands meant two, not so good things. One, since we had to dump our garbage overboard, sharks constantly accompanied us, and two, people.

We had to hide from other boats several times after stumbling upon people from one boat shooting at another. Patty ducked back behind an island just in time to keep us from being spotted.

There were more boats on this route, but at least we wouldn't starve or die of thirst. We also had several occasions when people tried to get us to stop and give them food or water. I always pointed to the islands and told them to go ashore to find water and to fish for food. Several, just wanted us to give them handouts, others wanted everything we had. A burst from my M4 from my provision boat seemed to ward them off quite well.

We only had to shoot at one boat to keep them from trying to board us.

The result was that they ran, and we ran, but it made us acutely aware that there were heavily armed pirates, so we sailed back to about five miles beyond the shelf until we needed fish or water.

Patty and I were on a long honeymoon, so we enjoyed the alone time. Life was great!

Patty was still planning to kill Carla if we ever ran across her sorry ass, but again this is a big world, and Carla would probably die in a pirate attack or starve to death. I told Patty that to make her happy.

Yes, we worried about Mary but knew there was nothing we could do to help her. Mary is a very strong person and can handle herself. She was with some strong people and should make it to their destination. I thought Mary would be fine in the post-apocalyptic world. She was one tough cookie.

Just when I thought that, everything couldn't get any better, I saw huge black clouds on the horizon stretching as far as the eye could see in both directions.

Patty saw the storm a few seconds later and yelled, "Lower the sails stow our gear and prepare to batten down the hatches. Let's fire up the auxiliary, and try to make for a cove along the barrier islands."

We completed our tasks and watched as the storm overtook us. The wind roared all around us, and the waves grew in size. We kept the auxiliary motor on and steered into the wind. Still our boat was tossed about like a feather in the wind. The storm lasted all afternoon and well into the night.

Both Patty and I feel this way about our little storm experience, scratch that off the old bucket list and never again. Were we frightened, hell no, we were terrified and knew we were going to die. I will never know how those little boats held together. Some time later, I was told that the drag boat actually helped maintain our heading into the storm, talk about babes in the woods.

After the storms passing, we slept the sleep of the exhausted and woke with the sun streaming in through a porthole. Scurrying topside, we were greeted by a beautiful day. Our bilge pumps had kept us afloat, but the Venture was nearly gunnel deep in a losing battle with Davy Jones.

Patty screamed out, "Oh, God, Matt, if she goes down we go with her. Let's get in the water and start bailing!"

"I've got this, Patty; you stand by with an ax while I bail. Oh, man, we cannot afford to lose that shit."

I dove in close to the Venture, and Patty threw me a pail. I started frantically bailing the water out. It took about twenty minutes to drop the level enough for me to get in and finish the task. The entire job took about half an hour.

I then made an inspection and found that she was in otherwise good shape and ready to sail.

The thought that in another five minutes the Venture would have gone down dragging us after her by the stern, scared the crap out of me. I didn't mention that part to Patty as I climbed back onboard with my shorts in my hand.

The next two days were uneventful until later in the evening on the third day, I heard Patty yell, "There's a boat up ahead. It's capsized, and I see people clinging to it."

I saw her looking at the horizon through binoculars and replied, "I'll steer wide so they won't see us."

"Matt, there are a couple of kids in the water."

"Patty, we can't save everyone."

"Please honey, we haven't yet saved anyone. This is our chance. We'll drop them off at the next island."

I saw the big puppy dog eyes and could not say no, "Okay, but watch them closely."

We steered towards them and took over 20 minutes to close the distance between boats.

When we were a hundred feet away, Patty yelled, "It's Antonio and his family. His sister in law is the bitch that sold me into slavery."

"Do you want me to turn away?"

"No, we'll save Antonio and the kids and leave her sorry ass in the water for the sharks."

A few minutes later the man yelled, "Thanks for stopping. We were dying of thirst. Hey, Patty, is that you? Thank God that you're safe. Why did you leave me?"

Yes, I'm alive, no thanks to your bitch sister in law. This is Matt, my new husband."

I pulled the two kids up onto the deck and then Antonio. I waited for Patty to say something about the hysterical woman.

Patty glared at her struggling to get on board and said, "Antonio, did you know that Carla sold me to a drug gang?"

"What? She told me you left on your own."

Patty pulled her pistol, aimed it at Carla's head, and said, "I'm going to leave you on your boat and let you die drinking sea water."

Carla begged for her life, but before Patty could tell me to sail away, Antonio grabbed the gun and shot Carla. She sank into the water leaving a red trail as she sank.

Sharks began stirring the bloody water almost immediately.

I grabbed for the gun, but Antonio was faster, and I felt a pain in my head.

As my lights, once again went out I heard, "Patty you are mine, and you will be with my kids and me forever."

***

I was barely awake and felt the tiny boat rocking. I couldn't remember where I was or even who I was. It was dark, and all I could see as I opened my eyes were stars to the south and the light show in the north. I felt around and found that I was in a small boat about 16 feet long. It had a mast so it must be a sailboat.

311

I passed out again and didn't wake until the sun was burning through my eyelids. The sun was high in the sky, and the wind was chilling me to the bone. I was damp even through a jacket and sweater. I found a bag with clothes and changed into dry gear.

My memory was slowly returning as I searched the boat. I quickly found the MREs, weapons, and bag with my treasure. It's funny how I remembered them, but didn't know my name.

I ate two packages of MREs, drank my fill of water, and raised my sail. I took a couple of aspirin and felt better in a couple of hours.

I found a compass and steered southeast heading that way because it felt good. I put a gun belt on with a Glock 17 and three magazines and placed the AR15 and Keltec Sub 2000 close by in case of attack.

I couldn't remember much, but I did remember being hit on the head by a man named Antonio. He took my boat and everything that meant something to me. I kept fighting to remember the rest of what happened to me.

I didn't remember Patty or Mary, The Flare or why I had a burning desire to head to South America to find... hell, I just didn't know at the time.

Yet, the drive to discover what I had lost burned with a fire I could not explain.

***

Well, it's about time to wrap up the first book in my series about my life after the Solar Flare. Yes, I decided to stop at what you might call a cliffhanger point in time; however, back then life was a series of cliffhangers. "Life is a bitch and then you die," kind of world.

I plan to travel to New Washington tomorrow and see if I can get Book I published by a real publishing company. It's about 1,300 miles from home and we have never traveled to the New USA or New Washington. The wife and kids are looking forward to the adventure.

There are daily flights from our home in Ecuador, but we call it New Israel, yet we decided to drive on the Washington Expressway so we can see the beautiful mountainous country and drive along the Pacific Ocean.

Well, I'll keep writing, and I hope you enjoyed my story. Oh, by the way, I named Book II "Adventures in the Apocalypse.

Matt Jones

The End

If you like my novel, please post a review on Amazon.

Thanks   A J Newman or should that be Matt Jones?

To contact the Author please leave comments @:

www.facebook.com/newmananthonyj   Face Book page.

To view other books by A J Newman, go to Amazon at my Author's page:

★

Books by A J Newman

America destroyed: After the Solar Flare
Alone in the Apocalypse   Adventures in the Apocalypse*
*To be published late spring 2017

After the EMP series:
The Day America Died New Beginnings
The Day America Died Old Enemies
The Day America Died Frozen Apocalypse

"The Adventures of John Harris" - a Post-Apocalyptic America series:
Surviving   Hell in the Homeland   Tyranny in the Homeland
Revenge in the Homeland....Apocalypse in the Homeland   John Returns

"A Samantha Jones Murder Mystery Thriller series:

Where the Girls Are Buried   Who Killed the Girls?

Books by A J Newman and Cliff Deane

Terror in the USA:

Virus: – Strain of Islam

These books are available at Amazon:

http://www.amazon.com/-/e/B00HT84V6U

Also from A J Newman

After The EMP

The Day America Died New Beginnings - Zack Johnson is stranded on the west coast when an EMP attack destroys the Grid. He must get home to find and protect his daughter. This is a tale about what he has to do to get home and survive. It's also a story about the people he meets along the journey. Many are great people, but some are thugs that have to be dealt with.

The Day America Died Old Enemies continues the story with Zack and his family encountering disease, attacks from enemies and friends and a dictator trying to take over the community that has been his home. Zack's team also comes up with some hacks that improve life and put them on the way back to a more modern lifestyle.

The Day America Died Frozen Apocalypse has Zack and team starting over after being driven from their homes to a hideout in the woods near their hometown. The USA was attacked with nuclear EMP weapons has no power and food is in short supply. The government has not helped, and there is a power struggle between the forces of good and evil. It is now mid winter, and while Zack and his friends prepared for survival, many of their neighbors are cold and starving. The new mayor has taken control of the food supply and only doles it out to his supporters. What can Zack do?

http://www.amazon.com/-/e/B00HT84V6U

The Adventures of John Harris:

This series of Post-Apocalyptic novels tells how John Harris leads a group of survivors through the chaos of a country that has fallen apart. Rogue US Government officials and a coalition of Third World Leaders have launched a major nuclear and EMP attack on all of the major powers and killed over 100 million Americans. The grid is down, and water and food are scarce. The USA is in chaos with criminals and thugs attacking innocent citizens while the DHS is placing millions in relocation camps. John and his team fight back!

http://www.amazon.com/-/e/B00HT84V6U

Also from A J Newman

A Samantha Jones Murder Mystery Thriller

A teenage girl solves a series of kidnappings and murders of young girls. The teen girl is stalked by her mom's boyfriend and almost killed by a high-ranking political figure. How are the two crimes linked? This unlikely crime fighter solves the puzzle of "Where the Girls Are Buried."

In the next novel in the series, she solves "Who killed the Girls?" Was it the high ranking politician or was it his son? Who is behind the attacks on their families? Why don't they want these crimes solved?

http://www.amazon.com/-/e/B00HT84V6U

Books by A J Newman and Cliff Deane

Virus: - Strain of Islam

Three years ago, CIA Agent Max Owens was captured and tortured by the Taliban because they thought he had information concerning a bioweapon the Saudis were developing to use against them. Several hundred villagers died and then nothing happened.

Now a biological attack on New York City leaves thousands dead and millions hospitalized in several countries. The USA is terrorized. No terrorist group claims the attack. Was this the major attack or a sample of things to come? Was this the end of the attacks or the first that leads to a worldwide apocalypse?

In this bioterrorism thriller, radical Islamic terrorists use genetic engineering to develop a deadly strain of virus based on the Ebola and Zika viruses. Their goal is to eradicate non-Muslims, bring forth the Twelfth Imam, and begin the World Caliphate.

Can Max Owens and his team of CDC and CIA operatives find and stop this terrorist group before they unleash this Strain of Islam and kill billions of people?

http://www.amazon.com/-/e/B00HT84V6U

About the Author

A J Newman is the author of over a dozen novels that have been published on Amazon. He was born and raised in a small town in the western part of Kentucky. His Dad taught him how to handle guns very early in life, and he and his best friend Mike spent summers shooting .22 rifles and fishing.

He read every book he could get his hands on and fell in love with science fiction. He graduated from USI with a degree in Chemistry and made a career working in manufacturing and logistics, but always fancied himself as an author.

He served six years in the Army National Guard in an armored unit and spent six years performing every function on M48 and M60 army tanks. This gave him a great respect for our veterans who lay their lives on the line to protect our country and freedoms.

He currently resides in Kentucky with his wife Patsy and their three tiny mop dogs, Sammy Cotton and Callie.

Made in the USA
Monee, IL
11 October 2023

44374134R00177